4.50
6/23

THE Death Certificate

STEPHEN MOLYNEUX

D1500656

The Death Certificate
STEPHEN MOLYNEUX
Copyright © Stephen Molyneux 2019

The right of Stephen Molyneux to be identified as the Author of this Work
has been asserted by him in accordance with the
Copyright, Designs and Patents Act 1988

Published 2019 by Sites To Suit Limited
publishing@sites-to-suit.co.uk

All rights reserved. No part of this publication may be reproduced
or transmitted in any form or by any means, electronic or mechanical,
including photocopy, recording, or any information storage and retrieval
system, without permission in writing from both the copyright owner and the
above publisher.

The names, characters, places and events in this publication are either
products of the author's imagination or are used fictitiously. Any resemblance
to real persons, living or dead, is purely coincidental.

ISBN: 978-0-9576059-2-3

Cover design by The Art of Communication
artofcomms.co.uk

Also available as an e-book.

ABOUT THE AUTHOR

Stephen Molyneux, amateur genealogist, lives in Hampshire and the South of France with two metal detectors and his long-suffering wife.

The Death Certificate is Stephen's second novel. His first novel is *The Marriage Certificate*.

To Sarah

PROLOGUE

LONDON, 1841

Samuel Jupp, locally known as 'Lucky Juppy', was a tosher. He made his living searching for jewellery, coins, and other valuables in the network of sewers under the streets of London. Although an illegal trade, he managed to earn a few shillings a day when conditions were right and access could be gained. He made enough to maintain his wife, Eleanor, and three-year-old son, Moses, in relative comfort. They had a roof over their heads, clothes on their backs, and sufficient to eat and drink. They lived in one room in a crowded tenement – rented, of course – but it wasn't shared and their situation was far better than most.

Entry to the sewers was prohibited. The outfalls into the River Thames were closed off with bars and locked gates. Samuel overcame this setback by cutting and modifying the bars of one of the outfalls. It allowed him to hastily remove and replace a small section. It was a clever system, using bolts and concealed brackets that enabled his 'door', when in position, to pass any cursory inspection.

It was half-past nine on a warm muggy Saturday evening in early July when Samuel and his new apprentice, nephew Jake, kept close to the wall, so as not to be observed from above. The ebbing tide had turned an hour before and exposed part of the foreshore. There was just enough light remaining to see that the effluent discharging from Samuel's adapted outfall, on the north bank between London Bridge and Blackfriars, was shallow and flowing slowly. It hadn't rained for weeks, which meant conditions were ideal. They had about six hours.

Samuel was in his early forties; a stocky man with a bushy black moustache that dominated his swarthy complexion. Jake, aged sixteen and by contrast a rather skinny individual, greatly admired his uncle and was grateful for the chance to learn 'the trade'.

"Here, gimme the spanner," Samuel whispered to Jake, "and keep lookout."

Jake was carrying most of their equipment. He handed the tool to his uncle, who quickly loosened four bolts before lifting aside the modified door. It was just big enough to allow each of them to step through.

Samuel entered first. He turned to receive two long, stout wooden poles with hoe-like ends, a pair of miners' lanterns, two small shovels, a canvas apron for each of them, and a couple of large, circular sieves. Jake then followed and Samuel replaced his door as quietly as he could. No one seemed to have heard. He indicated to Jake to be silent while he listened for a moment. There was no shout of alarm from any nearby police constable or nosey lamplighter.

Satisfied they hadn't been observed, he divided the equipment. With a shovel and sieve hanging from each of their belts, and carrying the poles, they proceeded into the sewer, sloshing through the mire for some thirty feet. Samuel signalled a pause so that he could light their lanterns, which each had suspended from a hook on the shoulder.

"Can't light up further in," explained Samuel, "there's gases what a bare flame might explode."

"Blimey, the smell's awful bad," responded Jake. "I ain't hardly able to breathe."

"You'll get used to it. Come on, just do as I say."

Samuel knew his most productive walks, where the pickings were good. His knowledge of the streets above and the sewers below enabled him to navigate to parts of the metropolis where the effluent entering the sewer was from prosperous areas or in the vicinity of busy markets. The chances of decent finds were even better on Saturday nights. A busy day around the market stalls with plenty of cash changing hands, and drunken or tipsy revellers losing trinkets and valuables while returning home made the prospect of lucrative finds even more likely.

The two progressed prudently and steadily through the damp confining tunnels, their lights dancing and flickering off the wet brickwork. At times, Samuel would pause to bend down and examine crevices in the brickwork.

"Always look in places like this," he explained to Jake. "It's holes and gaps where the small goodies get caught and stuck." With that, he gave a grunt of satisfaction and hooked out a silver groat, worth four pence.

They came to a junction and Samuel knowingly selected the right-hand channel to assure Jake that he was confident of the direction he'd chosen. "See here," he said, "mind your footin'. You need to poke and feel the muck with your pole. The bottom's not good and you don't want to fall into a hole nor trip on somethin' buried."

At the extremities of their lighting, they could see the shapes and shadows of rats scurrying away from them, disappearing into nooks and cavities.

Some of the rats were surprisingly large to Jake. Legend had it of a giant Queen Rat that ruled the sewers. Samuel chose not to mention the myth, it being his nephew's first experience below.

Mostly, they could walk upright, but where the tunnel was partially obstructed or reduced in height, they had to bend and pass their poles through to each other. Fortunately, due to dry weather, the sewage was shallow and didn't come over the tops their boots.

"Look out, lad, and hold your nose," warned Samuel. The remains of a dead cat lay just above the stream; bones and fur for the most part, but still a feast for fleeing rodents.

Jake did as instructed but didn't feel entirely at ease. "What's that rumblin' I keep hearin'?"

"That's just life goin' on as normal up top," said Samuel reassuringly. "There's wagons and carriages goin' by all the time. It's a warm Saturday evenin', don't forget. There'll be plenty of folk about and the traders'll be sellin' everythin' from food to fans."

"The roof won't collapse, will it?"

"Course not, lad. We're safe as houses down here, don't you worry."

After a short while, they reached the first of Samuel's walks: a thick clogging mass of sludge and watery slurry, two feet deep and twenty yards long. It lay below a large surface grid about four feet above them.

"This whole pile of muck is some of the drainin's from Gracechurch Street. Providin' no one else has been here for a while, we should get some nice pickin's. Watch me first to see how it's done, but cover your lamp a bit; we don't anyone up there reportin' us. Then, you start on that side over there and make sure you show me anythin' you find that's metal. Sometimes, good things can look like rubbish when they're covered in filth."

"Uncle Sam, looks like there's a shillin' just lyin' on the top!"

"Well spotted, lad. See what I mean," said Samuel, slipping it into his pouch. "I know the best places. Like as not, some unlucky devil dropped that this very evening."

They started to dig. Following his uncle's guide, Jake soon got the hang of it, shovelling and sifting the muck for coins and valuables. The slurry was mainly horse urine and its comparative liquidity made it useful to scoop into their riddles to soften and dilute the sludge. After a couple of hours, they had one spoon, several coppers, and a silver florin to show for their efforts.

Samuel held the spoon under his lamp and turned it over. He spat and rubbed it near the handle. "Can't see any marks on it, but by the weight I'll warrant it's silver!" He chuckled. "I'll take it to Foundry Tom. He'll tell me if it's good or not," he added, before ensuring it was safely tucked into a deep trouser pocket.

Jake was impressed. "I'd no idea there was so much down

here. Is it always like this?"

"It is if you stick with me! Come on; let's get off to another of my little spots."

They retraced their steps to the main tunnel and resumed their course through it, all the time moving deeper into the network and further from the outfall entrance. Ignoring several more tunnels, Samuel eventually chose one on the right and Jake dutifully followed.

"Any idea what the time is, Uncle?"

"Approachin' midnight, I'd guess…We've a few gratin's to pass under on this stretch. We're near several churches so listen out for the bells and don't forget to cover your lamp when you pass under the openin's. We don't want someone informin' on us; there's a five-pound reward offered if we gets caught."

As if on cue, they heard a church bell strike twelve times. Jake was impressed.

The bell fell silent and Samuel turned to his young apprentice. "Right, you know what that means?"

"No, Uncle, what does it mean?"

"It means the tide will turn in under two hours, so we've an hour or so left before we head home. We want to be out before people start gettin' about."

They reached a section where the tunnel narrowed sharply and the ceiling dropped much lower. Jake was becoming an old hand. He didn't need his uncle to explain the procedure. The partial restriction was short in length, so he waited for his uncle to get through before handing the tools to him. Jake followed and found that he was able to stand on the other side. They were in a small chamber with two channels leading away from it.

"We'll take this one on the left. It's a dead end. It climbs a bit first and finishes at the bottom of Stockcross Road. There's always big crowds: locals and visitors. It's right by Spitalfields. Makes for rich pickin's, lad! Come on, we're nearly there."

When they reached the end of the sewer, Jake could see why his uncle liked this spot. He could discern the underside of a very large grating with a temptingly large heap of muck below it. Jake also noticed that he couldn't see anything through the grating. The bars above appeared to be covered over with straw and other detritus.

"Why can't we see up through the grate, Uncle Sam?"

"Ah, well this is a low point and the streets drain down this way, so straw's probably got washed down and blocked it over from the last time it rained. The good thing is, we ain't got to worry about them up in the street spottin' our lamps and calling the Peelers!"

Jake, happy with the explanation, set about helping his uncle; once more, they scraped and sifted the muck for its valuables. He noticed that it was much drier than at their first location. The top layers crumbled and flaked, proof of the lack of rain in recent weeks. They worked steadily, pausing regularly to share their excitement each time one of them found a coin.

Apart from the all-pervading stench, it was hot work. The sultry evening temperature seemed to have penetrated that part of the sewer and soon their endeavours brought each of them out in a heavy sweat. Jake removed his apron and top garments and laid them to one side. Bare-chested, he set his lamp nearby and carried on. A short while later, he felt a drop of moisture splash upon his shoulder. He flinched and looked upwards to the grating. "Look, there's drips of water coming down on us!"

Samuel chuckled. "More like horse piss, I'd be thinkin'! Pay no attention, lad. Someone's waterin' his horse close by, that's all. A little bit longer and we can be off with a good night's gleanin's, I reckon."

The two laboured and sweated as droplets of liquid continued to ooze through the straw above and dribble onto them.

Up on the surface, the muggy air had been replaced by the coolness of a sudden rain storm of intense ferocity. It had caught out many of those returning home late. A single clap of thunder some distance off had announced the storm's approach and within minutes the rain was torrential. Pedestrians sought refuge wherever they could, in doorways, beneath awnings, and under

6

arches. Those already soaked struck out for home, sploshing through running streams of water; avoiding, where possible, the growing number of large puddles.

At the bottom of Stockcross Road, deep water collected. Fearful of flooding to their basements and properties, nearby occupants hurriedly dressed and emerged, wondering what to do.

"It's the drain what's blocked!" one inhabitant shouted. "It's clogged up with straw."

"Do you know where it is?" someone else asked.

"I do," answered a young boy pointing across the large growing pool. "It's over there in the corner near the lamp post."

"We need to find it," asserted an off-duty constable. "Form a line, each man a yard apart, and wade slowly down towards the corner...see if we can feel it with our feet."

Six men took off their shoes and stepped tentatively into the dirty brown water. Within a few yards, it was above their knees. They linked hands and advanced cautiously towards the bottom corner of the street, anxious to keep their footing. As they proceeded, slowly the depth increased until it reached their waists.

"I've got it!" exclaimed one of them. "I can feel it, all mushy like, but with bars underneath!"

"That must be it!" the off-duty constable confirmed.

Jake looked towards Samuel. "I just heard voices, Uncle." He pointed upwards. "I think someone shouted somethin' about bars?"

Samuel looked up at the underside of the grating. It was rocking slightly as if someone was loosening it. The drops of liquid seemed more frequent.

"Let's pack up here, lad. Quick, move everythin' away from the openin'. We don't want to be seen."

Above them, the men broke their line and congregated around the individuals standing on the grate. Collectively, they scraped their feet and jumped up and down in an effort to clear the blockage. Suddenly, a series of large bubbles erupted, followed by a gurgling sound. A deepening spiral formed as the water gushed through the grating down into the sewer.

"That's it! Look at it go!" shouted the off-duty constable. "Well done, men, it'll be gone in no time."

Below the grating, as Samuel and Jake were shifting tools and clothes, a deluge of water knocked a shovel from Jake's hands and swept him off his feet. His lamp was knocked over and extinguished as soon as it fell into the water.

"What's happenin'?" Jake cried as he regained his footing. "We're goin' to drown!"

"Grab your pole!" ordered Samuel. "Leave everything else. Quick! We ain't hangin' round here, it's like a bleedin' waterfall!"

Unhooking and holding the remaining light aloft, Samuel led the way back down the shallow incline towards the main sewer. Initially, the current pushed them along, surging through their legs and making it difficult to stay upright. They then met rising water. Panting with exertion, they waded into it. By the time they reached the small chamber where the left and right channels joined, the water was well above their waists. A torrent was pouring in from the other tunnel too and the chamber was filling. Their escape through the narrow restricted exit was already cut off.

"I can't swim!" cried Jake.

"Nor me!" Samuel shouted with the first note of panic in his voice.

"What we goin' to do?" asked Jake, close to tears.

"Here, hold the lamp while I show you. With your back against the wall, push the end of your pole onto the bottom. Wedge the top against the roof...like this. Raise your arms, grab the pole with both hands, and pull yourself up. If you can, bend your legs; use the wall to grip your feet. We'll have to stay like that till the water goes down..." He took the lamp from Jake and looped it over his thumb. "I'll try to keep my light out of the water."

It was uncomfortable for Jake to press his bare back against the rough damp brickwork, but a sensible idea. However, Samuel knew in his heart that their chances might be slim. Maybe his luck was about to run out. He'd no idea for how long, nor how hard it had been raining.

Lashin' down, he surmised, *to send such a surge into the sewers. Will I ever see Moses again? Will I ever get to teach him the ways of a tosher?*

Inexorably, the water level continued to rise. It soon covered their poles and then reached Jake's neck. He was shorter than his uncle. Terrified, he started to cry.

"Push yourself higher up on the pole, lad," urged Samuel, "but keep your weight to the wall. I'll try to hold on to the light."

Jake followed his uncle's instructions and found that his head was a few inches clear of the water, but nearer to the chamber's roof. He soon realised that his breathing space was reducing and that they might not have enough air. If that wasn't bad enough, the light flickering off the shiny claustrophobic brickwork illuminated something even more frightening. The surface of the water flowing in from the other chamber was alive with rats and they were swimming towards him.

"There's rats comin' on us!" Jake screamed out.

The verminous wave reached them in seconds. The rodents swarmed upon their shoulders and heads, seeking refuge, biting and squealing as they scrambled to escape the rising water.

Samuel and Jake cried out in panic and horror, shaking and twisting violently from side to side in their efforts to dislodge the repulsive hoard. In chaos and terror, Samuel lost hold of the lantern and it fell into the water. Everything went black, but the darkness gave no respite from their torment. Not until, that is, the water covered their heads and each had no choice but to give up his fight to stay alive.

PART ONE

CHAPTER 1

Warm and cosy in his little Fiat 4x4, on a cold October morning, Peter Sefton drove along the narrow, twisty, country lanes flanked by trees, pasture and, best of all, ploughed fields. With a left turn here, and a right there, to a stranger or townie the high banks topped by neatly trimmed hedges would have seemed like a maze, but not to Peter. He was at home in the beautiful Wiltshire countryside, using his knowledge of the local back ways and shortcuts to avoid the main roads and the school-run bottlenecks.

His choice of music that morning was the familiar compilation of soul and Motown, kindly downloaded for him by a friend who knew how; proof that Peter's playlist and technological abilities were both a bit last century. Still, he cared not. Reluctant to fiddle too much with gadgets, his smartphone, or new software for his computer, he was content with surfing the Net, and the default settings on his metal detector.

Detecting was something he'd enjoyed for nearly thirty years. Despite plenty of leg-pulling from friends and family about his 'anorak' hobby, most were genuinely impressed when they saw and handled some of the items he'd found: coins from Celtic to modern, Roman brooches, rings, beautiful little buckles and buttons. It took perseverance, patience, cunning, and luck to be successful. Alone with his detector, Peter was a hunter, reading the landscape and recognising signs of previous human activity.

His online research had revealed that the large field he hoped to detect that day covered the bottom of a small hidden valley.

The sides of it were steep and covered by stands of woodland, interspersed with grassy slopes that provided good grazing for sheep. The incline at the eastern end was more gradual and its base was once the location of a small hamlet, with only the farmhouse now remaining.

Maps of the wider area showed evidence of man's influence going back thousands of years, with prehistoric burial mounds and ditches not too far away. It truly was a fantastic detecting site, at least in theory, and Peter's anticipation of what he might extract from the soil had kept him awake for most of the night.

An early breakfast, with time to make sandwiches and fill a flask, not forgetting to take a cup of tea up to his wife, Felicity, had enabled him to leave just before eight o'clock for his prearranged rendezvous with the landowner, a farmer named Norman Coles. *Rendezvous* wasn't exactly the right word; more a case of, "Well, if you come by about quarter to nine, I should be back from feeding the pheasants."

Peter was looking forward to meeting Mr Coles, slipping him a bottle of whisky by way of thanks, maybe getting some background information on what he might find and, more importantly, being told exactly where he could detect. He really wanted it to be the large field that his research had identified.

As to the farmer, Peter hadn't been able to find out very much. His name and phone number were all he had, provided by a friend who knew him and who had cleared it with him for Peter to carry out some detecting. The electoral roll suggested the farmer lived alone. The only definite piece of information Peter could find was a link to a tractor preservation society that showed him to be on the committee. He had also discovered that the small hamlet down in the valley was called Oxenhope, as was the farm owned by Norman Coles.

Online satellite views had revealed one substantial house with a few largish outbuildings. The whole site looked isolated, and Peter wondered how productive the farm was. He doubted whether there was enough land to make the business viable, but he knew that hiring out to pheasant shoots was highly lucrative.

City boys paid thousands for a day's sport. The downside of that, he thought selfishly, was that he'd probably spend the entire day digging up the brass ends of spent shotgun cartridges.

As he turned off the metalled lane onto a muddy track, Peter tried to put any negatives to the back of his mind. Thinking again of the history in the area, and its previous inhabitants, he hoped there would be something good just waiting to be found, but would he be the first to detect there? Would the valley yield any of its secrets to him? Only time – and, no doubt, an awful lot of digging – would tell.

He crossed an ancient bridleway, which stretched away across the ridge to his left and right, before descending and entering a shady beech wood. A particularly muddy and slippery section of track focussed his attention on controlling the car. Leaves had fallen, covering the ruts and tramlines of other vehicles. He aimed for the centre and it seemed firm enough. It was steep at times, causing the car to slew a little. Peter imagined what it must have been like to guide a heavy wagon with a team of oxen or horses up or down such an incline.

It occurred to him that perhaps he'd turned off too soon, but a quick glance at the survey map on the passenger seat reassured him that he was still where he ought to be. Through the trees on his right, he spotted a telephone pole carrying a single black wire; surely the connection to the farm. Further confirmation came in the form of numerous pheasants on the track before him; some with a death wish, for having moved out of his way, they turned around and ran back across his path. Fortunately, they seemed to scatter unscathed. Pleasingly, as the trees ended at the bottom of the hill, he found himself looking through a slight mist across acres and acres of freshly ploughed field.

Peter stopped the car, turned off the music, and lowered his window. The air was damp and cold, heavy with the unmistakable smell of freshly turned soil. He breathed in deeply and exhaled slowly, enjoying the earthy aroma. A pheasant screeched somewhere back up in the woods; its call amplified within the dark confines of the trees that still retained their autumn canopy.

The early morning sunshine illuminated his windscreen, but the other end of the valley was still in shadow. He could just discern the farmer's brick and flint farmhouse; the smoke rising almost vertically from its chimney on such a beautiful calm morning.

Magical, he thought, *as if time is frozen and I'm gazing upon a scene from hundreds of years ago.*

He put the car into gear and followed the track around the perimeter of the field towards the house. Shortly, he approached a gateway formed by a pair of brick piers. One of them leaned precariously. The missing gates were lying nearby, their wooden boarding damp with moss and covered by the remains of the previous summer's weeds and grass. It was obvious that they hadn't hung in place for many years.

Passing through the entrance, and avoiding some deep ruts, Peter finally pulled up in front of Oxenhope Farm. He parked next to a very scruffy work-scarred Land Rover and got out of his car, aware of a humming sound. It was the noise of a generator coming from somewhere on the far side of the farmhouse.

Peter approached the front porch. Freshly split logs for an open fire were scattered haphazardly, almost blocking his way. He had to sidestep them in order to get to the old, heavy-looking dark oak door. A large iron ring hung upon it, suspended by some orange hay-baling twine. Peter grasped the ring and rapped loudly, consolidating the dent where previous callers had marked the wood.

Inside, at least two dogs barked. Peter, being not particularly brave when confronted by angry dogs, hoped that they wouldn't be as fierce as they sounded.

"Coming...coming," shouted an approaching male voice. "Hang on, just a minute, just a minute." The occupant tugged and pulled at the door from the inside before it grudgingly swung inwards, scraping on a brick floor. Thankfully, rather than ferocious, two wildly excited Springer Spaniels were released, along with a stale warm fug of wood-smoke, damp, cooking, and wet canines.

"Hello Mr Coles, I'm Peter Sefton."

The man looked vacant for a moment.

"I rang you last week and arranged to come over to do some metal-detecting."

An enlightened expression followed. "Oh yes, you're John Carter's friend, aren't you?" He offered a calloused and dry hand; proof that he was indeed a hard-working farmer.

"That's right," returned Peter, "pleased to meet you." He gave the hand a firm shake and tried not to be distracted by the farmer's scruffy appearance. It was coordinated scruffiness, however unintentional. Grey hair, thinning and uncombed, along with several days' growth of stubble, matched a thick grey woolly jumper with patched elbows. The farmer's dark-blue baggy work trousers obviously hadn't seen a washing machine for a while. They were held up by a thick leather belt, which also struggled to contain a hefty paunch. Nevertheless, the farmer had a friendly face, with a ruddy weather-beaten complexion.

"You found us then…I mean, people are always getting lost around here." The dogs were making a dreadful racket. "Shut up you two!" he shouted. Almost immediately, they calmed down and turned their attention to sniffing Peter's ankles.

"Yes, just about," replied Peter, doing his best to ignore the dogs while at the same time exuding a non-threatening indifference that he'd read was the way to calm dogs. "Thought I'd taken the wrong turning at one point, coming down the track, but I stuck with it and what a view when I reached the bottom… just amazing this morning."

"You're right. It's the land that time forgot down here; just how I like it."

Peter could detect a hint of the local accent in his voice.

"So, you going to find some treasure for me then?"

"I doubt it," replied Peter, half laughing and adopting a 'don't get too hopeful' tone. "More like World War Two bullets, bits of lead, buttons, and maybe some worn coppers, but it's always possible. That's the thing about detecting…you never know!"

"How long have you been doing this detecting thing?"

"Oh, about thirty years."

"Found much?"

Not wanting to raise expectations Peter kept it low key. "I've found one or two nice bits and pieces."

"Well, I doubt you'll find much here, you know. This valley was pretty much abandoned about a hundred and fifty years ago. There were buildings over there."

Peter turned towards where the farmer had inclined his head. He could see some moss-covered brick walls a foot or so above the weeds, obviously the vague outline of a former construction.

"That used to be a cottage. There's more ruins up towards the trees behind the stables, near the pheasant pens. I wouldn't go over that way though. It's dangerous...unmarked wells, you see. Few years ago, a lady was picking blackberries and she fell down one. I had a job getting her out. She'd stepped on an old wooden cover. It was hidden in the undergrowth and rotten. Fortunately, she didn't fall right to the bottom. The biggest part of the cover somehow got wedged about ten feet down with her still on it. I heard her shouting and panicking. When I saw what had happened I managed to lower a rope and was eventually able to pull her out...had to use one of my tractors in the end, though. She was a big lady! No doubt all the blackberry pies she liked to make! Anyway, afterwards I made it safe by closing it off with a strong steel sheet. Before I did, I chucked some bricks down the shaft just to see how deep it was. It was second or two before I heard them hit the bottom. That well was quite deep. There was no splash though, not nowadays. That's because the water table's gone down since the water company abstracted millions of gallons."

Peter was anxious to get on with the landowner and so he managed an impressed nod. He was interested, though, because ruined dwellings meant people, a community, and that meant metal losses, which he hoped to find.

"So, were there many cottages?" he asked.

"I'm not sure, exactly. Apparently, there were several families here up until the 1890s, but there'd been a depression in farming in the 1880s. Gradually, the inhabitants moved out, especially the young. They left the countryside, you see. I suppose they were attracted to towns like Swindon and the railway work there. It's only about twelve miles away. They never returned and the cottages became empty and fell into disrepair. It's very remote here, you know. It suits me, but it's not for everyone."

"So where can I detect then?" asked Peter, trying to pull back the conversation to the present. "I'd imagine this field used to be divided into smaller ones." He indicated the large single ploughed field.

"That's right...used to be four or five fields, I think, before the days of mechanisation. My grandfather ripped out the hedges back in the thirties, when he got his first tractor. They're my passion, you know, tractors. I've a bit of a collection in the barns."

Not wishing to be sidetracked by tractor talk, Peter ignored the reference. "So can I go anywhere on the ploughed or harrowed part?"

"Yes, no problem...go where you like. You got time for a cuppa?"

"Well, can I say no, if you don't mind, only I'd really like to get started."

The farmer looked slightly disappointed.

Peter felt a bit awkward. "I tell you what, though; you've just reminded me...I've got something for you. Just a moment."

Peter quickly trotted over to the car, closely followed by one of the dogs. He returned with the bottle of whisky. "Please have this...It's really good of you to let me do some detecting. I do appreciate it."

"Well that's very kind, thank you. I didn't expect anything."

Peter shrugged his shoulders. "It's the least I can do. I'm a bit of a detecting nut, you know, so I'm always grateful for somewhere to search. Obviously, if I find any treasure, we're on a fifty-fifty split."

"Yes, OK, sounds fair...Good luck."

CHAPTER 2

LONDON, 1849

"What's your name, boy?" asked the magistrate speaking directly to the ragged-looking urchin standing in the dock.

"Moses Jupp, sir," he quavered. He'd never been in front of a magistrate before. To him, they were the most powerful men in the world.

"Speak up, boy. Are you Moses Jupp?"

"Yes, sir," he replied, trying to lift his voice towards the bench.

"M'lud," began the clerk, reading from his notes, "on Wednesday last, at approximately nine o'clock in the evening, Moses Jupp is accused of stealing coal from a barge belonging to Mr Buxey of Wapping. Police Constable Thurgut saw the accused and another youth skulking between a pair of barges moored and aground at low tide, just below Southwark Bridge. He had reason to believe they were in the act of stealing coal. The older boy had a bag, which he began to fill with large coals from one of the barges. He passed it down to the accused who was filling a basket with coals, having covered them first in water and mud to give the appearance of them having been overboard and in the river for some time.

"Constable Thurgut disturbed the fellows in their work of plunder and they fled, leaving the bag and basket on the foreshore. The constable secured the other youth and, having handed him over to another constable, pursued the accused. After a long chase, he overtook him in Upper Thames Street. The accused exclaimed, 'Do you mean to take me?' to which Constable Thurgut replied that he did. The accused said that he would have some trouble to do that, and after a severe struggle with the constable, he got away and made for the waterside. The constable pursued him again, whereby the accused ran through the mud and boldly took to the water, where he swam away. Constable Thurgut tried to swim after him, but unfortunately got into difficulties and had the luck to be rescued by a passing waterman. By the time he was safely aboard, the accused had made his escape.

"On Tuesday night, the constable found the accused sleeping under an arch and took him into custody."

The magistrate held a monocle to his left eye, peered at Moses, and then turned back to the clerk. "What became of the other boy?"

"M'lud, Mr Lovegrove imposed one month's imprisonment with hard labour."

The magistrate looked sternly at Moses Jupp. "How old are you? What do you say for yourself?"

"I'm eleven, sir, and I wasn't thievin', sir. We was gleanin', sir, collectin' coals in the mud, like we does. Coals what was already lost in the mud, sir, what gets spilt from the barges."

"And why would you do that?"

"For money, sir."

"For money? Who would want to buy wet coal covered in mud?"

At this point the clerk intervened. "M'lud, the accused is a member of a class of scavenger commonly known as a mudlark. There are bands of them, winter and summer, who forage the river foreshore at low tide, searching the shingle or raking the mud for anything they can sell: old rope, copper nails, clothing, buttons, the odd coin, bones, that kind of thing."

"I ain't a bone-grubber!" yelled Moses.

"Silence!" The magistrate banged his gavel. "You will speak only when asked to do so. Do you make a living from this activity?"

"I sells a basket of coal for a few pence and I ain't never had help from the parish."

"I see…And when the tide is high, what do you do then?"

"We entertains the swells, sir."

"Swells? Entertain? What do you mean?"

"The ladies and the gentlemen, sir. We does cart-wheelin' or stands on our heads; tricks like that for money, or we sweeps the road so that they can cross without gettin' muck on their shoes. Sometimes, they likes to stand on the bridge and throw us coins in the mud so that we can find 'em. If we do, we keeps 'em."

"So what does your father, or mother, say about you being a *mud*lark?" The magistrate laid particular emphasis on the first syllable.

"They're gone, sir, both of 'em. Mother got taken by the fever, and my father died before I can remember him, sir. My Aunt Agnes told me he drowned in the sewer. He was a tosher, one of the best!"

"And your mother died how long ago?"

"'Bout six years ago, sir."

"So who's been looking after you since?"

"My Aunt Agnes took me in. She lost her son when my father drowned. They were together at the time. She was a widow and was kind to me, but she married someone else a couple of years ago and I didn't like him, so I left and I've looked after myself since."

"I see…" The magistrate considered what he'd heard. Perhaps the lad deserved a touch of leniency. "Well, I don't believe you were looking for stray coal. If you were innocent, you wouldn't have run away and tried to evade the constable. It seems, however, to be your first offence. I've a mind to commit you to transportation to the colonies, but I'll let you have a chance to mend your ways and perhaps teach you a lesson…Fourteen days' imprisonment with a whipping!" he declared, slamming down his gavel with a flourish.

CHAPTER 3

Peter set off from the car and worked his way slowly and methodically to the far end of the field, sweeping the head of his detector from left to right. The ploughing was quite shallow, enabling him to walk over and along the furrows without too much trouble. Midway, he jumped in surprise when he disturbed a hare. It had been so still and well camouflaged that he'd been unaware of its presence. He was almost upon it as it bolted. He paused to admire the manner in which it effortlessly covered the hundred yards to the safety of the hedge.

Looking down at the ground, he resumed his concentration, scanning the surface for signs of former use, hoping to identify a likely area in which to concentrate. Brick, pottery, small fine stones, and soft dark soil were all good indicators, along with the sounds coming from his headphones. At times, the field was quiet; at others, he would hear the pops, spits, and crackles as he swung his detector across pieces of unwanted buried iron. Peter, though, was patient. It was rather like fishing: waiting for a firm take was just like waiting for a signal with a sweet and steady tone.

Experience had taught him to anticipate from sound what an object might be. He always dug a strong signal, and sometimes ones that weren't too clear. It was hard to explain why, but if there was something right in the tone, however faint, then he would dig it. Less distinct signals usually turned out to be small pieces of lead, or perhaps a fragment of broken button.

Occasionally, weak signals revealed themselves as something really special. If he ignored an iffy one, he found he couldn't shake the feeling that he might have missed a good find.

During the first two hours, he dug up about twenty targets. His finds pouch became heavier with a few buttons, several brass shotgun cartridges, some scraps of lead, and a few small pieces of unidentifiable bronze. No coins, unfortunately, but the bits of bronze interested him. They had a lovely dark patina that made him feel hopeful. They were old, certainly more than five hundred years, and their presence in the soil could mean that the land had been occupied, perhaps cultivated, for a very long time.

At lunchtime, he stopped for a break. The sun had burned away the mist, revealing the entire perimeter of the field. He turned off the detector, removed the headphones, and sought out a good spot to eat, noticing a nice sunny bank just in front of a hedge.

He sat down and, looking behind him, saw that the hedgerow still bore a few late fruits, with elderflower berries, sloes, and blackberries quite abundant.

Perhaps I should pick the sloes to flavour some vodka for Christmas, he thought.

He made a mental note to bring a plastic bag, should he return, so that he could collect some.

Peter opened his backpack and took out the flask of hot chocolate and some sandwiches. He sat in the sun sipping his hot drink, eating, and reflecting on the pleasure for him of metal-detecting. It took him out into the countryside, to remote areas, which few bothered with or were able to visit. It truly was a privilege to be given permission to search in such a beautiful place. He thought ahead to his return home, looking forward to a nice evening meal and relaxing afterwards in front of the fire. Normally, he had little to show Felicity, not that she was particularly interested, and most of what he dug up usually went into the dustbin. Occasionally, he was lucky and managed to pull out an object that was really old and exciting...well, exciting to him, even if Felicity was generally underwhelmed.

Luck – that was it – you needed some luck. You had to walk over an item to detect it. A few inches either way, you missed it. His grandmother used to say, "Let me rub your palm for gold." Amazingly, once, it had actually worked! The day after he'd seen her, he found his only gold coin to date: a beautiful Celtic stater, more than two thousand years old – every detectorist's dream! Sadly, his dear old grandmother had long since passed away. He'd tried to invoke similar good fortune by asking Felicity to rub his palm, but generally the gods of the field had not been that kind.

Maybe, just maybe, today will be the day, he thought. Although, realistically, he knew that a bag full of junk would be the most likely outcome.

Peter finished his sandwiches and peeled a banana. As he munched, he lay back on one elbow to survey the field. He noticed a slight hump in the land about a hundred yards away. He had read accounts of how hoards were discovered where the finder had concentrated on a noticeable high spot. It seemed as good a place to try as any. After packing away his lunch, he slung his backpack over his shoulders, picked up his detecting kit, and set off to investigate.

The soil did seem darker and softer there. The flint and pieces of chalk were smaller and less coarse too; hopefully, as a result of hundreds of years of ploughing.

His first signal was loud and clear and he could tell that something lay within an inch or two of the surface. He pulled out a pinpoint probe from its belt holster, switched it on, and pushed it gently into the surface of the soil, moving it around in a circular motion. The continuous beeping it produced told him that the object was just under its tip. Then, he took his small archaeologists' trowel and carefully retrieved the metal item. It was a coin; his first of the day!

He recognised it immediately from its size and thickness to be a Georgian farthing, probably from about 1800. Unfortunately, as was so often the case with copper coins, the chemical fertilizers used in modern farming had corroded any detail. It was little more than a flat copper disc. Still, it was a coin. He placed the farthing into a small plastic box kept for coins and interesting finds, and recommenced his search.

Ten minutes later, he heard a familiar soft tone from the headphones. He swept his detector to locate the centre of the target, and then took his shovel and dug out a hole about four inches deep, placing the soil at the edge of the hole. He checked the hole with his detector. The signal had gone, but returned when he swept the earth he had removed. He knelt down and pushed the pinpoint probe through the loose dirt. It beeped, but he couldn't see anything made of metal. Puzzled, Peter scooped up a handful of the soil, and with the probe checked the contents of his palm. The machine gave a beep. The object was his hand! He carefully rubbed off some of the dirt and checked again. It was still there. He opened his palm and slowly moved the probe through the remaining soil. Then, he saw something: a small thin disc of dark-grey metal with some damp earth sticking to it. It was a silver halfpenny, struck by hand rather than machine, and he knew it was at least five hundred years old.

Still kneeling, Peter straightened up and took a deep breath. Whenever he found a really old coin he always asked himself a few questions such as, how long had it been lying there waiting for him? Who was the last person to handle it? He was thrilled and triumphant as he carefully placed the coin into a separate compartment in the plastic box. He'd rinse it off and examine it later to see if any detail would allow him to identify the monarch and therefore determine its actual age.

He took a yellow plastic tent peg from his backpack and marked the spot. Then he picked up his detector and began to search methodically in the immediate vicinity. It was unlikely, but there could be other coins close by, especially if someone had lost a purse full. Years before, he'd found six medieval silver coins in roughly the same place and believed that they had been lost together. No luck this time, though, and after a quarter-hour of meticulous searching, he moved on to another part of the field.

The afternoon followed in much the same pattern as

the morning, with the field producing mainly mundane and uninteresting finds. However, shortly before three o'clock, Peter found himself holding a small Roman bronze coin with some detail still remaining. He was ecstatic! That could take the history of the valley back about two thousand years! Perhaps there was a villa nearby. Peter's imagination went into overdrive. He calmed himself and regained his concentration, hoping he had found a hotspot and the coin was not an isolated loss. Once again, he searched the immediate area carefully, but found nothing more that could be associated with it.

Thinking that he'd soon need to pack up for the day, he decided to head back to the Fiat, now some distance away, detecting as he went. His next decent signal was loud, meaning the object was close to the surface. In shape, he could tell that it had length rather than the roundness of a coin. He was correct. When he recovered it, he saw it was an old spanner. He put it into his finds bag and carried on.

Several pieces of rubbish later, he received another encouraging signal through his headphones. Expecting to find another Georgian copper coin, he was delighted to see that he'd come across another Roman bronze coin. This one was much larger than the first. It was thick, weighty, and quite worn, but the profile head of an emperor was vaguely discernible. It was too big for his plastic box, so that too went into his finds bag.

Back at the car, Peter opened the rear and removed his muddy boots and leggings. The farmer spotted him and, accompanied by his two excited dogs, came over to see how he'd got on.

"Found the treasure then?" He laughed.

"Well not quite, but I have found a couple of nice coins."

"Really?" he said, sounding surprised.

Peter pulled out the small plastic box and opened it up.

The farmer studied the small silver halfpenny. "That is small. Your detector found that? Must be a good one." Then he looked at the small Roman coin. "Ah, I've seen these before. My father had a few of these in a drawer in his study. They used to pick them up sometimes when they were out in the field."

"Really? There might be more then?"

"Well, I'd say yes; you've obviously found another one."

"Would you like to keep them?" Peter asked. He hoped desperately that he'd be allowed to take them home, but consoled himself with the knowledge that there should be more to find, if the farmer did want them.

"No, you can keep them both."

"Thanks," said Peter, delighted with the farmer's response.

He cleared a space on the mat in the boot of his car and tipped out the rest of his finds. He had to push back the nose of one of the dogs. It was sniffing and showing great interest. He felt he ought to show the farmer the large Roman bronze too, and picked it out to show him. "Did they ever find any bronze coins like this one?"

The farmer didn't answer. He was transfixed by the sight of the muddy old spanner among the rubbish. "You find that out there?" he asked, gently lifting it from the mat and turning it lovingly in his hand.

"Yes, do you know what it is?"

"That, my friend, is part of the toolkit from one of my vintage tractors: an Allis-Chalmers, an American model from the 1930s. These spanners are as rare as hens' teeth and virtually impossible to obtain anywhere nowadays. My father lost that back in the fifties, so it's been missing from my old girl's set of tools ever since. I've been deducted points at tractor rallies for that, but not anymore."

Peter was delighted. "It's yours. Would it be OK, then, if I come back another time?"

"No problem, course you can, and you can keep that big bronze coin too."

Great, thought Peter. "Shall I just turn up or would you like me to ring first?"

"Probably best to ring because we'll be shooting from November to the end of January – not every day, mind, but you can't detect when the guns are about. Also, I'll be drilling seed in April if it's dry enough. Then it'll be under crop till the end of July."

"Thanks, that's very kind of you. In the meantime, I'll probably visit the county archives to see what they have regarding Oxenhope. They might have an old tithe map; it would be interesting to see how many dwellings there were, and whereabouts they were located."

"Yes, that would be interesting."

"I'll say cheerio, then, and look forward to next time."

"Yeah, cheerio, and well done for finding this," the farmer said, looking happily at the spanner.

They shook hands and Peter got into his car. He waved goodbye as he drove off, and was escorted by two madly barking dogs until he'd passed through the brick piers at the entrance. Just before he reached the trees and the climb up and out of the valley, he paused to take in the scene. The front of the farmhouse had now caught the last of the late afternoon sunshine. It was another world down there in the hidden valley. It had revealed some of its secrets, and Peter wondered if maybe next time it would reveal more.

CHAPTER 4

LONDON, 1851

Moses lay awake, the other boys around him sleeping. It was a dark February morning, with daylight possibly still an hour away. He reflected on his circumstances and good fortune. He was no longer sheltering under an archway, shivering because of winter cold and hunger. He now lay on a clean, dry board with a simple rug to cover him, within what seemed, to him, to be a large room, with space to accommodate about ten boys. The fire from a central stove provided some much needed warmth. He'd food in his belly from last night too; with everyone given a six-ounce loaf. What luxury it felt to be inside a building that wasn't a prison.

A week before, everything had been quite different. Climbing the stairs from the foreshore, his basket of scavenged coal scarcely half-full, his stomach empty, his bare feet cold and wet, his clothes filthy and torn, he had encountered an elderly gentleman who said he was from the London City Mission and wanted to help him.

Naturally wary of strangers, Moses had almost avoided the man, but was halted by something kindly in his manner and more so by his offer to take him to a bakery in order to get something fresh and warm to eat.

"But what shall I do with my gleanin's, sir?" he'd asked.

"How much do you expect to receive for them?" asked the

gentleman, regarding the half-starved destitute wretch before him.

"At least tuppence, sir."

The gentleman considered the matter for a moment. "Well, I'll give you tuppence for them and a halfpenny for the basket. What do you say? Would that be enough?"

Moses nodded. He held out his hand and pocketed the coins he was offered.

"Set it down and leave it here. Come with me."

Inwardly, Moses was thrilled. He knew he'd have been lucky to even manage a single penny for his coal, and the basket was worthless: similar ones were easy to find and replace.

They set off up Fish Street Hill, the gentleman leading the way. It was mid-morning and plenty of people were about. Moses knew the area well and was not unduly concerned. He'd money in his pocket and the promise of food was enough to make him content to follow along for the time being.

"What age are you?" asked the gentleman.

"Thirteen, sir."

"Where do you sleep?"

"Anywhere I can, sir. Sometimes on the barges or under an arch."

"Can you read or write?"

"No, sir."

"What about counting? Can you count up?"

"A bit, sir."

"And do you go to church or sing in the choir?"

"No, sir, never."

The gentleman made no comment, but seemed satisfied with the boy's answers. They turned right and entered the first bakery they encountered. Moses hung back, trying to remain out of sight from the baker's wife behind the counter.

"Yes, sir?" she asked.

When the gentleman looked down to ask Moses what he would like, Moses realised that the baker's wife had also noticed him.

"Why if it ain't that little tea leaf what was in 'ere last week makin' off with two of my pies!"

Gathering her skirt, she started to make her way around the counter, intent on catching Moses, but he was too quick. Anticipating trouble, he shot towards the door but was blocked by a large male customer who was entering.

"Stop 'im! He's a thief!" shrieked the baker's wife.

The man grabbed Moses by the ear and twisted it hard causing him to cry out in pain. He was firmly held and had no way to escape.

The elderly gentleman looked somewhat alarmed and unnerved by the commotion. "I'm sorry, madam, I had no idea," he managed to say. "Thief, you say...Has he stolen from you?"

"Bleedin' right he has," she shouted, her finger in Moses' face. "The brass neck of him! How he dares to show 'imself in here. He owes me threepence!"

The gentleman looked hard at Moses for a moment. "All right, madam," he said calmly. "I'll pay for the pies," then addressing the other man, "Would you let go of him, please, sir."

The male customer released Moses, who stood sullenly rubbing his ear.

The baker's wife returned to her side of the counter, straightening her apron and struggling to assume her former manner. "Now, what was it you wanted, sir?" she tried to ask calmly.

"I'll have a large fresh loaf, please, and take what you need for the pies," he replied, handing her a shilling.

"Here you are," she said, "it's still warm...You watch out for 'im, though," she added as she handed back some change. "He'll as likely pick your pocket, given 'alf a chance."

"Oh, yes, well, thank you; thank you for the advice." With that, the gentleman, accompanied by Moses, left the shop.

"She had it in for me," Moses explained as they walked towards the river. "I never pinched nothin', only what was old and goin' stale."

"Well, let's not dwell on it. Come on, there's a bench over there."

Once they were seated, the gentleman offered the loaf to Moses who tore off half and greedily began to eat. He was famished and the warm fresh bread tasted magnificent. He licked his lips with pleasure.

"What do your parents say to you scavenging in the mud?"

"Ain't got none...both dead," Moses managed to say between mouthfuls.

"What happened to them?"

"My mother got fever and my dad drowned in a sewer. He were a tosher, one of the best he were, but he got caught by a flood."

"So what's your name?" the gentleman asked, uninterested in further details of Moses' parents.

"Moses Jupp, sir."

"Well, young Moses, have you heard about the Ragged School in Field Lane?"

"I might have heard talk of it, but it weren't no concern of mine."

"Well, I'd like to make it your concern, because I think you could do well there. You seem like a bright boy to me and I think you would benefit from some schooling."

"I'm not sure about that, sir. I needs to be down there on the shore." He pointed towards the river.

"Not if you were learning how to read and write. I've room in my house to accommodate seven boys overnight, until we finish converting the old smithy under the school into a dormitory. Then we'll be able to take a good deal more. You'd be given shoes, clothes, a warm dry place to sleep, and some regular food. There'd be no more sleeping on barges. How do you like the sound of that?"

"But why do you want to help me? Why would anyone teach me and feed me, sir?"

"Because some of us who have been blessed with sufficient means are worried about boys and girls like you. We don't want you to get into trouble with the law and end up in a prison, or a reformatory. We'd like you to learn to read, and know about the Bible and to love God. We want to help you become productive and not have you fall into a life of begging and crime."

33

"Would there really be somewhere dry to sleep, and food to eat?"

"Yes there would, I promise you," replied the elderly gentleman.

"What's your name, sir?"

"My name is Mr Chambers and I am a member of the committee which runs the ragged school. I have met several young boys like you and taken them to the school where, I'm pleased to say, they've been much happier than before and benefitted greatly from some education. What do you think? Would you like to come with me now and enrol?"

"Enrol, sir?" Moses thought he'd got the gist of most of what Mr Chambers had been telling him, but he was unfamiliar with a word like 'enrol'.

"It means joining the other boys and girls at the school."

Moses thought about the proposal. He didn't want to appear too eager, but deep down he couldn't believe his luck. Food, shelter, and clothing were his priorities, his necessities. He thought back to his time in prison. The whipping had been painful, but he'd been fed and clothed while he was there. Here was someone offering to provide what he needed most, so why not 'enrol'?

"Would I be able to leave if I didn't like it?"

"Of course, but hopefully you'll find it agreeable and want to stay."

"In that case, Mr Chambers, sir, I'd like to enrol."

That had been a week ago, and Moses was brought back to the present by the sound of loud banging on the bedroom door. It was Carruthers, Mr Chamber's valet; a big burly man who demanded obedience. He was quick to cuff any pupil who dared to defy him.

"Come on, come on, you lazy lot, up you get! Come on, it's seven o'clock."

Moses stood and stretched. Around him, boys groaned at being disturbed from their slumber. He was used to getting up early. His previous life had been ruled by the tide, for the best pickings were made by those who were on the foreshore as the tide receded.

He washed his face and couldn't resist running his hand over the back of his head. His hair was so short and still felt strange. On his arrival, Carruthers had insisted that he have his head shaved, such was his filthy state. He dressed and put on his boots. They were the first boots he'd ever owned and he'd still not grown accustomed to the pleasure of wearing them. Neither the boots nor the clothes were new, but they were clean and without holes or tears.

The routine was so different to his former life. He still couldn't believe that he, along with the other boys, was given breakfast before they walked the short distance to Field Lane.

Moses had noticed that the candles burning in the wall-mounted sconces did little to improve the light whenever they entered the schoolroom to find a place. Girls had separate lessons in another part. The boys, numbering about a hundred, had to sit squeezed tightly together on long wooden benches. It was overcrowded, but at least it was warm with so many bodies in close proximity.

Unfortunately, it was not so pleasant for Mr Pilbeam, the schoolmaster, when he arrived. "Open some windows, for goodness' sake," he would say. "The air in here is foul and stifling!"

Before lessons started, the boys sang a hymn and listened to a reading from the Bible. Then writing slates were distributed and teaching began. Some boys found it hard to concentrate or pay attention. Those who misbehaved received a thrashing with the cane across their backsides. Moses, however, was keen to learn, anxious to avoid the embarrassment of having to wear the dunce's cap, but even his mind drifted occasionally.

"Moses, boy! Are you listening? Not good enough for you here? Prefer not to have any education and end up in jail or a prison hulk with your only schoolmaster being the prison chaplain?"

"No, sir."

"Well pay attention!"

"Yes, sir. Sorry, sir."

Winter gave way to spring. Having stood up to the bullies and ignored those intent on disruption, and having joined a group of boys who wanted to learn and were blessed with the intelligence to do so, Moses made good progress at Field Lane.

One afternoon in early April, just before the lessons were due to end, Mr Pilbeam read out a list of ten names, asking them to stay behind at the end of lessons. His announcement caused a great deal of verbal speculation: some jocular and some rather unpleasant and rude. The master had to wave his cane threateningly before order was restored. After the final bell, the boys on the list remained, wondering what it was they'd done. The answer came shortly from the school superintendent, who had entered the room, accompanied by an older stranger. He told the boys to sit down before stepping forward to address them.

"Have any of you heard about Prince Albert's involvement in organising a grand exhibition here in the metropolis, to show to the nation and the world the magnificence of our engineering skills and achievements?"

Several of the older boys nodded. One of them asked, "Isn't that going to be in the giant glass palace they're constructing in Hyde Park?"

"Precisely!" the superintendent exclaimed. "Full marks to you boy, absolutely correct! This will be no ordinary exhibition. No, this is going to draw people from all over the nation and from all over the globe. The universe will have never seen the like. This will go down in history."

The boys looked impressed.

"You're probably wondering why I'm telling you this," continued the superintendent, "and why should it concern you? Well, let me enlighten you. When the exhibition opens next month, London will be at the heart of a great influx of visitors, thousands upon thousands of them. Many of them will be wealthy individuals who pride themselves on their smart appearance.

"Now, I'd like to introduce Alderman MacGregor here, one of our trustees. He has come up with a marvellous suggestion

36

that will give you boys the chance to be part of an enterprise we intend to establish. We are going to form a Shoeblack Brigade and you boys have been selected to become shoeblacks. You are all thirteen, and over, so are due to leave the school later this year."

The boys turned to each other, looking a little mystified.

Alderman MacGregor observed their expressions and smiled. He took his turn to speak.

"You will be given uniforms and the equipment to be able to perform a valuable and important function, namely a shoe-cleaning service. Pitches will be established and allocated by the police at a number of metropolitan thoroughfares, where high numbers of potential customers are anticipated. The tariff will be decided beforehand and part of the takings will be kept for you by the school in your own name."

The superintendent interjected. "You have been chosen because we believe you have the discipline to work hard at the task we are going to equip you to undertake. Mr Pilbeam here," he said, indicating the schoolmaster, "tells me that you have all achieved sufficient competency in counting to be able to take money and give change correctly. You will be expected to maintain a smart appearance, keep your uniform clean, and be civil and polite to the customers. As we speak, wooden blacking boxes-cum-footstands are being constructed. These will be used for storing your materials, and for the customers to rest their feet while you shine their shoes. Any questions?"

"Will we really be able to earn some money for ourselves?" asked Billy Nunn.

"Yes, indeed," replied the superintendent. "The Shoeblack Brigade, for that is what we are calling it, will have its own accounts. A bank will be established by the committee. It will be administered by someone appointed to ensure that each of you will receive, into your own individual account, a sum directly related to the extent of your own endeavour, less a deduction for the cost of providing you with your lodging, uniform, and cleaning equipment. You'll be the first recruits but we hope the brigade will number about seventy shoeblacks when fully up to strength."

"Has this been tried before to see if there are enough customers?" asked Moses.

Alderman MacGregor replied. "Yes, in Paris, two years ago, and it was very successful."

Everyone's attention was suddenly diverted to the door of the classroom. Someone was knocking loudly.

The superintendent looked at the schoolmaster. "Mr Pilbeam, that should be Darius Mills. Could you let him in, please?"

"Certainly, superintendent."

The schoolmaster opened the door and allowed the young man to enter. He was dressed in a red jersey, over which he wore a black apron, and he carried a large wooden box.

"Welcome, Darius. Come in and set up over here please." The superintendent pointed to a spot and turned back to the boys. "Darius is going to give you a demonstration on how to clean and shine a customer's shoes."

Darius set the box down on the floor. "Boys, as you will observe, the box has a storage compartment containing polish, cloths, and brushes, and a small compartment for takings. It also acts as a footstand. Mr Pilbeam, would you care to place your foot on the box?"

The schoolmaster did so, and Darius set to work. The superintendent proudly explained that Darius was a former pickpocket, and now a fine example to all at Field Lane of a reformed pupil. The boys looked on eagerly and were impressed by Darius's efforts.

One of the more business-minded boys decided to risk asking a pertinent question. "How much will we charge each customer?"

"That is to be decided," answered Alderman MacGregor, "but we anticipate a standard charge of one penny per customer."

One penny, thought Moses, *just for some easy work like that.*

"What about our schoolin', sir?" asked Sydney Ellwood, a boy Moses knew from mudlarking.

"You'll be back here for night school on three nights a week," replied Mr Pilbeam firmly.

Alderman MacGregor explained more details. "If you wish to join the brigade, you'll be given training next week. Once completed, you will be issued with a red jacket, red jersey, a black apron, and black corduroy trousers. You will each be assigned a number and this will be embroidered onto your jacket collar, as well as on a sleeve. The police are looking into the allocation of pitches, but you can expect to be working in areas like The Strand, Piccadilly, Holborn, and the Royal Parks. This is envisaged as a summer activity to begin with. You will be housed in a new hostel near Leicester Square. We have appointed Inspector Gilchrist to keep an eye on you when you start your work as shoeblacks. Raise your hand if you would like to join the brigade."

All ten hands shot up.

"Very well, we'll make the arrangements. You'll need to be measured for your uniforms. You can expect to move into your new hostel in the next few days."

With that, the superintendent and the alderman left the room, followed by Darius Mills. The boys turned to each other, chatting excitedly about what they'd just learned.

"Well done, boys," smiled Mr Pilbeam as he began to herd them out of the room. "What a splendid opportunity for you all. I just hope you make the most of it and don't fall back into the deprivation you used to know."

CHAPTER 5

As soon as Peter got home, he couldn't wait to show Felicity the medieval silver coin and the Roman bronzes he'd found.

"How did you get on today?" she asked.

"I found a few coins that I need to clean up. They're a bit muddy."

"I hope you're not going to make a mess in the kitchen sink."

"No, don't worry; I'll use the one in the utility room."

Peter went to the car and unloaded his detecting gear. He tipped out the contents of his finds bag and picked out the coins and the pieces of patinated bronze for keeping before putting the remaining rubbish in the dustbin. He took the coins back inside and ran them under the tap. The mud soon washed off.

As expected, the Georgian copper was flat and corroded, but the small Roman coin retained enough detail to make identification possible, although it would need some research. The large bronze – a sestertius – was another matter. He was surprised to see that it had a hole near the edge, suggesting that someone had worn it. The hole was oval and had achieved that shape through wear. Peter imagined that a leather thong may once have suspended it around the neck. The obverse had the barely discernible silhouette of a Roman emperor, but it was the reverse which really excited him. Someone had used a hammer and punch to make a series of dots which crudely spelt the name, *M A JUPP*.

He dried the coins and took them into the living room to show Felicity.

She turned each of them over. "Very nice…looks like you've had a good day. You'll have to give John Carter a ring and thank him for asking the farmer."

"Yes, of course I will, but have a look at this," he said, picking out the sestertius. "It's a Roman coin, which at some time in its life has been worn as a necklace. It also has what I assume to be an owner's name punched on it."

Felicity examined it closely. "Do you think you might be able to research this name?"

"Well, it is unusual so it might be possible. I've never heard of anyone called Jupp before. I'll have a look in a minute; see if I can get a match."

"Did the farmer say you could go again?"

"Yes he did. He was absolutely thrilled with an old spanner I dug up on the way back to the car."

"Really?"

"Apparently, it was part of the toolkit from one of his vintage tractors. He wasn't interested in the coins, which is great because hopefully I can find some more."

Felicity handed the coins back to Peter. He took them upstairs to his study and switched on his computer. He considered where best to start. The Roman sestertius was heavily patinated, even the dots, so it had probably been lying in the field for at least a hundred years. The owner would have been long dead, so he decided that a search of the death records might be worth a try.

He logged on to his favourite genealogical website and searched the death indices. He chose to concentrate on the period from 1840 to 1890; when the farmer had said that Oxenhope Farm was still inhabited. There was little point in searching later, and any earlier tended to be more difficult. He split the period into decades. His suspicion that Jupp was quite a rare surname proved correct. His first few attempts produced no likely matches, apart from a Martha Jupp from Hungerford. That wasn't too far away, but Peter felt it more likely that the wearer of the bronze coin was male. It was hardly a delicate piece of feminine jewellery.

During the decade covering the 1870s, he found only four

deaths of males with the surname Jupp and first name beginning 'M'. When he looked at the district in which each of those deaths occurred, he knew straight away that one of them was his man. The event took place in the second quarter of 1871 and was registered in Marlborough, Wiltshire, England; the correct registration district for Oxenhope. The name of the deceased turned out to be Moses Arman Jupp. He was thirty-three years old.

Peter sat back from his computer with a sigh of satisfaction. He was certain that the owner of the Roman coin lying next to his keyboard was Moses Jupp. It felt a little spooky as he picked it up and held it in his hand, because he realised that it was the first time he'd ever recovered an old object for which he'd managed to identify a previous owner.

Two minutes later, he'd ordered a copy of Moses Jupp's death certificate. He preferred to have the certificates mailed to him rather than to download a PDF file, so he would have to wait a couple of days longer before it came in the post. He pondered what more he would learn when it arrived.

CHAPTER 6

Moses' training at the new hostel in Leicester Square was short and simple. A boot seller had been co-opted to assist the organising committee. He showed the boys exactly how to remove the mud and the horse manure they were likely to encounter on customers' shoes. He explained the finer points of applying the blacking, before brushing and buffing to produce a polished shine.

"We should have the blacking boxes tomorrow, along with your new uniforms. Until then, I suggest you share the two boxes we have and take turns."

The boys set about practising and soon had the hang of it. It wasn't difficult. One or two of them had encountered teasing and unkind remarks from other boys who'd heard they'd been selected for the brigade. Most of it was jealousy, but it was also true to say that some of those not chosen regarded the activity as being too belittling for someone of intelligence.

However, the thought of their potential earnings soon dispelled any doubts the brigade members may have had. As promised, the uniforms and the blacking boxes were duly delivered the following morning. The cost of the uniforms was covered by several philanthropic ladies who were supporting the committee's efforts.

A novelty for the brigade was that the uniform included a cap. Excitedly, and with much joshing and ribbing, the boys got changed into their livery. They looked very smart indeed. They were also provided with waterproof capes.

Later on in the afternoon, Alderman MacGregor called the boys together to meet two police officers.

"This is Police Inspector Sutton and Sergeant Thurgut. They will explain how pitches have been identified and how they will be allocated." He stepped to one side and Inspector Sutton took over.

Moses felt sick. Sergeant Thurgut was the policeman who'd arrested him for stealing coal two years before. He was an ordinary constable then. Moses cast a quick glance at him, not wishing to make eye contact. The man looked a little older than he remembered, but there was no mistaking him: six feet tall, broadly built, full head of dark hair, with a sharp protruding chin and a stern expression.

Moses hoped that his own clean appearance and smart uniform would make him unrecognisable. He struggled to keep his attention on what the inspector was saying.

"Looking at our maps, we have chosen ten locations where you will be permitted to set up your blacking box. Each pitch is on a major thoroughfare, with plenty of passing trade. You must stay in your allocated station and must not move or operate elsewhere without our express permission. Do you understand me?"

All the boys mumbled their agreement, nodding their heads at the same time.

Moses risked raising his eyes to look directly at the police sergeant. Their eyes met and a slight change in the officer's jawline confirmed to Moses that he had been recognised. He recalled the rough handling he'd received from the constable when he had been taken into custody.

"We intend to change your pitch to a new location every week, so that all of you will get a fair chance to work the most lucrative spots," the inspector continued. "You will charge each customer as per the tariff that Alderman MacGregor and I have agreed. This will be shown to each customer and approved before you start. There will be no deviation from it. You will return here at six o'clock each evening and you will deposit all of your takings to Alderman MacGregor's clerk. A third of what you take will be kept to cover your keep, a third will be deposited into an individual savings account for you, and a third will be given back to you.

"The brigade will be known as the Central Brigade. You will be officially recognised as legitimate shoeblacks. If you see any independent shoeblacks, please report the matter to a policeman as we intend to discourage them. We have numbered the pitches from one to ten to start, but there will be more when we are fully up to strength. Today, we will allocate them on a strict alphabetical basis. The committee has given me your names."

He handed a list to Sergeant Thurgut, who cleared his throat before speaking. "Aylott, you come first alphabetically so for the first week you will take pitch number one on the corner of Regent Street and Piccadilly." He continued through the list. "Jupp, you will take pitch four on the corner of Strand and Bedford Street."

Moses barely took in his instructions, so concerned was he at the thought of Sergeant Thurgut being involved.

Having reached the last name and allocated all of the pitches, Thurgut enquired if anyone was uncertain as to where they would be stationed. Everyone seemed happy and so he stepped back to allow Alderman MacGregor to address the brigade once more.

"Thank you Inspector Sutton and Sergeant Thurgut for your assistance. I must say, boys, that you all look extremely neat and colourful in your uniforms. Let's hope that the populace overcome their modesty and take to the fashion that is commonplace abroad of having their shoes cleaned in public. The Great Exhibition is due to open next week. We expect a large number of visitors. That will give you a little time to hone your skills. I want you to give each customer an exemplary service. You must at all times be civil, and I expect discipline in the way you behave. You must, of course, maintain your clean appearance and uniform.

"Each evening, you will return here with your takings, which my clerk, Mr Hunt, will record in his ledger. If you need further supplies of cleaning requisites, you will ask him to issue them. You must use only those provided by the brigade. He will keep a note of what has been given out and this will be matched against the money you collect. If we suspect any shortfall or misuse then you will be dismissed immediately.

"While you are here at Leicester Square, you will conduct yourselves as you would at Field Lane. Disobedience of any kind will be dealt with in the first instance by Mr Forbes, your new hostel superintendent. He has full authority to use corporal punishment. Those guilty of extreme bad behaviour will have their case considered by the brigade's committee and may be expelled from the brigade and Field Lane. Anyone so expelled will have their savings forfeited. You will be out of here double-quick and on your own. Do I make myself clear?"

There was a murmur of agreement from the new team of shoeblacks.

"I hope you will help to make this scheme a success. You need to show that you have the right attitude and can work hard. The more money you bring in, the more will be saved in your savings account. We hope it will give you boys the chance to improve your future opportunities. That's all I am going to say for now. You will start tomorrow morning and be in your allotted position by eight o'clock. The weather is set fair. Good luck to you all."

The next day, Moses arrived at his pitch in good time. As he looked about him, he was pleased to see plenty of people, mainly men at that time of the morning, hurrying past about their business. Opposite, there were some shops and a coffee house.

Surely I'll get a few customers, he thought.

He set his blacking box down on the pavement and took out the card displaying the tariff. He propped it up in a prominent place. Nothing much happened for a while. One or two men glanced at him as they strode purposefully past. Most people seemed to have other matters on their minds. A hackney coach drew up, and an elderly lady descended. She walked in Moses' direction and was passing by when his red jacket caught her attention.

"Young man, what is that uniform you are wearing?"

"I'm a Central Brigade shoeblack, madam," he replied. "Would you like your shoes cleaned?"

"Good gracious, no!" she exclaimed. "How vulgar…In the street…Whatever next!" She marched away muttering to herself.

Moses began to feel a little anxious, wondering if Alderman MacGregor's idea of shoeblacks would be a failure. Presently, he noticed a well-dressed man, about twenty yards away, regarding him with interest. The man approached. "Are you a member of this new shoeblack brigade I've heard about?"

"Yes, sir."

"How much?"

Moses pointed to the price on the card. "One penny, sir."

"Show me what you can do."

The man raised his foot and placed his boot on top of the box.

He was a tall, portly man and Moses was impressed by the size of his footwear. Reaching into the main compartment, he removed a small scraper and his polishing materials. First, he removed the mire around the heel before applying a generous coat of blacking. Then he buffed off the excess with a brush, finishing with a soft cloth. The result was a highly polished boot.

The man looked down and grunted with satisfaction. He removed his clean boot and placed his other on the box. Moses repeated the process.

"That'll be one penny, please, sir."

The gentleman felt in his pocket and produced the coin. "There we are, young man."

Moses touched his cap. "Thank you, sir. Good day to you, sir." He felt elated at having his first customer. It had been so quick and so easy to earn a penny!

By the end of the morning, he knew that Alderman MacGregor had been right. He'd earned seven pence. Five more customers and he'd have a shilling, which would give him four pence to spend and four pence in his savings account. He'd soon have more money than he could ever have dreamed of.

He waited patiently, hoping soon to have another customer. He couldn't help but think of the future. Some of the boys reckoned they were going to save enough for a sea passage to New York. He imagined what he might do. He thought he might buy a horse, if he could make enough. He'd need to learn how to ride though. He'd never been further than ten miles from London Bridge. He'd heard there were other great cities to see, like Manchester and Bristol. Maybe he could make his fortune in places like that, but by doing what, he'd no idea.

During the afternoon, the sun came out and the mud under the pedestrians' feet started to dry. Eight more customers were confident that the weather conditions would make it worthwhile having their shoes cleaned. Once or twice, while he waited, Moses couldn't resist a sneak peek into the box's little cash compartment, marvelling at the silver threepence he'd accepted and given change for. Threepence was equivalent in value to the cost of a night in a lodging house, something that Moses could never afford when he was mudlarking.

All was going well and he felt himself growing in confidence, until he spotted Sergeant Thurgut looking intently at him from across the street. His confidence turned quickly to anxiety and dread as he watched the policeman leave the pavement opposite and stride purposefully towards him, the passing traffic halting respectfully to allow him to cross. Moses was so distracted that he almost missed a customer asking to have his shoes cleaned. He turned back to the job in hand, trying hard to give it his full attention. The man was quite elderly and a little frail. He made polite conversation, to which the young shoeblack did his best to maintain, but throughout the exchanges Moses was aware of the sergeant's nearby presence.

As soon as the customer had paid and left, Sergeant Thurgut came up to Moses, and bending down, hissed into his ear. "Plenty of customers then, let me see your takings."

The sergeant's breath smelt horribly of stale tobacco.

To Moses, his height and build made him seem enormous. Reluctantly, he gathered up the coins in his box and showed them to him.

"My, haven't you been a busy little blighter? Not bad for your first day. I think I deserve a little recompense from you, seeing as you nearly drowned me."

Thurgut turned to look around. No other persons were particularly close. He put his large right boot on the box. "Better give my boots a quick shine too," and then, in a low voice so as not to be overheard, "When you've finished, I'm going to pretend to pass you a coin and you're going to give me that threepence as change. Do you understand?"

Moses gulped with fear and disappointment. He understood all too well.

CHAPTER 7

Five days after ordering Moses Jupp's death certificate, Peter was on his computer tracking his share investments when Felicity shouted from downstairs.

"There's something for you in the post. It's just come."

"What is it?" he shouted back.

"You'll have to come down and see!"

Peter left his computer and rushed downstairs, knowing that Felicity was teasing. Of course, his certificate must have arrived. Sure enough, there it lay on the table next to the phone, the familiar envelope bearing the address of the General Register Office on the reverse.

He quickly opened it and unfolded the certificate. Expecting to see some form of illness as the cause of death, he was surprised to see that Moses Arman Jupp had died as the result of an accident, but what an unusual and horrible accident it was.

The death certificate had been issued by the coroner for North Wiltshire on 26 May, 1871, following an inquest held three days after the death had occurred in Oak Meadow Field, Oxenhope. Moses Jupp's occupation was shown as 'fogger' – *whatever that is*, Peter wondered. He read the cause of death again, and then went into the kitchen to find Felicity.

"Listen to this," he said. "Cause of Death…Injuries to the thighs, legs, arms, and neck accidentally received from the knives of a mowing machine, drawn by a pair of runaway horses, the leader of which, the said Moses Jupp, had been holding."

Felicity pulled a face. "That sounds pretty gruesome."

"Exactly...What a dreadful way to go, eh?" agreed Peter. "That might account for me finding a Roman coin with his name in the middle of a field."

"How do you work that out?"

"Well, what if the knives of the machine cut the thong, chain, or whatever it was that he wore to suspend it, and it got flung to the ground? It says here that he had injuries to his neck. It's possible. Don't forget, this occurred at the end of May, probably haymaking time, so it could have been hot and he might have been shirtless. There's another thing, too..." he added, with a grim expression. "The accident might have happened in that part of the field where I found the coin, which isn't a very nice thought."

"Yes, I see what you mean. Poor chap. Was he married? Did he leave a widow?"

"I don't know just from this because it's a coroner's death certificate. Usually, you'd have the name and address of the informant; normally, a spouse or close relative. In this case the coroner is the informant. There might be a newspaper report somewhere, with a few more details. Perhaps I could even find an inquest report. Do you want to use the computer for the next hour or so?"

"No, you carry on. I've got some things to do later, but I can use my laptop."

"OK, I'll go back upstairs and have a look."

CHAPTER 8

As the weeks passed, life at the hostel was generally good and Moses made some friends. Not all were orphans; some had one parent. Others came from large families with many siblings whose parents struggled to feed and clothe them.

In the evenings, the shoeblacks exchanged tales of unusual or amusing customers they'd encountered. Billy Nunn showed them several foreign coins he'd been deceived into accepting from overseas visitors. Moses made them laugh when he described the old soldier with one leg who'd insisted on paying half price!

The benefit of being a shoeblack was that they could earn money and save, and continue with their education. Monday, Wednesday, and Thursday evenings were spent at Field Lane. Moses was making excellent progress with his reading. Mr Pilbeam had loaned him a book about Horatio Nelson and the Battle of Trafalgar. It was a little advanced for him at first, but he managed to make steady improvement and discovered that history really interested him.

Sergeant Thurgut found time to visit him quite regularly. Moses decided to thwart him by hiding some of his takings in his boot. The policeman took only a proportion of what was in the blacking box; no doubt hoping that enough remained to keep Mr Hunt, the ledger clerk, happy. In fact, Mr Hunt had already noticed that the sums given to him by Moses, to be recorded in the accounts, were less than those of most of the other Central Brigade members.

There was only one member who was bringing in less than Moses and that was Henry Riddiford. Mr Hunt was certain his poor performance was mainly down to his timidity, not helped by being the hapless victim of a gang of boys who'd mocked his uniform and called him a 'cardinal'. They spat and threw flour at him, spoiling his smart appearance. He spent too much time being vigilant, fearing the gang's return, rather than looking cheerful and assured as a means to attract customers. Mr Hunt was prepared to allow him time to improve and become more confident, for he brought in just enough to cover his keep. Looking back at the small number of packets of blacking paste and dusters issued to him, the clerk could see that his problem was a lack of customers.

Moses Jupp, however, was a different matter. Mr Hunt compared the cash returned by Moses against that returned by the other shoeblacks from the same pitch during the preceding weeks. He'd had more packets of blacking issued to him than any of the other boys and yet his revenue was below theirs. Something was not right. He asked Central Brigade's Inspector Gilchrist to keep an eye on him.

Moses realised that the amount of money he took back to the hostel each evening was consistently less than most of the other boys, who were always comparing and boasting about who could earn the most. Thurgut now took more money, and despite Moses hiding cash in his boot, his daily returns were still below par. He also knew that Mr Hunt had a record of how much blacking paste he'd been given. The only solution, apart from reporting Thurgut, and he knew no one would believe him, was to buy extra blacking himself and make what he had go further.

He overheard two of the shoeblacks whispering something about making blacking with sugar-candy and soot. They were ingredients which were easy and cheap to obtain, but he had no means of processing them, nor anywhere to do it, because evenings were spent at either Field Lane or in the hostel. So, he set himself the objective of cleaning as many boots as he could in a day, but using the blacking as sparingly as possible. Even with Thurgut taking a cut of the earnings, Moses hoped that he'd still be able to keep the ledger clerk happy. It was a tall order, yet during the first week of July, despite the policeman fleecing him of nearly ten shillings, he'd matched the performance of the boy who had preceded him at the same location.

Moses was unaware that Inspector Gilchrist was monitoring him; at times using a spy-glass to observe him. Mr Hunt had suggested to the inspector that perhaps Moses applied blacking too liberally and that explained the shortfall in his revenue. The inspector was soon able to confirm from observation that, if anything, Moses tended to be rather economical with its application.

One morning, during the second week of July, Inspector Gilchrist discreetly followed Moses from the hostel to his allocated pitch for that week in Regents Park. He always wore plain clothes on observation duties. On the way, he was interested to see Moses enter a bootmaker's shop. He waited out of sight and saw Moses leave the shop with two packets of blacking paste, which he slipped into his trouser pocket.

"Gotcha!" he said gleefully to himself. "You'll be doing extra customers off the books, I'll be bound!"

The inspector decided to watch a little more, again using his spy-glass, before he confronted Moses. He passed the morning counting the number of customers. Just before midday, he discerned a brief furtive movement whereby Moses looked around to see if anyone nearby was watching. He then slipped something from the blacking box into his left boot. The inspector decided to act upon what he'd just witnessed and made his way quickly over to where Moses was stationed.

"Right Jupp, let's have a look at your takings, shall we? Come on, boy, let's have a look!"

"Hello, sir, course you can, sir."

Moses tried to remain calm and as normal as possible. He handed the inspector one shilling and tuppence, the equivalent of fourteen customers paying a penny each.

Inspector Gilchrist checked the takings. "Is that all?" he asked accusingly.

"Yes, sir."

Instantly, he grabbed Moses by the upper arm, almost lifting him in the process.

"You little thief! I've been watching you all morning. Saw you buy some extra blacking too, which you know is against the rules, and I counted twenty customers. That cash is sixpence short."

Moses was so shocked he was almost dumbstruck. He couldn't think of anything to say that sounded believable. "I ain't stole nothin', sir. Honest, I ain't!"

"I saw you put something in your left boot. Remove it at once and show me what you've hidden there!"

Moses put his boot on the blacking box and tried to shake his arm free. "I need both hands to untie the laces."

The inspector released his clamp-like hold, and Moses bent to remove his boot. An instant was all he needed. Quick as a flash, he ducked and then sidestepped the inspector before sprinting away across the park.

"Stop him! Stop him!" Inspector Gilchrist shouted.

Two police constables heard the commotion and turned to see Moses running towards them.

In his panic, Moses hadn't noticed them, not until it was too late. One of the constables was especially young and athletic. He had no problem in intercepting and tackling the runaway shoeblack. Down they both went; with such force that Moses' cap flew from his head and rolled on the grass.

Moses was badly winded and he struggled to inhale. By the time he found he could breathe again he'd been fitted with handcuffs.

The inspector joined the constables and all three stood over Moses.

"What seems to be the trouble, sir?" asked the older constable.

"I'm Inspector Gilchrist of the Central Shoeblack Brigade on plain clothes observation duty. I suspect this boy of theft. I have just checked his takings and found them to be sixpence short. I asked him to show me what he'd secreted in his left boot, at which point he tried to escape and evade me."

"Is that so? Well he can show us all now, can't he? Come on young man, off with your boot."

Moses had no choice but to obey. He undid his laces and pulled it off. He handed it to Inspector Gilchrist who looked inside and then turned it upside down. Nothing dropped out.

"It must be in his sock then," remarked the inspector. He looked at Moses again. "Remove your sock."

Moses did so.

"Here, hand it to me!" The inspector took hold of the sock and crumpled it. "Ah," he said with satisfaction. He turned it inside out and a sixpence fell to the ground.

Tears formed in Moses' eyes. He wanted to explain the real reason why he'd put some of his takings aside, but he knew it would be pointless. He knew he was going to be punished. At the very least, he'd be dismissed as a shoeblack. He thought fleetingly of his savings account, which he estimated held about three pounds – a fortune to him.

The inspector provided details that the older constable noted in his book, and then Moses, feeling even more miserable, was led away and taken into custody at Marylebone Police Station.

The holding cell was filthy and crowded. An older boy pinched Moses' cap, taunting him while passing it to other boys. Inevitably, a fight broke out, which resulted in a burly police official entering the cell to separate those involved.

The following morning, a bag containing Moses' old clothes was delivered from the brigade hostel to the police station. He was told to change into them and to put his uniform in the bag. It was taken from him. His short spell as an official shoeblack was over.

Later that day, he appeared before a magistrate. Inspector Gilchrist was the only witness. The evidence against Moses was damning: the inspector explained that the Brigade Committee had met the previous evening and had expelled him.

"Well? Do you have anything to say for yourself?" asked the magistrate.

"No, sir," replied Moses.

"I see. It seems to me, young man, that you had the opportunity to make something of yourself. You were selected to be an official shoeblack and yet you have repaid the kindness and generosity of the trustees of your brigade by stealing cash, which should have been handed in. You've done no good to the reputation of the brigade or to yourself. I think what you need is a spell on the treadmill at Coldbath Prison. That should make you see the error of your ways. I sentence you to a month's hard labour!"

♦

Ultimately, Moses went back to the life he knew: scavenging from the foreshore. He managed to find lodgings in a court off Shepherd Street, where he shared one small room with Ned, a rat-catcher; Ned's faithful little terrier named Jessie; and Fred, a lamplighter. It was cramped, but cheap, and the best he could afford.

His landlady, Grace Rushton, was a kindly woman. She had an unusual accent. She was not from London, but from the country. No one in Whitechapel spoke anything like she did.

Everyone in the lodgings referred to her as 'Mrs R'. She thought it was an abbreviation for Rushton, but it had its origin as a play on the way she said the word 'our' in her country accent. She pronounced it as 'air'. Even though her husband Arthur was from London, the nickname was used for him too.

Mrs R took an interest in Moses, appreciating that, as an orphan, life was harder for him than for most of the other boarders. Sometimes, she saved him some leftovers from her family's meal, perhaps some rabbit stew or a slice of pigeon breast. She and her husband were in the poultry and game trade so meat was always on the menu.

"Come on, young man, I've set something aside," she'd say warmly, and Moses would be given a plate with some food and a piece of bread.

"Thank you, Mrs R," he'd say gratefully. He was always

hungry and really appreciated her kindness.

"Now, if you're eating in front of me, then you need to learn some manners, my boy. Hold the fork in your left hand, and the knife in your right hand, and use the knife to cut the meat – not stab it!"

"What? You mean like—"

"Don't speak with your mouth full! Eat your food more slowly; it's not a race!"

Moses chewed obediently before swallowing. "Sorry, Mrs R, I forgot."

"Well don't you go forgetting again. One day, you might even be able to eat in polite company!"

"Thank you, Mrs R."

"So, what did you find today? Anything interesting?"

"Not really, just the usual. Some nice pieces of coal down near the gas works and quite a heavy piece of copper that must have fallen from the side of a ship. I sold everythin', so here's my keep for the next two weeks." Moses brought some copper coins out of his pocket and counted out sixpence.

Mrs R put the money in her purse and tucked it into the pocket in her apron. "Thank you, Moses. You're a good lad. Would you be interested in earning some extra money, when the tide's in and you can't get down on the shore?"

"Yes, course I would. D'you know someone who could give me some work then?"

"Yes, me! You can help to pluck and draw the poultry and game on the stall. I could do with an extra pair of hands sometimes. You could do some packing and wrapping for customers too. Think you could do that?"

"I'm sure I could, Mrs R, if you don't mind me still doin' my gleanin' as well."

"No, I don't mind. I haven't got enough work for you full time, but if you could help me when you're not on the river, that should be just about right."

So Moses began working at the Rushtons' market stall. It was smelly, menial, and repetitive work most of the time. Rabbits and hares were skinned. Poultry was plucked. Drawing guts and giblets was unpleasant, but Moses was tough and he took to the work with no problem. It was honest toil, which he would do when he couldn't earn from the river, and it meant that he could support himself more easily.

The stock was brought to the stall by handcart from a store situated nearby. Moses was shown where it was, and if Mrs R was running short of something, she would send him to get whatever she needed. While there, Moses noticed a small wooden lean-to on the back of the store. It appeared to be empty.

"Mrs R?"

"Yes?"

"You know that little wooden piece on the back of the store?"

"Yes?"

"Any chance I could store my tools and smelly damp clothing in there? What I use down on the river. I wouldn't need to bring so much back to the lodgin's."

"I don't see why not, but we'll need to agree on rent. I'll have to check with my husband first. I'll let you know."

"Thanks, Mrs R."

Mr R seldom put in an appearance at the market stall. He felt himself to be above that level of commerce, priding himself on his ability to be the wholesaler and supplier. His work, little as it was, was generally finished by mid to late morning. He was then able to pass the rest of the day supposedly dealing with business contacts in the trade. In reality, it meant sitting close to a bar, nursing a mug of ale. He'd generally return for the evening meal, count the takings from the stall – not, of course, forgetting the rent from the lodgers – secrete it all somewhere known only to him and consume the food prepared and presented by his wife, before leaving to spend the evening in his favourite tavern.

"I've asked my husband," Mrs R said to Moses the next day, "and you can use that lean-to for a halfpenny a week. Would that be agreeable?"

"Yes, Mrs R. Thank you."

"Well just you see you keep it tidy. I'd get a lock put on it if I were you. You can't trust no one down that way."

"I will, Mrs R, thank you."

Finally, Moses had obtained premises for his little enterprise. It was small and primitive, but it was a step up from Ned and Fred moaning constantly about the smell and clutter of his mudlarking equipment.

During winter evenings at the Rushtons' boarding house, the landlady, her children, and some of the lodgers frequently sat together after supper around a long wooden table. Mr R was usually out. The downstairs room was large and had two fire grates, one at each end, with candles providing light. It was always cosy and warm. Most of the lodgers, including Moses, congregated there when they could.

Mrs R often spoke fondly of her childhood on a Wiltshire farm. She said it was called Oxenhope and it lay in a sheltered, isolated valley where the weather was different to the rest of the county, and you could grow things that couldn't be grown elsewhere. Her family had been there for generations.

"My family owns the land, yer see."

"What? The whole valley?" It was Ned who asked with a hint of scepticism. As always, Jessie lay at his feet. He was cobbling an old pair of shoes and paused his hammering to hear her reply.

"Yes, it's been passed down through the family since the 1600s. We even had our own schoolteacher, cos what with the labourers' children, and our family, we had enough for a class."

"But what did you do for fun? Didn't you get bored being in the countryside?" asked Nellie, a young laundry worker and another of the lodgers. She was a pretty girl who spent most of her spare time knitting socks for a military charity.

"Bored? There weren't no time for that! You'd never imagine the things we used to do. Apart from helping with the farm work, like gleaning after harvest, stone picking, or planting out vegetables, we used to make camps in the hayricks and go rabbiting with nets and ferrets. We always had fresh food in the valley. Every Sunday, no matter what the weather, we walked two miles to church at Wyke. It meant climbing a steep path, crossing an old trackway, which the Romans used, then down into the village to the church. In spring, we picked primroses; in early summer, bluebells in the woods, cos they like it shady. In autumn, we used to find wild mushrooms in the pastures and pick blackberries, elderberries, and sloes from the hedges. We slaughtered our own animals, cured our own meat, and produced milk, butter, and cheese from our own dairy."

Mary, who was about seventeen, was fascinated. She wanted to know why their landlady came to London and why she hadn't stayed at Oxenhope.

"Because I married my husband, that's why. Father used to take me with him to Swindon cattle market sometimes. Thursdays, it was; a proper market. We used to sell our cattle and pigs there. Mr R used to come buying – it was the railway, see. It came to Swindon in forty-two, so butchers like Mr R could get out to the country to buy their stock. Mr R and my father used to do business together and, well, he took a shine to me and I to him. I was so impressed that he used to come all the way out on a train from the big city of London. I'd never been on a train. I'd always wanted to go to London. It sounded so exciting. So when Mr R proposed and asked my father for permission to marry me, I was overjoyed when he gave his blessing."

"Did you get married in the church where you went every Sunday?" asked Mary.

"Yes, we did. After the reception at The Fox, we had one night in the room upstairs before we caught the train to London the following day."

"Does your husband still go out to buy cattle from the country?"

"No, there's no need, cos he only sells game and poultry now. There's wholesalers in the market who can get them for him."

"Do you ever go back to see your parents, or brothers and sisters?" asked Nellie.

"No, never! And that's eight years we've been married. Mr R keeps saying we'll go back for a few days next year, but we're always so busy that we never gets round to it. Maybe it will happen and we'll go back to see everyone."

Mrs R sighed wistfully and let the conversation move on to another topic. She'd talk about Oxenhope again, if a letter arrived from her sister with some piece of news, or if someone commented on the quality of vegetables to be had from local shops.

Moses always enjoyed evenings in the large room on the ground floor. He never tired of hearing his landlady's childhood tales and was always a willing listener.

CHAPTER 9

Peter settled in front of his computer, intent on finding out more about the death of Moses Jupp.

He decided to search an archive of British newspapers. He first identified the name of the newspaper covering the Marlborough area back in 1871. He entered a few key details from the death certificate and then read through the results. One of them had a few lines mentioning Moses Jupp's inquest. He clicked on it and found himself looking at a copy of the original newspaper page from 1871, published on the day after the inquest. A column was highlighted. He zoomed in to read the details.

KILLED BY MOWING MACHINE AT OXENHOPE

On Tuesday afternoon, a shocking accident befell a man named Moses Jupp who lived at Oxenhope and was employed by Richard Turnbull in Oak Meadow field where haymaking was going on. Suddenly, the horses drawing the mowing machine took fright and knocked Mr Jupp down. The animals could not be stopped, and the knives had inflicted such terrible injuries on the poor man's body that he died almost immediately. The body was brought to the infirmary.

The inquest was held on Friday morning. Mr Maloney, assistant surgeon, in describing the injuries sustained by the deceased, said there were extensive lacerations about the neck and thigh. There was a compound fracture of the left arm and the first and third fingers of the left hand were torn off.

Elizabeth Jupp identified the body as that of her husband, who was thirty-three years of age.

Michael Prentice, head ploughman to Richard Turnbull of Oxenhope Farm, said the deceased and he were with a mowing machine in Oak Meadow, the deceased leading the front horse. The horses bolted and Mr Prentice, who was on the machine, fell, and was dragged about ten yards. When he got clear, he saw the deceased on the knives and the machine went on for about sixty yards before the horses halted. He then saw the deceased was badly cut. Mr Prentice said that the leading horse had bolted before, two or three months ago. Usually, the horses were pretty quiet. He also told the court that Moses Jupp was not used to working with horses. The jury gave a verdict of accidental death, coupling it with an expression of opinion that only those well able to control horses should be employed in such work.

Peter sat back from his desk and thought about what he'd just read. He wasn't sure why, but he sensed a connection between himself and Moses Jupp. It might have been no more than finding the worn bronze coin with his name punched on it, but on reflection, it was the death certificate that had really sparked his interest; the death was so horrible and unusual. Yet, there was more to it than that.

Yes of course, he realised, *the death certificate stated where the death had occurred and it had taken place on the farm where I've been detecting! That was a first, and what a unique if rather distasteful aspect it was.*

He decided to look online at the 1871 Census, taken in April and some weeks before the accident, to see if he could locate the Jupps at Oxenhope. He soon had the relevant transcription of the census on his screen and saw that both Moses and Elizabeth occupied a cottage: number 2, The Row. No children were listed. There it was again, his occupation shown as 'fogger'. He looked up the word and learned that the Victorian occupation of fogger – or fugger – was someone who fed and tended livestock. It seemed to be quite a humble position and ranked below more skilled jobs like carters, shepherds, or ploughmen.

Peter viewed an image of the original census entry that was also available, and was interested to see that the head of the household at the main farmhouse was Richard Turnbull, aged fifty-one. That tied in with the inquest report. He was described by the census enumerator as a farmer of 350 acres. He had a wife, one son, and four daughters. He also had an unmarried sister, two house servants – one being a cook, the other a nursemaid – as well as two plough boys. In total, there were twelve individuals recorded under his roof.

Studying the census image further, Peter counted fourteen households in the valley at the time. The occupations were typical of those found within a farming community: shepherd, ploughman, carter, under-carter, gamekeeper, with most listed as labourers.

The occupation of Cornelius Brown, 'schoolmaster', and head of household in one of the dwellings was particularly interesting. Peter had learned that it was not unusual for an isolated community like Oxenhope to have a teacher. Thinking about it, Peter decided that it probably paid Turnbull to provide education at Oxenhope, in order to attract families to live and work on the farm for him.

The census showed that of Richard Turnbull's five children, four were under fourteen and listed as 'scholars'. Among the other households, there were twelve scholars; and the schoolmaster and his wife had two young daughters, both shown as scholars too. That made eighteen children who were being taught by Cornelius Brown.

All of the inhabitants were born in Oxenhope or nearby, apart from just four individuals. The schoolmaster and his wife came from Surrey. Elizabeth Jupp was born in Berkshire. Most interesting of all was Moses Jupp's birthplace, recorded as Middlesex – Whitechapel, to be precise, in the heart of London!

Peter picked up the phone and called Norman Coles, bringing him up to date with the discovery of Moses Jupp's name on the large bronze coin and the information on the death certificate. Norman was very interested and Peter promised to show him the coin on his next visit.

CHAPTER 10

LONDON, 1853

By the time Moses reached fifteen years of age, he found that life was looking up. He still had his work on Rushtons' stall as a fallback. As for scavenging, his luck or maybe it was his skill, was improving. He no longer raked between the barges at low tide for pieces of coal. He had learned more about the Thames; its moods and movements, and had noted several locations where he could be confident of finding coins and small items of jewellery on a regular basis.

The river was controlled by the tide and by the amount of rain falling on the countryside to the west of London. This meant that the water level rose and fell, not only by the tides but also by season. It shifted and deposited the sediments, sands, and gravels that were carried along with it. Despite the filthy state of the water, especially in the summer when it stank, Moses got to know where parts of the river bed were exposed at certain low tides, and where there were firm clean areas of sand and shingle.

Learning by experience, he'd got a feel for the right sort of coarse sand and small pebbles with the weight and consistency to be associated with small metal objects. He knew where he could most likely find the more favourable areas of deposition; noting how, as the river meandered, the speed of the current was greatest on the outside of a bend and slowest on the inside. The bottom of the river changed constantly. It was not just a matter of studying the current, but looking for sections of the river where crossing points and outfalls would seed the very items he wanted to harvest.

One of his favourite spots was downstream of where Fleet Ditch drained into the river. After a storm, the throng would go out on the river in boats to collect floating wood and furniture, washed out from flooded cellars, but that was not Moses' method. He preferred to wait until low tide; to search for smaller objects washed down and stranded on the exposed river bed. He found that he was adding to his knowledge continually, and was careful to keep his theories and information to himself.

As his father had done, he usually took anything made of precious metal to old Tom Booth, just across the river in Southwark. He operated from a small workshop in a back yard off Mermaid Street. More locally known as Foundry Tom, he always kept a crucible ready on a slow fire for melting down metal. Tom could handle anything of value. He provided the means to convert all manner of items into hard cash: silver cutlery, candlesticks, and gold rings. He never asked any questions and consequently his 'services' were used not just by those who'd 'found' items of value, but by those who'd acquired goods through nefarious means. The problem with Foundry Tom was that his prices were low. They reflected the fact that he was really just a fence, providing a somewhat meagre return and, more importantly for some, the means to make items and evidence disappear.

Not only were Tom's prices disappointing, but also Moses never felt comfortable south of the river. He couldn't put his finger on it, but straying that way too frequently was asking for trouble. The Borough was notorious for pickpockets and thieves. The areas for the best pickings were controlled by gangs who actively discouraged any outside competition or threat to their livelihoods. Even the foreshore nearby was risky.

He'd once been intimidated on the Southwark side by two particularly unpleasant individuals. He was alone at low tide near Symons Wharf using a short rake to scrape the surface for any small objects buried just out of sight. It was a tight, confined patch of foreshore, sandy and firm, which had yielded several coins on his previous visit. He was engrossed in his task, but looked up when he observed two pairs of boots close to the end of his rake. He straightened to speak to the owners, but before he could say anything, the larger of the two men grabbed his collar and yanked his head to face them.

"This bit of shore is ours. Anything you find here belongs to us. Did you know that?"

"You can't say that. It's for everyone!"

The stranger tightened his grip and snarled in Moses' ear. "Listen, you filthy little urchin, you need our permission to search here, do you hear? And that means payment of threepence now!"

Moses found himself in a tricky situation. He only had a couple of farthings on him and even if he'd had threepence, there was no way he would have given them any money. He studied his potential extortionists. He guessed they were both in their mid-twenties; considerably bigger than him, and dressed well. They both smelt strongly of alcohol and must have been drinking in one of the nearby taverns. They'd most likely spent all they had and were looking for an easy way to get some more beer money. Moses had to think fast.

"My money's in a tin over there in that basket," he explained, trying to turn to point out where it was. They looked to where he indicated. It was about thirty yards away. They could both see that the route to the basket looked rather muddy.

"Well go and get it and bring it here then," ordered the other man.

Moses was released. He obediently left the men and crossed the mud to his basket. It contained a few coals but nothing more. He looked back and weighed up his chances. He knew that if he ran towards Southwark Bridge, they would be obliged to cut across a particularly muddy section in order to catch him. Not only was it muddy, but also the mud was deceptively deep. He acted quickly. He flipped the coal out of his basket and grabbing the wicker handle, along with his rake, he dashed off along the edge of the stream towards the bridge. The two would-be extortionists shouted in fury and set off diagonally to cut him off. His trap was set.

They sprinted across what they assumed was firm but shallow mud. Midway to catching him, they suddenly sank down to their knees. The momentum of the larger one propelled his body forward and he toppled face down into the unpleasant mire. The other came to an unsteady halt and just about managed to maintain himself upright. He cursed Moses loudly, as he offered a helping hand to his filthy, smelly, and dishevelled comrade.

Moses paused to look back when he heard the cursing. It was with some relief that he witnessed the amusing sight. It was one of the sweetest moments of his life. It brought to mind his escape from Sergeant Thurgut, who had chased him into the river and was forced to give up the pursuit on the point of drowning.

CHAPTER 11

Peter drove into the car park of the Wiltshire County Archives just after ten o'clock. He'd made good time and had enjoyed the trip down the motorway in his sports car, rather than the little Fiat he used for detecting. He was relieved to find an empty space at the end of a row, reducing the risk of his cherished vehicle being dented. He was always being ribbed by friends for being a bit of a pain when it came to parking.

He hoped his idea of visiting the archives would pay off and that he'd be able to discover some information about Oxenhope; material which might come in handy for any future detecting on the farm.

Once inside the modern purpose-built centre, he settled down in a quiet corner to see what records the archives held. His first objective was to find an old plan of the valley. He hoped it would show the arrangement of individual fields before the hedges were grubbed out by Norman Coles' grandfather.

One of the archivists showed him where to find the tithe maps and he was delighted to find one for Oxenhope. It was dated 1844 and showed the exact boundaries, and even the names of the former fields. Peter could see straight away that the slight hump in the field he detected on his first visit was in 'Cows Croft'. His small Roman coin had been found close to where a hedge used to divide Cows Croft and 'Long Lay'. The Roman sestertius with *M A JUPP* stamped on it had been found in 'Oak Meadow Field'.

That was the field named on the death certificate. So, poor Moses had died in the vicinity of where he'd found it.

Somehow, Peter didn't feel much satisfaction to be proved right as to where the accident had happened.

The tithe map also showed the distribution of dwellings down in the valley. Norman Coles was correct when he said that there had been about a dozen cottages at one time. Peter could see their locations; counting them, he made it eleven. There was a concentration near to the present-day pheasant-rearing pens, which were roughly behind the farmhouse, with one of the houses being nearly as large. He used the camera on his phone to take a picture of the map in order to record the layout of everything, assuring the archivist that he'd pay the standard copying fee before leaving. Next, he searched the digital index for any mention of Oxenhope. He turned up nearly two pages of results. Most of them were to do with the wills of individuals who'd died back in the eighteenth century, but two results interested him. The first was a mention of Oxenhope in *An Introduction to Field Archaeology* published in 1910. The other was a mention in *The National Field Club Book* of 1865.

Peter left his seat to locate them on the bookshelves and returned a few minutes later with the two publications. He was tempted to dive straight into the one concerning field archaeology, as this was closest to his heart, but he resisted and instead chose the Field Club book. He soon found the relevant page and what an interesting report it was:

There is in the possession of one Mr Richard Turnbull of Oxenhope in the county of Wiltshire, a forechine of pork 193 years old, which has always been in his possession or his ancestors, who have owned and resided on the same estate for upwards of 300 years.

The pork was undoubtedly cured with salt in the ordinary way and has till the last seven years been exposed to air. Now it is in a glass case and is perfect as far as the bone is concerned except that the fourth and fifth joints are slightly separating from each other. There is also some decaying flesh left on the bones getting into a state of dust, or somewhat resembling cheese when mites are about it. While repairing the house, his father put it in the granary unprotected, where some of it got eaten by mice. Before being put there it was in a sound state, both flesh and bone, and had been tasted in of course very small pieces, for curiosity sake, by many people before and after the mice had feasted upon it.

Two gentlemen called on Christmas Eve 1860 when he said he would give them for supper what no other person in England could do, pork nearly 190 years old and a dish of ripe white currants, which he went into his garden and gathered for them. The currants grew on an old large bush against a south-east wall and had not been protected in any way. One of Mr Turnbull's ancestors cut up the pig in 1672, the same day that two women were hanged in Salisbury for witchcraft. The gentlemen confirmed that they tasted the pork and found it to be palatable, as were the freshly picked white currants.

Peter put the book aside and picked up the one about field archaeology. The story it contained about Oxenhope was equally enthralling. 'Labourers Digging Drains at Oxenhope Find Roman Gold Coins' claimed the title:

18th August 1842: Two labourers in the employ of William Turnbull Esquire made a discovery of gold coins while digging in Oak Meadow Field at Oxenhope. During the course of trenching they uncovered part of an earthenware pot which contained twenty gold coins. They were found at a depth of about eighteen inches. The coins were delivered to their employer who asked Mr Jordan of the firm of Makepeace and Co, goldsmiths, to examine them. The discovery was reported to the Crown, and Mr Jordan deposed to the Coroner that the coins were Roman and of the Emperor Trajan. As the coins were found below the surface, the inquest jury returned a verdict of Treasure Trove and the Coroner accordingly took possession of them for Her Majesty.

Peter closed the books and considered what he'd just learned. The report of the coins being found on the farm really excited him. He pictured the shape of Oak Meadow from the tithe map and how it fitted into the valley as he knew it.

Everything seems to happen in Oak Meadow Field...how strange, he thought.

He tried to imagine where the find-spot might have been, and wondered if any more coins remained in the ground. He hoped so. He'd certainly concentrate his future efforts in that general area. Then, of course, he had the fascinating report of the pork and the white currants. Was it possible that the granary still existed and that the white currants still grew against a south-east wall?

He looked forward to asking Norman.

CHAPTER 12

LONDON, 1860

"Moses…Moses, you can't 'ave heard," shouted young Jimmy excitedly as he entered the cramped wooden shelter attached to the back wall of the poultry store where he and Moses kept their tools and sorted their pickings.

"Heard what?" Moses replied. He paused in examining his finds from the previous day and looked up expectantly at Jimmy, a mudlark who lived nearby with his widowed mother.

"George Hopgood's only gone and found some gold coins down near Barge House Stairs. There's supposed to be more what's comin' up. Everyone's headin' down there."

Moses stopped what he was doing and took a hurried look about him. He gathered up a pair of shovels, rakes, and sieves. "Grab these while I sort out a sack."

Jimmy was feeling quite proud that his news had obviously excited Moses. "How long we got with the tide, Moses?"

"About two hours if we're lucky, but it depends how near the stream he found 'em."

They set off towards the river. The weather had finally turned more agreeable, spring was in the air and there were lots of folk enjoying an afternoon stroll or going about their business. They dodged the walkers, the traders, and hawkers who'd set up their stalls to take advantage of the passing trade. They made their way as fast as they could, conscious of the need to get to the stairs as soon as possible. They were anxious to share in the spoils and beat the incoming tide.

When they reached the section of foreshore near Barge House, they were dismayed to witness a considerable clamour and commotion on the foreshore. Looking down, Moses counted at least fifty people, of all ages, and many dressed in squalid rags. Some were known to them, and most were armed with pickaxes and shovels. They were digging and sifting the stinking putrid mire washed out from the sewers.

Moses led Jimmy down the steps and they headed towards where the throng was concentrated. There were holes everywhere. Some of the older brawnier men were working in the fashion of grave diggers, creating corpse-shaped pits, which annoyingly were filling with ooze and water when no more than a foot or two in depth. The men shovelled out a sloppy concoction of mud and faeces, creating a feculent spoil for wives and children to pounce on in their frantic search for gold or silver.

A young boy found a silver coin and instead of putting it instantly into his mouth to conceal it, he held it high triumphantly and shouted his good fortune. It was a foolish indiscretion, for almost immediately he was pounced upon and pushed aside as someone prised it from him, while others moved in to take over his little patch.

Moses looked hastily about, trying to find some spot where they too could try their luck. More hopefuls were streaming down onto the foreshore all the time. He turned to look towards the centre of the river – the stream, as it was known. The tide had already turned and was steadily creeping back. There, he spotted George Hopgood. He was bent low, looking down into the shallow murky water at the edge, swishing aside the foam of raw sewage with bare hands, trying to see and feel among the detritus on the riverbed. They ran over to him.

"What you found, George?" asked Moses, in a voice just above that of a whisper. "We heard you had some gold coins."

"Sure have," George whispered, "but where I found 'em's been taken over by that lot." He inclined his head back towards the mob scrabbling in the mud. "I'm trying me luck here."

George was twenty-one, a year younger than Moses and six years older than Jimmy. He lived in a shabby, overcrowded hovel behind the Tower of London. Moses had known him as long as he could remember. They had something in common: each had lost their father to drowning and, consequently, each wore a medallion bearing their own name, so that should either of them succumb to the same fate, at least their bodies would be more easily identified.

Away from the mud-coated throng, Moses spied a short stretch of beach consisting of fine pebbles and shingle. It was close to the encroaching tide, but mercifully, clear of excrement and debris. He could also see that the stones looked small, about the same weight as a coin, although he kept this observation to himself. "Let's try there," he suggested quietly to Jimmy. "We'll have to be quick though cos it'll soon be covered. Come on."

Jimmy was happy to go along with anything Moses suggested, especially when it came to searching the river.

The two began shovelling shingle into their sieves. They worked furiously, filling the sieves, washing the contents at the water's edge, tipping out the rejected spoil, and then refilling. Meanwhile, the unstoppable creeping tide confined them to a slowly diminishing area. It was Jimmy who found the first coin. It was a sixpence, about as much as he could earn in a day as a coal-finder, even in deep winter when demand was high. Jimmy popped it into the corner of his mouth and looked towards Moses, merely raising his eyebrows to acknowledge his find. No one apart from his friend saw the sign, but both resumed searching with renewed fervour.

Moses struck next. Moving the small stones in the sieve with his fingers, rinsing and sorting, he spotted a tiny thin silver coin no bigger than his smallest fingernail. He too popped it into his mouth, savouring its coldness, aware of its sharp edge, and yet salivating on the food it might buy. He updated Jimmy with a barely perceptible nod.

Ten minutes later, Moses had another coin in his mouth, but

this was different. It was thicker, smoother, and heavier than the previous one. It was a different colour too, unlike any coin he had ever found. He didn't know how old it was, but he knew it was gold.

Within thirty minutes, their bountiful little patch was covered with water and they were forced to abandon their endeavours. Moses made a mental note of the spot, aligning it with buildings on either side of the river and the arches of the nearest bridge. He hoped to return at low tide the following day. They collected their tools and made their way to the stairs. Practice meant they could talk and laugh even with coins concealed in their mouths.

When they reached the level of the pavement, a well-dressed man approached them. "Any luck?" he asked. "I'm prepared to pay well, should you have any ancient coins or artefacts."

Neither Moses nor Jimmy was too sure what an artefact was.

"What, you mean curiosities an' the like, sir?" asked Jimmy.

"Exactly, my boy, exactly."

"No we ain't, but we get 'em sometimes," said Moses, hedging his bets.

"Can you read, either of you?"

"I can," replied Moses.

"Well look, here's an advertising token with my name and address. Now, don't lose it! The name's Charles Blackett and I'm a dealer in ancient coins and antiquities, which includes curiosities. I've a shop on Commercial Road. If you find anything old or interesting, you come and see me and I'll give you a decent price. Don't you go up to Westbrook's or Whelan's, you come straight to me."

Moses took what looked like a brass coin about the size of a penny. After giving it a quick look, he carefully slid it into his pocket. Although he held, in his mouth, a coin that he was sure would interest the dealer, Moses was no fool. He decided to make up his mind later on as to whether or not to offer it to him.

At that moment, a mud-spattered group of individuals ascended to street level and Charles Blackett turned away to put the same offer to them.

Moses and Jimmy moved aside, but paused to observe. One member of the group, an elderly woman, put a grubby hand into the folds of her filthy skirt. She fished for something in a hidden pocket and brought it out to show the dealer. It was a small gold coin, certainly smaller than a guinea. The boys couldn't identify it, but they detected Mr Blackett's excitement and then saw how he tried to conceal his eagerness. He hefted the coin in his closed palm to determine its weight and authenticity, put on a serious expression and, in a secretive huddle, commenced negotiations with the woman. Neither Moses nor Jimmy could hear all of the conversation, but they did see Mr Blackett put two half-crowns in her hand before dropping the gold coin into a small leather pouch attached to his waistband.

Jimmy was unaware that Moses had literally struck gold. "Did you see that?" he whispered. "Five shillings for one coin! Imagine finding something like that!"

"I might just have," Moses whispered. "Come on, let's get back. Once we're away from here, I'll show you."

CHAPTER 13

A few days later, Peter drove over to Oxenhope Farm to see
Norman Coles, with the results of his visit to the archives. He'd
managed to get two copies of the tithe map reproduced onto A3
paper.

Norman met him in front of the farmhouse. His jumper was
covered in bits of straw – they were in his hair too. He invited
Peter to follow him around to the rear to his office: a wooden
shed attached to the side wall.

"Come in, I've a table in here and you can show me whatever
it is you've got rolled up under your arm."

"Full marks for observation, Norman! How'd you guess?"

Norman laughed. They stepped into the office, where Norman
instructed the dogs to stay in their baskets. He used his forearm
to clear some space among the clutter of items on the table top;
mainly stale mugs, a dirty plate, a large key ring, and a box of dog
biscuits.

In the corner, two rusty filing cabinets supported an old
manual typewriter and a grubby telephone. Papers were piled
up everywhere. The waste bin was overflowing, and the only
window hadn't been cleaned in years. Thick cobwebs were stuck
to the upper part of the frame, where several happy spiders lived.
There was an old paraffin heater opposite the table. Peter couldn't
remember the last time he'd seen one, probably on an antiques
stall. Thankfully, it wasn't in use; earlier in the day, the sun had
penetrated the thin wooden walls and the air was still warm.

However, the smell from the dogs was nose-twitchingly strong.

"First things first," said Peter, handing Norman the bronze sestertius. "Here's the Roman coin I found with the name of Moses Jupp punched into it."

Norman took it and examined it closely. "M A Jupp? So you've found out the owner's name was Moses?"

"That's right."

"Bit spooky to think of someone wearing this, eh?"

"Yes, it is. I feel the same about rings too. Now and again I find a ring with the detector – not always valuable, I might add! But I never try them for size. I've seen others do it, but to me they're personal and it just wouldn't feel right."

"Know what you mean…Here, you have this back."

"Thanks." Peter put the coin into a pocket-sized container with some soft internal padding.

"Anyway, here's the death certificate of Moses Jupp, showing exactly how he died, and this is the inquest report printed from the local paper."

Norman carefully read the details. "Dreadful way to go, must have been agonising for him. I shudder to think of the pain, poor fellow. Some of those farm workers had rotten lives. So where's Oak Meadow Field?"

"Ah, well, the answer's here."

Peter unrolled one large sheet of paper, explaining that it was a copy of the 1844 tithe map.

"Hang on there…Let's weigh it down to keep it flat." Norman reached over to the narrow window sill and picked up several small fossils. "These often turn up in the field," he explained as he placed one at each corner of the map.

Peter joined the farmer in looking at the cartographer's handiwork. They agreed that it was beautifully drawn, each field having a name.

"Here's Oak Meadow," Peter indicated.

"This is really interesting," Norman said. "So the one field out there now was five originally, eh? I thought it was something like that. I know my grandfather changed it and knocked it all into the one that I've got now.

"You see these small oblongs and squares," Peter pointed out, "they're dwellings or cottages."

"Yes, I see those, and here's the farmhouse, the largest one," commented Norman, "exactly where it is today and where I'd expect to see it."

"What's this building here?" asked Peter.

"That's The Row, four derelict cottages now. It's just at the back of the yard."

"Four? I counted it as one, so that makes fourteen dwellings in total. Good, because that matches the number of households on the 1871 Census with sixty-five individuals living down here, including Moses Jupp. Richard Turnbull was the landowner at the time and according to the census he had 350 acres, five children, and even employed a teacher."

"Fascinating...fascinating..." murmured Norman. "Can't say I've ever heard of Richard Turnbull though. I suppose he could have sold the farm to one of my ancestors. I've only got 240 acres now, so some of the land must have been disposed of separately. The name doesn't ring a bell."

"I think he was a bit of a character, you know." Peter chuckled. "I've come across some references to him and to his father. Would you like to hear what I've found out?"

"Yes, certainly."

Peter showed him the stories he'd copied and printed, about the treasure trove of gold coins and the 193-year-old pork.

Norman was intrigued. He rubbed his chin thoughtfully. "I've never heard mention of any old pork...Kept in a glass case, eh? But we've still got the granary. I've got two of my tractors in it. Shall we go and have a look?"

"What about the white-currant tree?"

"Nah, that's gone...nothing there now on that side of the farmhouse. I'd have picked 'em myself if they still grew against the wall."

Peter followed Norman out of the office to a large yard with old stables and other outbuildings on three sides. Immediately behind the stables, he noticed the terrace of four small cottages which Norman had referred to as The Row. They were boarded up and most of the roof tiles were missing. The wooded hillside rose gently behind them.

"Those stables used to be for the heavy horses," Norman explained, "the ones that did the ploughing and farm work before we had tractors. That's the old granary, the one on the end."

They crossed the yard to a pair of large double doors. Norman pulled one open, and he and Peter entered the cool dark interior of the granary. When Norman switched on a powerful light, two beautiful classic tractors were illuminated. They occupied the centre of the building with space to walk around and admire them. Peter thought the interior was surprisingly tidy compared to the office.

Norman spent ten minutes showing Peter around the tractors, explaining their histories, and what he'd done to restore them. He pointed out some of his handiwork. Peter could see that they had been restored to an immaculate condition and was genuinely interested in what Norman had to say. He listened carefully, while at the same time glancing down to the old brick floor, wondering and imagining where the forechine of pork may have once laid. He noticed that the surface was reasonably flat, given the age of the building, but in one corner it looked as if a small section had been disturbed at some time. The tessellations in the brick pattern were not quite perfect.

Peter waited patiently until Norman had finished speaking. "Perhaps I could run my detector over parts of this floor some time. They used to bury things for safekeeping you know. I might get a signal or two. Look at that corner, for example. See that section of five bricks? They don't fit like the others."

"Oh, I expect they had to fix a bit of rising damp or something; but, yes, you're welcome to try."

"I've got my detector in the car. Could I get it and do it now?"

"Why not? I need a distraction...Anything to put off doing the paperwork!"

Peter shot back to his car and returned with his detector.

Norman watched carefully as Peter switched it on and hooked his headphones over his ears.

"Do you mind holding onto these while I give it a quick go over in the corner there?"

"No, of course not," said Norman, taking hold of a small archaeologists' trowel and screwdriver.

They walked over to the corner and Peter swept the head of the detector over the disturbed bricks.

"There's a signal here! Quite an extensive one too, meaning something bigger in size and shape than a single coin."

"Really?"

"Yes, it goes under at least two bricks. What do you think? Can we lift them? I don't want to spoil your floor."

"Yeah, come on, otherwise we'll always wonder what it is. I'm sure I can put them back carefully."

"Great!"

Peter swept the coil sideways and then forwards and backwards to confirm the centre of the signal. "Let's lift these two, if we can."

He set aside the detector and both men knelt so that they could see more closely. Norman had the tools, so he worked the screwdriver into the end joint between the bricks. There was very little mortar. He puffed a little, but got down far enough to gain some purchase. Then he levered up the end of the brick. Thankfully, it came away in one piece. Peter grabbed it and laid it aside, and then Norman removed the second brick.

The long rectangular hole they had created revealed nothing; only that the floor had been laid directly on earth. There appeared to be no damp course or gritty bedding.

"Let me run the detector over again to check."

"Is it still there, the signal?"

"Yes, it seems stronger now and coming from under the next brick along. Can we lift that one out too?"

"Yeah, no problem."

A minute later they had three bricks removed.

Peter checked again. "Yes, it's definitely here. Try the trowel to dig down a bit. I don't think it's very deep from the signal I'm getting."

Norman stuck the trowel in a little and scraped back some soil. There was nothing, so he tried again. "Hey, I felt resistance, like it's caught on something. Shall I keep going?"

"Yes, go for it, but do it gently; we don't want to damage whatever it is."

Norman pushed the side of the trowel in a little more and carefully pulled it back towards him. It stuck momentarily and then he levered the object up out of the earth and picked it up. It was about two inches across, roundish, metal, but dark grey with corrosion. He handed it to Peter.

"Any idea?" Norman asked.

"I'm not sure. It could be lead, but doesn't really seem heavy enough for that." Peter rubbed it, but it was difficult to make out any detail. "I think there might be something embossed on it, or some marks. I can feel some slight bumps and undulations." He gave it back to Norman. "What do you think?"

"Ooh, I don't know. I was hoping it might be treasure or something...Doesn't look particularly interesting to me."

"Let me check the hole to see if there are any more signals." Peter swept the coil over the soil. "Yes, we've still got a signal."

Soon after, Norman carefully levered out a second object of about the same shape and size. Peter's detector indicated that the signal was still there. They continued digging and checking. In the end, they extracted eight roughly similar metal objects from the hole.

"That's it, no more signals. That must be the last one."

"What do you think they are then, Pete?"

Peter noticed that it was the first time Norman had called him that.

"No idea, Norman. I think they need a good soak and maybe a gentle rub with an old toothbrush. That might reveal some detail. Failing that, I could try my electrolysis set at home, with perhaps a wire brush, but only with care. Do you want to have a go at cleaning them, or shall I?"

"I'm happy to soak them and brush them off. Leave them with me if you like."

"OK, thanks. Right, shall we put these bricks back?"

"Yeah, better had."

Using the trowel, Norman scraped and flattened the base of the hole. "I've got some sand out the back. Just a minute, I'll get some."

As Norman left, Peter picked up one of the objects and tried to work out what it was. It certainly wasn't made of precious metal. His best bet was that they were old horse brasses. Maybe cheap ones which were made of base metal rather than brass, but he wasn't sure.

Norman returned shortly with a bucket of soft sand and some tools. He expertly spread a layer of sand over the bottom of the hole and then lowered each brick, tapping gently with a mallet, until all three were flush with the level of the floor. He brushed some extra sand across the surface with his fingers, working it into the joints.

"There we are, good as new," he said proudly.

"Yes, nice job, Norman, very professional."

Norman dropped the objects into the bucket containing the sand. Peter picked up his detector and tools. They closed up the granary and returned to the office.

"You'd better take this map with you," Norman offered.

"No need, that's your copy to keep. I've got my own."

"Thanks. I might get it framed, you know. It'd look good mounted on the wall there."

"That's a great idea," agreed Peter, "but it's a shame we didn't uncover something valuable just now. I guess the treasure will have to wait."

Norman laughed. "Yes, I suppose it will...And no pork for my supper either!"

CHAPTER 14

Moses decided to visit Charles Blackett, Dealer in Ancient Coins and Artefacts. The address on the brass advertising token he'd been given a few weeks earlier was about fifteen minutes' walk from his lodgings. He was a little apprehensive. He had no idea what to expect from the coin dealer. He'd met him only briefly at the top of the stairs by the river.

Questions were spinning around in his head. *What sort of premises does he have? Surely, it won't be like Foundry Tom's? Was it a shop? Who did he do business with?*

It was all new to him. He felt fairly certain, though, that he needed someone like Mr Blackett to buy the coins he was increasingly successful in finding. He might be a more lucrative outlet.

Moses made his away along Commercial Road, looking at the numbers. He found the right address on the corner with Sidney Street. It was a real shop, narrow with a single bay window and a proper door, not a backstreet entrance guarded by a lookout. He approached nervously to examine the window and was immediately impressed. There were three tiers to the display. The top two presented coins, exhibited on dark felt within wood-framed trays. The lower tier held metal curios, comprising what were labelled as Roman brooches and a group of small flat lead objects, some quite intricately shaped, including a throne and a scallop shell. Moses was fairly certain he'd seen a similar scalloped-shaped object before, but couldn't recall when.

Everything was protected by sturdy steel mesh, painted black and fixed in place on all four sides. Although it provided security, it was not obtrusive. If anything, it gave an impression that here was a genuine business dealing in objects of value.

A sign was mounted on the middle shelf. The words 'Ancient Coins and Artefacts Bought and Sold' were painted in a neat white script on a shiny black background.

This is exciting, Moses thought. With trepidation, he took a deep breath to calm himself before turning the door handle and entering the interior of the shop.

A bell jangled above the door and Moses saw Mr Blackett look up from behind the counter. He came around to meet him immediately, but his manner was not altogether very welcoming. Moses recognised him as the man who'd given him the token. He was about fifty, portly in stature, with a round ruddy face framed by a formidable set of mutton chop whiskers, contrasting sharply with a bald pate. Moses noticed his eyebrows were misaligned and the bag under his right eye was significantly more wrinkled than the other.

"Goodness me, goodness me!" he exclaimed. "Have you come up from the river with a coin for me?"

Moses wondered how the dealer had worked out his reason for calling. *It must be the way I'm dressed*, he decided. He imagined Blackett's customers would tend to be wealthy and older.

"Yes, sir, I've got three to show you."

"Well, the first rule is that, if you come here, you knock at the entrance off Sidney Street. I can't have my customers observing me while I acquire stock. Now, out you go and make your way around to the yard. One of my servants will answer."

Moses felt slightly rebuked, but followed Blackett's instruction. He found a wooden gate within the side wall that screened the rear of the premises. It opened into a small yard containing a privy and a coal store, and gave him access to the back door. He used the heavy door knocker. Presently, he heard someone moving about inside, and the door opened to a parlourmaid who asked him his business.

"I've come to see Mr Blackett. He asked me to use this door."

"And what might be your name, sir?" she asked.

"Moses Jupp."

"Just a moment, sir. I'll tell Mr Blackett you're here."

She disappeared into the interior, but in the brief moment they'd met, Moses was struck by how pretty she was.

She returned a few moments later. "Mr Blackett will be here presently," she said.

Moses could hear approaching footsteps.

"Thank you, Bess," said Charles Blackett.

The maid turned and left. Moses was invited inside, and met more cordially.

"Moses Jupp, sir," he said as he shook hands with Charles Blackett.

"Pleased to meet you, Moses. Come through to my study and let's have a look at what you've brought to show me."

He followed Blackett through a scullery and into a room at the back of the shop. Blackett closed the door behind them, and then drew open a pair of thick dark curtains. Light flooded in through a large window with steel bars on the inside.

Moses brought out a handkerchief from his pocket that he unfolded to reveal the tiny gold coin and two silver ones. Moses had no idea what they were, only that they were old and not like any of the coins in general circulation.

Blackett carefully took the handkerchief to a table just under the window to get the best light. "Mind if a take a closer look?"

"Course not, sir."

The dealer picked out the gold coin first. It was smaller than the nail on his little finger. He closed one eye and squinted through a magnifying pendant with the other. He examined the coin carefully, turning it over in order to see both sides. "Do you know what you've got here?"

"Not exactly, but I've some idea," Moses lied.

"This coin is Saxon, you know. Probably about a thousand years old. A good find because these are difficult to spot. Where was it found?"

"I'd rather not say, sir, if you don't mind. We likes to keep our best spots to ourselves."

"Yes, I understand. I daresay you do, but you can't blame me for asking."

Blackett laid the gold coin on a square of dark-green velvet and turned his attention to the silver coins. They were both wafer thin, the smallest about half the size of the other. He managed to grip the larger one between his fingers and brought it up to his magnifier to study it closely.

"This one's medieval, a silver penny...an Edward III long cross, minted here in London."

"How can you tell, sir?"

"Look at the cross lines from side to side and top to bottom. See the writing running around the outside?"

"Yes, I see it."

"There are only two words. Can you make out the word 'civitas'?"

"Yes...but what does that mean?"

"It means 'town' in Old English, and the other word is 'London'."

"Yes, I can read that."

"Well, there you are then. That's how you can tell. Sometimes it's other places like York or Durham."

Moses nodded his head knowingly, but really he'd never been outside of the small part of London he frequented.

Blackett placed the coin onto the velvet with the gold one. He tried to get hold of the third and smallest coin, which was tiny. After several unsuccessful attempts, he licked the end of his finger and touched the coin. It stuck, and he brought up for examination.

"This one's medieval too, silver, but heavily clipped, I'm afraid. It started out as a halfpenny, but there's not enough writing left to tell its age accurately."

"What do you mean 'clipped'?" asked Moses.

"In medieval times, they used to cut small slivers of silver from around the edge of the coin. If you snipped a little from enough coins, you could accumulate quite a bit of silver, which could be melted and turned into an ingot or a valuable object like a ring. It was stealing. Merchants used to weigh the coins to check the quantity of silver and that's how we got the pound, which was originally just a measure of weight."

Moses was riveted. He'd enjoyed history at ragged school and envied Blackett's knowledge.

"So, what do you want for them, if I buy all three?"

Here, Moses was on uncertain ground. He thought he'd get about five shillings from Foundry Tom. He was determined to make at least twice that. "They've got to be worth two pounds, sir, I should've thought."

Blackett rubbed his chin thoughtfully. The coins were nice and he already had a collector in mind for the gold one. He would probably get five pounds for it and several shillings for the other two. He felt sure he could buy the lot for about ten shillings. However, something about the young man made him wonder. He might bring more coins if he paid what he would think to be a generous amount.

"Tell you what," he said, "I'll give you one pound. How does that sound?"

Moses was thrilled, but careful not to show it. "Could you make it just a little more, sir? I've worked hard for many hours to find them."

"Last offer then, take it or leave it...I'll increase it by one shilling to a guinea."

A guinea was a fortune to Moses. He'd rarely heard of anyone earning that much from items recovered from the river. He shook Blackett's outstretched hand. A deal was struck!

Mrs R was lighting a fire in the main room when Moses arrived back at the boarding house. She noticed the smile on his face.

"What ya' been up to then, Moses?"

"I've just sold some coins I found, to a dealer. One of them was a thousand years old."

"Good Lord! You're going up in the world. Time was when

91

it was pieces of coal and copper nails, but ancient coins now, eh? Well done, my lad, good for you."

Moses put his hand in his pocket and gave her a shilling. "Here you are, go and treat yourself Mrs R, you're always good to me."

His landlady was genuinely touched by his generosity. "I can't take that, Moses."

"Please Mrs R, go on, get somethin' for yourself."

"That's very kind of you, Moses. Thank you, very kind. Now sit down and I'll pour us some ale."

Moses settled in a chair and smiled contentedly to himself. The other boarders were still out at work.

Mrs R disappeared for a minute, and reappeared with two brimming mugs. She always collected a large jug of ale on her way home from the stall.

"Here you are, Moses." She took a chair next to him and they relaxed. "Did I ever tell you about the gold coins they found at Oxenhope?"

"No, never," he replied, his interest immediately aroused.

"It was the year before I got married to Mr R. My father was still alive, running the farm then he was. Two of his men found a pot of gold coins when they were digging."

"Really? What happened?"

"Well, the authorities said they was treasure trove and belonged to the Queen. I think the local museum took them. I know we couldn't keep them, which was a shame, but there we are."

"Has anything else ever been dug up?"

"Well, my grandfather did keep some old coins in his study that he said were found on the farm."

"Were they gold?"

"No, they were dark green. I think they'd been in the ground a long time."

Moses knew exactly what she meant. He loosened the top buttons of his shirt and pulled out the leather thong holding the old Roman coin with his name on it. "Were those coins the same sort of colour as this? It was a coin once."

"Yes, just like that, but nowhere near as big."

"I think they were probably Roman."

"Where did that one come from then? Was it the river?"

"That's right…came out just below Execution Dock. Soon as I found it, I thought it'd be perfect for a medallion to put my name on. Did it myself, too, with some tools I borrowed."

"Mmm, very nice too."

The conversation drifted on to Mrs R's other memories of Oxenhope. Moses, however, would never forget the story of the gold coins.

CHAPTER 15

Peter pushed himself to get up to date with things he needed to do so that he had some spare time to research Moses Jupp. Obtaining the death certificate had really brought Moses to life, which Peter realised was somewhat oxymoronic. He chuckled to himself and thought Felicity might groan a bit when he told her that one.

Moses Jupp had rekindled his interest in genealogy. It was at least ten years since he'd spent many hours researching his own family. There were a few brick walls remaining, but he was reasonably content with where he'd got to. He'd made some interesting discoveries and managed to go back eleven generations.

Since then, he'd been drawn into investigating a marriage certificate he found in an antiques shop. That had been really exciting and stimulating at the time, but afterwards he'd lacked inspiration and direction about where to go next with his genealogy research.

Metal-detecting had taken over, and he frequently found there were sources to research or investigate that improved his chances of digging up something worthwhile, but Peter was definitely feeling the genealogy buzz again. Even better, the death certificate of Moses Jupp was directly linked to his passion for detecting. What a perfect combination! There'd be no holding back; he was going to find out as much as he could.

But the particular question bugging Peter was how did a man born in Whitechapel end up on a farm in a remote valley in

Wiltshire? Oxenhope was about eighty miles from the capital. Generally, in those days, people didn't move far from where they were born. He realised that he hadn't actually looked for Moses Jupp's birth. He soon found it; the name was unusual. It occurred during the first quarter of 1838, in Whitechapel. He ordered the birth certificate. Then he traced young Moses, aged three, on the 1841 Census. He was living with his parents in what he imagined was probably a slum off Tenter Street; an only child. The census showed that his father Samuel was born in Whitechapel and his mother Eleanor came from Ireland. Peter identified Tenter Street on a map of the time. It was near to the docks and the Tower of London. It was Samuel's occupation, however, that really grabbed Peter's attention. The enumerator had written 'Scavenger'!

What on earth was a scavenger?

Thirty minutes of research later and Peter knew a little about the life of a scavenger in Victorian London. As the Jupps lived near the Thames, with its foreshore and sewer outfalls, it seemed quite plausible.

He next searched for Moses on the 1851 Census, taken in March. Another surprise was in store because this time the entry for thirteen-year-old Moses recorded his occupation as 'Ragged Scholar'.

What does that mean?

Peter could hardly believe the twists and turns the trail was taking. The census page was particularly interesting. There were six other boys aged between nine and fourteen at the same address in Southampton Row and all listed as ragged scholars. The head of the household was Thomas Chambers, a sixty-four-year-old architect. Living with him were his wife, two female servants, a male servant, and the seven male scholars. It was the relationship between Mr Chambers and the boys that Peter found most intriguing. Against each name was written 'Inmate'.

The terms 'inmate' and 'ragged scholar' puzzled him. He searched online for information and was swamped with references to Field Lane School, Clerkenwell, London; one of the first Ragged Schools, established by benefactors in 1842 to give free education to destitute children. Many of the pupils were orphans and strays. Further research found a copy of a newspaper report from 1858 entitled 'Our Homeless Poor'. It described observations during a visit to the Field Lane School and it closed with a list of those responsible for running and administering the establishment. Among the members of The Managing Committee was one Thomas Chambers of Southampton Row. A quick check on the address of the school and the residence of Mr Chambers confirmed their proximity. It seemed logical that Moses and the other boys stayed overnight at the home of Mr Chambers as 'inmates' because they weren't working and couldn't pay for lodgings, as someone classed as a 'boarder' would. With Mr Chambers' connection, they must have been educated as ragged scholars at Field Lane.

Peter paused to reflect on what he'd just learned. *Moses may well have been an orphan in 1851, if he stayed at an address as an inmate and attended a school for destitute children. He made a note to further investigate his parents.*

He looked forward to telling Felicity about what he'd discovered. He thought she would be equally interested since she'd only recently retired from primary school teaching. He wondered if she'd ever heard of a ragged school. He passed the next hour reading all about the ragged school system and how it spread as more schools opened. He learned that it was supported by charitable donations and religious organisations.

Next, Peter turned his attention to the 1861 Census. He quickly identified Moses, aged twenty-three, single, and a lodger at an address in Whitechapel. Nothing unusual there, but again, it was his occupation that was surprising. Despite some education, Moses, like his father, was a 'Scavenger'.

Is that a family trade? Peter wondered, *or was it more a case of necessity and the need to survive?* He had no idea, but he was truly intrigued.

The other lodgers – or more correctly 'boarders' as they were termed on the census – came mainly from London or Ireland. The head of the household was named as Arthur Rushton, a poultry and game dealer. He was born in Whitechapel, as were his two daughters, but the place of birth for Grace, his thirty-nine-year-old wife, was recorded as Marlborough, Wiltshire.

Peter's mind raced. *Could it be that Grace had some association with Oxenhope? Was she somehow a clue as to why Moses had left London and moved there?*

He felt it important to investigate her too. From the marriage records, he soon found a marriage for an Arthur Rushton to a Grace Turnbull in 1843, and registered in Marlborough. He remembered that Turnbull was the surname of the farmer at Oxenhope, so was certain that Grace was related to him. He worked out her year of birth as around 1822. He went back to his notes on the 1871 Census and calculated that Richard Turnbull's birth year would have been about 1820. Peter was pretty sure that Richard was Grace's older brother.

He reasoned that the 1841 Census would prove their connection, so looked up Oxenhope, but annoyingly, due to remoteness of location perhaps, it was missing from the census. Omissions of that nature were quite common. Instead, he ordered a copy of the Rushtons' marriage certificate to confirm the name of Grace's father.

By now, Peter's connection with Moses Jupp had grown considerably. Their paths had crossed – literally – albeit with a gap of about 150 years, but crossed they had. Now Peter realised, there was more to it, and not just a connection to the farm. Moses was a scavenger. Wasn't Peter himself a scavenger too, when he went out searching with his detector? In a sense he was. Like Moses, he searched for lost and discarded items – items which were hopefully of value – although, in Peter's case, those of historical interest were just as important to him. There the similarity ended. For Moses, the circumstances must have been entirely different. Scavenging was most likely an essential means of making his living, a way of life he had little choice in taking up. For Peter, metal-detecting was a hobby, a pastime, something enjoyable to do when he felt inclined.

What options did Moses Jupp have at a time of such poverty and hardship back in Victorian London? Peter could only wonder.

There was so much more he wanted to find out about the life of Moses. He checked for the births of any siblings, but drew a blank. He found what he thought were the deaths of his parents and it looked as if Moses had been orphaned by the age of five. He ordered death certificates for Samuel and Eleanor Jupp to prove that his suspicion was correct.

Recalling from the newspaper archive that when Moses died, he'd left a widow named Elizabeth, he decided he needed to know about her as well. How did she fit into his life? He had no idea of her background or what she did before she married. He searched the index to marriages and found what he thought was the correct marriage in the first quarter of 1870. Her maiden name was Doggett. He ordered a certificate for that event too.

Peter made a list of all the certificates he'd ordered. He hoped they'd fill in some of the blanks in his suppositions and theories concerning the life of Moses Jupp. How much more would he learn when they arrived? He would just have to be patient to find out.

CHAPTER 16

When the tide made it impossible for him to work on the foreshore, Moses continued to help out at the meat stall.

Old newspapers and periodicals were used for wrapping meat sold to customers. One day, he noticed that the sheet of paper he was about to use had illustrations of items termed as 'being of archaeological interest'. He glanced at the sketches and recognised some of them as similar to the curios he'd seen in Charles Blackett's window. The paper was part of a periodical magazine titled *The Gentleman's Magazine*. He put the remains of it aside and used another newspaper instead. Later, when trade slackened, he asked Mrs R if he could keep the periodical.

"Course you can, there's plenty more old newspaper over there, just use that."

After supper, when the Rushton family and their lodgers were gathered around the long table, Moses nipped back up to the small room he shared and brought down the periodical his landlady had said he could keep. Fortunately, it was almost complete.

Considering it was three years old and had been bundled up with string, it was still in good readable condition. Moses turned to the illustration that had first caught his interest. It was of an object described as a 'St James Scallop Shell Pilgrim Badge'. The text underneath explained that they were cast in lead alloy, small enough to clasp in the hand or be sewn onto a garment. Pilgrims brought them back from holy shrines as souvenirs.

Although Moses' historical knowledge was sketchy, he knew enough to guess that the item was a few hundred years old. It closely resembled the one he'd seen in Blackett's window, and then he remembered where else he'd seen one. The previous year, a mud-covered object had been shown to him by another scavenger who'd just found it on the foreshore. They'd decided between them that it was nothing more than a strangely shaped piece of lead. It was thrown into a basket with other bits and pieces of lead, all intended for melting down.

Moses was sitting beside Ned, who was illiterate, but Moses would help him by reading out announcements from the newspaper of forthcoming ratting events, in which dogs killed rats for sport. Ned provided the live rats. Apart from the ones he caught, he also had contacts in the countryside, so that he could also supply fresh farm rats. They had a reputation for being stronger and more difficult opponents.

Moses showed Ned the illustration he was studying. "You any idea how old somethin' like that would be? It says it's late medieval."

"Ain't got a clue, but you could ask Cecil in the corner, over there. He's new here, and he was tellin' me how he works in a bookshop."

Moses took the periodical over to Cecil and introduced himself. "I was wonderin', what with you workin' in a bookshop an' such, whether you'd know how old somethin' would be, if it was late medieval."

Cecil looked at the illustration. "Well, you're lucky because I happen to be interested in history. Let me see…late medieval would be roughly from the fourteenth to fifteenth century. It ended when the Tudor kings came to the throne. You've heard of Henry the Eighth? He was a Tudor."

Moses nodded. "He's the one with lots of wives!"

"That's him. Well, this pilgrim badge would probably be four or five hundred years old."

"I wondered if it might be somethin' like that."

"Are you interested in history then?"

"Yes I am, but I don't know much."

"Well, I'll tell you what, if any tatty history books come in that we can't sell, I'll bring them back here for you. We don't just sell new books; we also deal in second-hand ones.

"Thanks, that's very kind."

Cecil was true to his word, and regularly brought back history books for Moses. The books became important to him and he passed any spare time he had studying and learning. He particularly enjoyed reading about the period beginning with the crusades up to Elizabethan England. Whenever he came across sketches of ancient objects, he studied them carefully, committing them to memory, hoping that his growing knowledge might one day be put to use in identifying something he recovered from the river.

It wasn't an artefact, but another coin that caused Moses to call on Charles Blackett with the intention of making a sale. It had come from one of his favourite gravel beds, one that normally produced modern spendable coins. However, on a recent search, it had given up an old-looking silver coin that he didn't recognise. Using his growing library, Moses had identified it as French. He wasn't sure how to pronounce its name, but he suspected it was an unusual find and hopefully of more value.

Between the pattern of the tide, and working on the stall at busy periods, he found time, one afternoon, to make his second visit to the dealer's shop. Before setting out, he'd washed and spruced himself up. He'd put on a clean shirt, jacket, smart trousers, and black cap, all of which he'd recently bought second-hand, but in excellent condition. He'd given his boots a polish too.

He hoped that he might be shown in again by Blackett's parlourmaid. There was something about her that he hadn't been able to forget. During the fleeting moment they'd met, she'd made a very favourable impression on him and he'd even imagined walking out with her on a Sunday afternoon.

He reached Commercial Road and made his way along it until he reached the dealer's shop. He decided to spend a few minutes examining the window display. Instead of looking at what he considered on his first visit as mere curios, this time he recognised many of the items from his history books and further copies of *The Gentleman's Magazine* salvaged from the market stall.

Of the coins on the top two tiers, he now appreciated that they were organised into classes, based on age. There was a tray with four silver coins labelled 'Celtic', and next to it, two trays of bronze and silver coins marked 'Roman'. Another was marked 'Saxon'. The tray that contained the most coins was labelled 'Medieval'.

On the lower tier, the artefacts included two examples of Roman nail cleaners made from bronze, each with a lovely shiny dark-green patina. They were about three inches long. There was even a tiny bronze ear-scoop for removing wax. There were several more lead pilgrim badges and some dark-coloured medallions too. Nothing was priced, so he decided, if given the opportunity, he'd ask Mr Blackett to give him some idea of values. He felt sure that there was no reason why he shouldn't turn up objects like these himself. It was a matter of recognising what was worthwhile and also what sort of price he could expect to receive from the dealer.

During the few minutes he was studying the contents of the window, a gentleman entered the shop. The bell jangled as he did so. Moses observed what took place as discreetly as he could. It was obvious that the dealer knew the man, for they shook hands warmly. He watched as Charles Blackett reached into the window and removed the tray with the Roman bronze implements. A few minutes later, the gentleman left the shop. Shortly after, the dealer replaced the tray minus the ear-scoop. He spotted Moses and indicated to him to go to the back entrance.

Moses tapped the door gently. He was disappointed not to be let in by the parlourmaid, for it was Blackett himself who met him. They went through to his study.

"Hello Moses, have you something else for me?"

"Yes, sir, an old French coin, I think."

"Really? Let's have a look then, shall we?"

Moses pulled out a slim brass tin from his pocket. The hinged lid was decorated with the stamped impression of a ship under full sail. It was a recent find from the river, which Moses thought had probably been lost by a sailor who'd used it for snuff. Disappointingly, it had only contained mud when found, but its size and shape made it ideal to hold interesting coins. He'd polished it and lined the interior with a small offcut of dark-purple velvet he'd been given by Nellie. It certainly improved the impression he wanted to create to the dealer. He opened it to reveal his discovery.

Blackett took hold of the coin carefully, and turned it over under magnification. "Yes, you're right," he acknowledged. "Very nice too, and quite rare...Another one from the foreshore, I assume?"

"Yes, sir, that's right."

"So how did you know it was a Frenchie then?"

"I've been learnin' up on history. I've got my own set of history books and I've been readin' *The Gentleman's Magazine*."

"Have you indeed? I'm impressed."

"I was hopin' to ask you about some of the things in your window. I want to learn about them, in case I find somethin' similar down on the river."

"Well, I usually indulge in a glass of sherry about this time. What say we take a glass now and we can have a chat about what you want to know?"

"Yes please, sir. That would be most agreeable," said Moses, using a phrase taught to him by Mrs R.

Charles Blackett went to the fireplace and pulled a cord at one side. Moses heard a bell ring somewhere in the interior of the premises. Shortly after, there was a gentle knock and the parlourmaid entered. She was just as Moses had remembered: average height, and probably about the same age as him. She had a pretty face, and beneath the edge of her white cap, he noticed a wisp of fair hair. Her white apron was spotless, and the way she filled it hinted that she had a nice shapely form.

"Bess, please bring some sherry for myself and Mr Jupp."

"Yes, certainly, Mr Blackett." She nodded gently and left the room.

"So what would you like to know about the items in the window?" Charles Blackett asked Moses.

Moses' mind was on Bess, but he registered the question and quickly switched his attention to reply. "Well, sir, if I found a pilgrim badge, how much could I expect you to pay?"

"They're fairly common, but I've got collectors who are always keen to acquire an unusual one. As a guide, something which is worn or battered would be a shilling, but in good condition and with the details still clear and legible, and preferably indicating the shrine from which it originated, I'd probably give you two or three shillings."

"And those medallion things on the bottom shelf in the window?"

"They're from the time of the crusades. I might pay up to three shillings if you find a good one."

Moses did his best to hide his excitement. "So, what about Roman ear-scoops, or somethin' like that?"

"Well, nail cleaners, ear-scoops, toothpicks, and also bronze tweezers if you can find them, up to two pounds each; tweezers, maybe three pounds because they tend to break and complete ones are rare."

Moses took in as much information as he could. He was quite envious of the dealer's knowledge and listened carefully.

They were interrupted by another tap on the door. Bess came in carrying a tray with a white linen cloth, on which stood a bottle marked *Jerez* and two sherry glasses. She set it down on a table near the window.

"Thank you, Bess. Could you pour for us?"

"Very well, sir." She carefully filled the glasses and presented them on the tray to Moses and her employer.

Moses took his glass, taking the opportunity to make eye

contact with her. "Thank you," he said. He was even more struck by her beauty.

"Leave the bottle on the table, please, Bess."

Moses could barely take his eyes from her.

"If that's all, sir?"

"Yes, thank you, Bess."

She nodded, almost imperceptibly, and left the room, closing the door after her.

Moses had never before been offered sherry from a tray. He watched Blackett and copied how he took a small sip each time there was a pause in their discussion. The dealer gave no hint that he suspected his guest was unaccustomed to taking sherry every afternoon in similar fashion. Moses resolved to ask his landlady for more advice on how to act in what she called 'polite company'.

They continued with their conversation. By the end, Moses had a pretty good idea as to what the dealer was keen to buy.

"So," Blackett continued, "how much do you expect me to pay for this Frenchie? It's a double patard, by the way, from about 1470."

"I was hoping to get about fifteen shillings, sir."

The dealer pondered for a moment. "I'll give you twelve. How does that sound?"

It sounded like quite a lot to Moses. "Very well, sir." He put out his hand and they shook to confirm their agreement.

"You hang on here for a minute and I'll get your money." Blackett left the room.

Moses waited patiently and looked around. A large tall bookshelf took up one wall and was filled with an impressive number of books. A clock ticked loudly. He wondered whether he'd be likely to see the parlourmaid again before he left.

Blackett returned. "Here you are, young man, twelve shillings."

"Thank you, sir."

"Keep me in mind if you find anything else of interest won't you?"

"Yes, sir."

"Good. Now I need to get back to the counter. Wait here and I'll call Bess."

The dealer left the room. Presently, there was a tap on the door and Bess came in. "I'm to see you out, sir. I'll just collect the tray and glasses."

"Thank you," Moses replied nervously.

She picked everything up from the table. "If you'd care to follow me, sir."

Now was his chance.

When they reached the yard, he finally summoned his courage. "Are you doing anythin' this Sunday afternoon, miss? I've a mind to watch the female Blondin. I wonder if that might be a spectacle you'd like to watch with me."

"Is she Madame Genevieve, the tightrope walker?" Bess asked.

"That's right, miss."

"I'm not sure; I don't know you."

"Please, miss, it would be a great pleasure for me."

"Very well," she said quickly. "Meet me on the corner outside the shop at two o'clock."

Moses only had time to nod his agreement before she said goodbye and closed the back door.

On Sunday afternoon, Moses waited anxiously by Charles Blackett's shop. At two o'clock precisely, he saw the wooden gate in the wall open and Bess come out, shutting it quietly behind her. She wore a light jacket over a blouse, with a straw hat; just right for a warm August day. Moses thought she looked lovely. He was thrilled that she had agreed to pass the afternoon with him.

"Hello, Mr Jupp," she said formally.

"Moses, please call me Moses...Can I call you Bess?"

"Yes, of course."

He touched her gloved hand awkwardly.

"So what have you planned?" she asked.

"I thought we'd take a stroll down to the river and make our way along to the Cremorne Gardens at Chelsea. That's where one end of the tightrope is fixed. The other's over at Battersea. You haven't seen her before, have you? She's due to cross at three o'clock and four o'clock."

"No I haven't, and she is someone I'd very much like to see."

Moses offered Bess his arm, which she took, and the two of them set off towards the river. He thought they made a nice couple, he being of average height with Bess a few inches shorter.

"I think we'll be in luck with the weather, as long as it stays calm like now. The Blondin can't make a crossin' if it's too windy."

When they reached the Thames, Moses escorted Bess down to the pier at Tower Stairs. Waiting for them there was an old waterman whom Moses knew well.

"Hello Linus, this is Bess."

Linus and Bess shook hands.

"I thought we were walking up to Chelsea," said Bess, slightly confused.

"Ah, I've organised this as a surprise. Linus is a good friend."

Linus offered an arm to steady them as they stepped down into his wherry. After his passengers were seated at the stern, side by side, he unhitched and skilfully sculled out to midstream. He turned towards London Bridge, pulling on the oars with long powerful strokes.

"Have you been out on the river before?" he asked, making conversation with Bess.

"Only on a steamer, but that's all...not like this. It's completely different being closer to the water."

"Good job it's been cool, with plenty of rain recently to keep the river high, or you might have needed to hold your nose." Linus laughed.

"Yes, but not as bad as during the Great Stink," Bess replied.

"No, that's true, but it still gets smelly sometimes."

"Linus is going to take us right up to where Madame Genevieve will make her crossin'," Moses told Bess. "We should have a terrific view, much better than watchin' from the banks with all the other people, and for us it'll be free!"

Linus chuckled. "If she does fall off and take a duckin', let's hope she doesn't die of poisonin' from the river."

107

"Oh my word! I hope not," replied Bess, "but this is so exciting."

Moses could see that Bess was enjoying herself. She'd settled back in the seat and appeared to be appreciating the view.

As they came under the span of Battersea Bridge, they saw the female Blondin's rope strung across the river from bank to bank. On each side, hundreds of spectators were gathered where the ends of the rope were connected to metal platforms. A band could be heard on the Chelsea side playing popular favourites.

There were several steamers with their decks packed with day trippers. Pleasure craft and small boats were anchored. Others were jostling, and milling about, trying to hold station in the best viewing positions.

Linus rowed under the tightrope and spotted a ferry he knew well. The captain threw down a line so that they could tie up alongside. They had the perfect view.

The excitement in the crowd grew on the Battersea side, and Madame Genevieve could be seen climbing to the platform to commence her crossing. Her husband handed her a long balancing pole. As Big Ben struck four o'clock, she stepped onto the rope and took a few careful steps. The band fell silent.

Bess raised her hand to cover her mouth. She hardly dared look as the rope took the weight of the intrepid woman.

Madame Genevieve adjusted her balance to the sound of gasps from the crowd and then began to walk slowly but confidently across the wide span of the river. About a third of the way across, she paused to lower herself and kneel on the rope. She maintained her balance, much to the crowd's amazement. Then she rose and continued amid wild applause. As she passed the halfway mark and began to approach the Chelsea side, she came closest to Linus's boat. They could see her clearly as she paused again. This time she lifted one foot to the side and maintained her balance on her remaining leg. The spectators located on the water and on the land cheered and clapped to show their admiration for such an astonishing feat.

"How does she do it?" asked Bess in amazement.

"Good balance, I suppose, and bravery," said Linus.

"Or she's mad!" added Moses.

Meanwhile, Madame Genevieve was negotiating the last part of the crossing and climbing the slight incline to reach the anchor platform on the Chelsea bank. When she reached it and stepped onto it, an assistant took the balancing pole from her. She turned to take applause from the crowd below and from the starting point. The ferries and steamers sounded their horns and whistles. The band struck up again. Everybody cheered. It was a carnival atmosphere.

"So where would you like me to put you ashore?" asked Linus on their return journey.

"Somewhere near Temple Pier, if it's no trouble," replied Moses.

"Course not."

"Have you two been friends for a long time?" asked Bess.

"Oh yes, a good few years I'd say, eh Moses?"

"That's right, must be at least seven or eight. Linus sometimes sets me down on shoals and banks, which you can only reach at low tide with a boat. I've made some good finds from places like that and we split the proceeds, don't we Linus?"

"We do indeed. I generally leave him for a while and then come back for him before the tide returns."

"So is that right then, Moses, that you make a living from what you find on the foreshore?" asked Bess.

"Yes I do. I know it's not a very respectable occupation, but I manage all right. When I can't get down to the river, I help my landlady. She has a stall sellin' poultry and game. She's a lovely person. I like her a lot."

"He's been findin' some nice coins and artefacts recently," added Linus, trying to improve any impressions Bess may have been forming about Moses.

Moses was slightly embarrassed.

"I know Mr Blackett only deals in quality pieces," she

said, "so if you're selling to him then you must be finding some special items."

"Here we are," announced Linus. He expertly brought his boat alongside some stone steps leading up from the river, and put a rope through an iron ring to hold it steady.

Moses stepped off and held his arm out to Bess so that he could guide her up safely. "Thanks, Linus." He winked at his friend.

"Yes, thank you, Linus," added Bess. "It was most enjoyable."

"It was a pleasure. Enjoy the rest of the afternoon."

When they reached the top of the steps, they turned to watch Linus cast off. As he rowed away, they waved and shouted goodbye.

"What time should you be back?" asked Moses.

"By eight o'clock. Mr Blackett's a bit of a stickler. He's not a bad employer, but he wouldn't approve if he heard me coming in too late."

"So, shall we have somethin' to eat?"

"I ate at midday, thank you, but I'm sure I could manage a glass of lemonade."

Moses looked around and spotted some street vendors positioned to catch the attention of any thirsty and hungry passers-by.

"Let's try one of those. Do you like jellied eel?"

"Yes, especially in spice. I'd never tried it until I moved to London, but I've got quite a taste for it now."

"Two lemonades and two jellied eels, one with spices, please," requested Moses.

"Here you are, me darlin'," said the lady stallholder, passing over the food and drink. "That'll be threepence, please, and leave your glasses on that table afterwards."

Moses and Bess found a low wall nearby to sit on while they enjoyed their snack under the pleasant afternoon sun. They watched folk strolling by. They amused themselves swapping opinions on what the people wore, especially the ladies, and trying to guess what they might do in life.

On their walk back to the shop, Moses asked Bess about her childhood and how she became a parlourmaid.

"I was born, and went to school, in a small village called Theale. It's near Reading, in Berkshire. I say that because most people haven't heard of Theale. I've got two brothers and a sister. I'm the oldest and my father is a broom maker."

"What, like sweepin' brushes?"

"That's right: besoms."

"Sorry, I interrupted. Please carry on."

"The schoolteacher suggested I go into service, and my parents also thought it would be a good idea. I'd always wanted to come to London and so I looked in the newspaper and answered some advertisements. Mr Blackett's was the first interview I had. I thought he seemed kind, and so when he offered me the position of parlourmaid, I accepted. What about you, Moses?"

"I didn't have much choice, I'm afraid. I was five when my mother died. I don't really remember my father. He drowned when I was three."

"I'm so sorry. Who cared for you after your mother died?"

"My Aunt Agnes…for a few years. She was a widow, but she got married again and I didn't like her husband. I left when I was eleven and managed to look after myself, findin' things on the foreshore to sell like coal and copper nails. Then one day, I met a man who helped me enrol at the ragged school. I've got him to thank for my readin' and writin'. I was in a shoeblack brigade during the Great Exhibition."

"Were you really? Did you wear a uniform?"

"Course I did!" Moses laughed. "You should have seen some of my friends in the brigade though, when they got pelted with flour and eggs!"

"Really? Who would do that?"

"Oh, gangs of ruffians, those who hadn't been selected… Jealous types."

"Oh yes, I can imagine. So what happened? I'm sure I read somewhere that some boys saved up enough for passages overseas."

"I was doin' all right, but we had our pitches allocated by a police sergeant. He took a dislike to me and made life difficult, so I left and went back to workin' the river."

Moses didn't want to tell Bess what had really happened. He thought the afternoon had gone really well and didn't want to put her off.

He delivered Bess to Blackett's shop in good time before eight o'clock.

"Thank you, Moses. I've had a lovely afternoon."

"Do you think we could do somethin' like this again?" he asked.

"Yes, I'd like that very much."

"Next Sunday, then, same time?"

"Yes, that would be a pleasure."

Moses touched her gloved hand. He didn't feel brave enough to give her a peck on the cheek. Hopefully, he could save that for next time.

They parted and wished each other a good evening. He watched and waited until Bess was safely inside before turning and setting off for his lodgings. It was going to be a long week.

Moses continued to court Bess on Sunday afternoons, at least twice a month. They became increasingly fond of each other. He soon knew he was in love with her and had considered asking her to marry him, but fearing rejection, he decided he dare not because of his lowly means of earning a living, and the uncertainty of relying on the river to provide.

Apart from Mrs R's stall, his earnings were dependent on what he scavenged. He couldn't take on the responsibility of a wife, and ultimately children, with such a precarious income. He wanted to be able to provide a home, not a room in a boarding house. How could any woman like Bess consider him as a suitable husband?

He sought ways to improve his situation, and hopefully his appeal to Bess. In addition to the job at the stall, he assisted Ned at ratting contests. Although he found the events distasteful, he needed to make whatever money he could, but neither job gave him the opportunity to earn large sums. He consistently found more from the river than most other scavengers, but there was no certainty.

CHAPTER 17

The following week, when Peter had got home from the local supermarket, he opened the front door and was delighted to see some more envelopes from the General Register Office scattered on the carpet.

It was lunchtime, so now he had a dilemma. He was starving hungry. Felicity was out for the day, so she wouldn't be fussing over whether he'd eaten or not. Should he have some lunch first or open the post? He decided to eat, and then he could relax and savour the pleasure of discovering any fresh information the certificates might provide. He always felt a definite thrill when holding any certificate for the first time. It was the anticipation of what would be revealed. Certificates brought him closer to the characters he researched.

When he finally settled at his desk, about an hour later, he wasn't sure what to expect as he opened the envelopes and gathered the certificates together. The first one he studied was Moses' birth certificate. He was born on 4 January, 1838 to Samuel and Eleanor Jupp. No surprises there. Then he looked at his parents' death certificates. Eleanor had died in 1843 at the address in Tenter Street. 'Febris' was stated as the cause of death. Peter had never heard of it. A quick search online gave him the answer: *febris* was Latin for fever.

Samuel Arman Jupp's death was an unusual one. The cause of death was recorded as 'Drowning Accidentally by an Overflow of Water when in the Sewer'. He was found dead on 5 July, 1841, in the sewer near Custom House Stairs. Under the column for Rank or Profession, the Registrar had written 'Scavenger'.

Peter contemplated what he'd just learned. *If Samuel drowned in a sewer, he was probably a more elevated scavenger, known in slang at the time as a tosher: one who specialised in recovering valuable items from the sewers.*

He calculated that Samuel had died about four weeks after the 1841 Census, and what a ghastly death it must have been. With Eleanor passing away too, the certificates confirmed that Moses was an orphan by the time he was five. That would explain why he became a pupil at the ragged school.

The last two were marriage certificates. The first recorded the correct marriage of Moses Arman Jupp to Elizabeth Doggett, on 29 January, 1870, at the parish church in Theale, Berkshire. Moses' profession was entered as 'Scavenger' and Elizabeth's was blank. Their fathers' professions were recorded as 'Scavenger' and 'Broom Maker'. Underneath Samuel's name was written 'Deceased'.

The name Arman was new to Peter. He concluded that Samuel and Moses shared it as a family name. It was disappointing that Elizabeth's profession was not shown, but that was not unusual for marriages of that era.

Peter turned to his computer and checked the 1861 Census to see if it might help him. He was pleased to find an Elizabeth Doggett listed. She worked as a parlourmaid within the household of Charles Blackett, a dealer in ancient coins. The address was in Commercial Road. Another quick check online confirmed to Peter that Commercial Road was not far from Rushtons' boarding house.

So, he thought, *Moses and Elizabeth lived reasonably close to each other. That might partially explain how they met.*

Another possibility was that Moses may have done business with Charles Blackett. Scavengers and toshers often found coins. If they were ancient, he surely would have used a more specialised means of selling them.

He then looked at the second marriage certificate, concerning

Arthur Rushton and Grace Mary Turnbull. It had taken place in October 1843 at Saint Martin's Church, Wyke, Wiltshire. It was the nearest village to Oxenhope, and he knew it well. He and Felicity often ate at The Fox country pub, in Wyke. The restaurant had a good reputation. Grace's father was shown as William Turnbull, farmer. With one of the witnesses named as Richard Turnbull, Peter was certain that he was not only Moses Jupp's employer but also the brother of Grace – if not, then a cousin. It really didn't matter, though; more importantly, it proved that Grace Rushton was the connection between Moses and Oxenhope.

Peter mulled over what he'd learned from the census returns and various certificates. In 1861, Moses was a scavenger like his father. At the time of his marriage in 1870, he was still a scavenger; yet a year later, he was a lowly fogger tending livestock at Oxenhope. It was a big change in his situation, and the reason for it baffled Peter.

PART TWO

CHAPTER 18

LONDON, 1865

Sergeant Thurgut tapped gently on his superior's door and was told to enter.

"Ah, Harry, I've a little job for you. You're pretty well informed as to what goes in Whitechapel?"

"I'd like to think so, Inspector."

"Heard if any ratting goes on down there?"

"Well, there are rumours but, these days, activities like that tend to be kept a bit quiet, sir."

"I'm sure they are, but the fact is our own superintendent, no less, has been made aware by an influential member of parliament that the practice of killing rats for amusement is still taking place in Whitechapel. Do you know the Katherine Wheel public house? Apparently, that may be a venue for it."

"I know where it is, sir; certainly, the class of establishment where I could imagine such practices to continue. Of course, I've never been in there."

"No, that's good. I'd like you to pay a visit, but we don't want you being recognised. Make sure you disguise yourself – wear plain clothes – and see what you can find out. Report back to me. I want to know exactly what goes on. Then I'll decide whether we take the matter further."

"Yes, sir. I'll go this very evening, although depending upon the frequency of such activity it may be a week or two before I witness any such occurrences."

"Yes, I understand, but do your best. If nothing's happening at the Katherine Wheel, try to find another local place where these so-called sporting events might be held."

"Very good, sir."

"Thank you, sergeant. You may go."

Thurgut returned to the small office he shared with two other sergeants, one of whom was there at the time.

"George, you heard of any establishments with a rat pit?"

"Can't say I have, Harry, but I think there's one over in Whitechapel."

"Does the Katherine Wheel ring a bell?"

"Yes, that's it. Landlord's a stocky fellow, if he's the same one. I think his name was Kimber. It's a rough crowd that gets in there."

"I don't doubt it."

"Why are you asking?"

"The inspector wants me to do a bit of snooping, in plain clothes."

"Lucky you...I have to keep the old trouble and strife happy of an evening; not like you, all single and fancy free."

"It does have its compensations," laughed Thurgut.

"So what's it all about then, Harry; this plain clothes business?"

"Seems our masters are taking an interest in ratting."

"Oh, there'll be no fun left with the likes of them. Good job there's still plenty of the gentry among the dog fanciers to thwart them. So where do you stand on ratting?"

"Me? Never really thought about it. We used to have a little terrier when I was a nipper. He killed a rat or two, I can tell you. Rats is vermin I suppose."

"Exactly, so why bother trying to stop it?"

"No idea. Still, that's not my concern, is it? I've just got to pass an evening down there and report the facts."

Thurgut entered the Katherine Wheel, a tavern of unremarkable appearance, just after eight o'clock. He glanced about him as he made his way through the noisy, smoky, crowded atmosphere to the bar and ordered a jug of beer.

Customers, predominantly male, were gathered around tables, shouting and laughing, with tankards and jugs of ale before them. A few were entertaining lady friends; prostitutes, in fact, for no respectable lady would ever frequent such a place. A buxom pot-girl ran the gauntlet of straying hands as she attempted to clear empty jugs. In a snug corner, a group of hags sat huddled together, joking and cackling, worse for wear, clutching beakers of liquor.

Thurgut could see that the establishment was popular; its brown-stained ceiling witness to years of pipe-smoking, added to by the fumes emitted from the coal-fired brazier standing in the large hearth.

A fellow he assumed to be the landlord took his money without comment. He sampled his ale and nodded good evening to a customer who'd turned to look him over. He broke eye contact and scanned the room as far as he could see.

Good, he thought, *no one I recognise immediately, so hopefully no one here who knows me either.*

He took out his pipe and lit it, before turning back to the bar to watch the landlord. He was a portly individual with strong muscular arms. Thurgut could imagine him more than capable of slinging out those who got involved in a brawl or became unruly. He was deep in conversation with a rough-looking man, both leaning across the bar from their respective sides, heads together, speaking in low tones with cupped hands.

Behind the bar, a narrow counter ran. At the end of it, a trough overflowed with dirty mugs and glasses. The poor overworked young wretch washing them was struggling to keep up. Among the empty bottles on the counter, he noticed a well-thumbed book. He was close enough to read the title: *Champion Prize Fights.*

That's mainly boxing, he thought, *but it implies someone has an interest in fighting sports. Would that include ratting?*

He sipped his ale and looked nonchalantly around the room not wishing to attract any attention.

Can't see any sign of a rat pit. If it does take place here, then maybe they use another room, out the back somewhere.

He spotted a black and white bill pinned to a substantial door on the far side. He made his way over, casually, in order to read it. It was freshly printed and couldn't have been in place very long.

At Mr Kimber's Katherine Wheel, Katherine Wheel Court, Whitechapel, sparring every Monday and Saturday. Young and Bentham to take on all comers. Tempting prize money.

On Wednesday next, some excellent sport is announced. Two dogs are matched to kill two dozen barn rats each, for three guineas a side, neither to exceed 20 pounds in weight. A good supply of fresh barn rats and the rat pit always ready for gentlemen to test the quality of their dogs.

So, this confirmed the landlord's name and that the Katherine Wheel had a rat pit. Probably the door he was facing led to the where the sparring and the ratting took place. He tried the handle. It was locked.

"What you after then? Tryin' to find your way upstairs?"

Thurgut turned towards the female voice. She looked no more than twenty and her straw bonnet dressed with colourful ribbons set off nicely what was a pretty face.

"I thought it might lead to outside. I need some fresh air."

"What, too warm are you? Need me to come out with you and unbutton your coat?"

Thurgut thought about it for a moment, but decided he couldn't take the risk.

"Perhaps another time," he muttered reluctantly. He drained his ale before she could say anymore. She looked at him in a coquettish way, but he brushed past her and left by the door through which he'd entered.

Thurgut arrived a little earlier on his second visit to the Katherine Wheel. It was the night billed for the ratting. As before, there were plenty of customers. He bought a drink from a barman, not the landlord this time, and surveyed the scene while he supped.

He saw three men enter the pub and go directly through the large open door at the far side of the bar area; the door that had previously been locked.

A few minutes later, another group entered and did the same. Thurgut picked up his drink and followed them over to the doorway. A man stood at the side taking money. "One and sixpence each, please gents."

Thurgut joined the end of the line and paid the entrance fee. He followed the group through a further door, which took them outside into a dimly lit yard. Immediately, he became aware of shouting and whistling near at hand.

"Sounds like we're in for a good evening," said the leading man, opening a door on the other side of the yard. The source of the noise was immediately evident. The group, now including Thurgut, entered.

He found that he was in a rustic building with wooden beams extending upwards to the tiles on the roof. *It must have formerly housed city milking cows*, he thought. It was quite large and the interior was lofty enough to accommodate the boxing ring, with tiered seating for spectators on three sides.

Thurgut was struck by the smelly atmosphere. It was a concoction of stale beer, smoke, sweaty people, rats, and dogs. Gas lights provided illumination. He tried to identify the mixture of sounds. There were shouts, shrieks, and cheers; also the noise of barking from excited and aggressive dogs.

The ring, with ropes and canvas, was directly before him. He looked up to observe a man seated at a table, his back to him. On the far side, he realised there was a gap between the ring and the first row of seats. As he moved around, he saw that the gap was occupied by two rat pits. He estimated each to be about eight feet square with chest-high wooden sides. It was hard to be sure, because the sides of both pits were obscured, surrounded by a tightly-packed wall of men, about twenty-five to each pit. They were shouting encouragement and cheering the dog in the pit below them. "Go on, Dandy boy, go on! Just five more!"

From the other pit, "Show 'em you're a good'un, Judy, come

on gal," followed by a loud cheer.

A short blast from a hunting horn announced the first dog to kill its quota of rats. Thurgut could now see that the man at the table, up in the ring, was Kimber, the landlord. He was clearly in control of the scene below, seated with a timing clock and brass horn. It became apparent that he was referee and timekeeper.

"Judy wins with twenty rats in three minutes and twenty-seven seconds," he announced. There was a further cheer.

Those who'd placed their money on Judy jumped and shouted in jubilation. Those around the other pit were disappointed, but keen to see how their dog would do, their attention returned to the scrap before them. Their hooter sounded at four minutes and ten seconds.

A queue formed at the side of the ring, for those who were due winnings. The landlord was joined by another man who scrutinised the bets and paid out accordingly. Meanwhile, the dogs were retrieved and a young urchin jumped into each pit to remove the dead rats.

Judy was held aloft for all to see. She was badly cut around the eye and mouth, but her owner seemed unconcerned; just ecstatic to accept hearty congratulations and the prospect of his prize money.

Thurgut looked over towards the other pit. The owner of Dandy was fitting a muzzle to his dog. Its ears were bleeding profusely. Several spectators commiserated, wishing him better luck next time.

Thurgut found the whole thing intensely exciting. He wondered why anyone would want to prevent such sport. He had no sympathy for the dogs; no thought of any cruelty. It was in their nature to kill rats, which of course were mere vermin. Hopefully, there'd be more bouts to follow. Maybe he could even place a wager or two for himself?

The landlord sounded his horn again and announced that the next competition, open to all comers, would take place in twenty minutes. It would be for dogs around twelve pounds in weight to take on twenty-four rats. He encouraged the spectators to avail themselves of a drink from the ringside bar and invited any two gentlemen, who wanted to enter their dogs, to sign up and weigh in.

Thurgut relit his pipe and joined the queue to buy a beer. He listened hard to the conversations around him, trying to glean any information which might help him to choose his dog.

From the back of the room, two young dandies approached the ring with their dogs. The two animals were small terriers: one almost completely white, the other black and tan. The men were well dressed in velveteen coats with large shiny buttons, over black trousers and silk shirts. The landlord came down from the ring and each dog was weighed on a substantial pair of scales. The weights were noted.

The landlord climbed back up onto the canvas and invited the two men with their dogs to join him.

"The match will be between the white terrier called Snowy and the black and tan whose name is Jack," he called out.

There was excitement among the spectators. The owners were invited to parade the dogs around the ring for all to see, causing a great deal of discussion and speculation in the crowd. Thurgut thought he heard someone say they'd seen Jack before at another venue and he'd despatched twenty rats in less than three minutes.

"We've a good supply of barn rats, this evening; fresh in from the country, with full sets of teeth," the landlord continued. "The rules of this class govern that any dog over twelve pounds will take on an extra rat for every four ounces of excess weight. Jack weighs in at twelve pounds five ounces and will therefore have one extra rat, making twenty-five. Snowy weighs twelve pounds eleven ounces and will therefore fight two extra rats, making twenty-six. The prize is set at two pounds to the winning side. Any dog failing to kill its quota of rats within six minutes will be disqualified and all wagers forfeited."

Thurgut decided that he liked the look of Jack and elected to throw caution to the wind. He put five shillings on Jack to complete the task, in less than two minutes forty-five seconds. His odds were 6–1. It was a lot of money to stake, but the excitement was intoxicating and he was enjoying himself immensely. He puffed contentedly on his pipe while watching the proceedings closely.

Up in the ring, the landlord tossed a coin and invited the dogs' owners to choose heads or tails. He turned back to the spectators. "Jack will take the pit on my left and Snowy the pit on my right."

Thurgut left his drink on a seat and pushed through to get a place at Jack's pit. Men squeezed in around him, but he had a good view. On one side of the pit was a platform that was level with the top of the pit wall. Upon it was a cage full of rats squeaking and scratching to get out.

"Let's have twenty-five in Jack's pit and twenty-six in Snowy's pit," ordered the landlord.

A handler wearing a leather glove fearlessly thrust his hand into the stocking-leg mouth of the cage and grabbed rats by their tails, flinging them out into the pit.

Thurgut recognised him as the man who'd been in close conversation with the landlord on his previous visit. The fanciers and spectators around the walls counted them in unison as they were thrown in. An assistant stood by him. He went off to bring a further cage to the platform to complete the tally. Thurgut thought he recognised the man, but wasn't sure where from.

"Mr Wheeler, our scrutineer, has overseen the count," announced the landlord, turning to Mr Wheeler. "Do you confirm that Jack will face twenty-five and Snowy twenty-six?"

"Ay, I do."

"Very well…On the count of three, the dogs will be put to the rats and I will start timing." He paused for a moment, and checked with the owners that they were happy for the competition to commence. They nodded their agreement. He picked up the hooter and began the count. "One, two, three…" The crowd counted with him. He honked the hooter and the dogs were dropped over their respective pit wall.

Thurgut was captivated. He'd never seen such ferocity and carnage. Around him, the spectators yelled encouragement, banging the wooden sides with their hands and feet to startle any rat seeking to shrink back.

Jack was so fast that he'd killed ten rats within the first minute. At two minutes, there remained four rats, but Thurgut could see that the dog was tiring, and one of the rats had clamped its teeth to his ear. The dog shook his head violently and dislodged it. Two minutes thirty seconds and two were left. One he killed decisively, but the last ran quickly around the internal perimeter of the pit. With five seconds left, Jack caught it and tossed it triumphantly into the air.

The rat fell dead just as the landlord sounded the horn. "Two minutes, forty-three seconds for Jack," he announced.

Thurgut cheered along with everyone else. *What sport! And I've just won thirty shillings – a week's wages!*

Meanwhile, in the next pit, Snowy had still to finish. The three-minute mark went past, then four minutes and five minutes. The noise around the pit diminished. Thurgut couldn't see, but he surmised the dog was tiring. At six minutes, the horn sounded, and a cry of anger went up from those who'd forfeited their wagers. There was no thought for the dog or the rats. Men moved way murmuring and disgruntled. Thurgut looked over the side. Two rats were still alive, but Snowy, the white terrier, was covered in bloody bites. A rat clung to his eyelid and he lay still, barely breathing. He would have to be put down.

Nothing, however, could dampen Thurgut's spirits. He presented his betting ticket and watched with glee as thirty shillings plus his five shilling stake was counted out and handed to him. He placed the winnings into his inside coat pocket. He debated whether to leave or stay for the next contest, the one advertised, between the dogs in the twenty-pound class, but was enjoying himself so much, he decided to stay.

By the time Thurgut decided to leave the Katherine Wheel, he had acquired nearly four pounds in winnings.. He patted his pocket contentedly. Unfortunately, he'd barely left Katherine Wheel Court when he was struck from behind. Stunned, he fell;

landing face down on the cobbles.

When he recovered consciousness, he rubbed his head. He felt a bump forming. Then he remembered where he was. His first thought was his money. He fumbled in his coat pocket. It was empty! His winnings had gone. He, Sergeant Thurgut of the Metropolitan Police, had been robbed!

He got up onto his feet feeling groggy, but aware enough to feel misery and anger. Whoever had taken his money must have seen him winning, and watched where he'd put it. Somebody who was there that evening was responsible. He vowed to himself that if ever he got hold of the culprit, he'd exact his revenge.

The following day, Thurgut presented his report to the police inspector.

"I attended a ratting event at the Katherine Wheel in Whitechapel yesterday evening, sir. I observed several fights which involved dogs killing rats within a rat pit. They have two rat pits. From what I could ascertain, these fights are held regularly on the first and third Wednesdays each month. Soon after leaving the establishment, I was struck from behind and robbed."

"Any permanent injury?"

"No, sir, just a nasty bump on the head."

"Sorry to hear that Thurgut, but well done for getting the information. It just goes to show the sort of criminal element that this type of activity attracts. How many persons would you say were there to witness this so-called sport?"

"I should say forty to fifty around the rat pits, mainly of the lower orders. There were more seated, including some gentlemen with their grooms and coachmen, so about seventy in all."

"Anybody recognise you?"

"I don't think so, sir."

"Good, what about you? See anyone you knew?"

"No, sir," but as he said it, Thurgut recalled the assistant who'd brought in the other cage of rats and suddenly realised who he was.

He's grown up since I last saw him. How long is it? Must

be fourteen years, but there's no mistaking that spikey hair with a touch of ginger, and the freckles...Moses Jupp. Could it have been him that robbed me?

"Who's the landlord?"

"Wilfred Kimber, sir."

"I know the superintendent's keen to get ratting tested in court. When's the next ratting night?"

"In two weeks' time...Wednesday the twenty-first, sir."

"Right, we'll call in at the Katherine Wheel on the twenty-first. I intend to take the lead, but you will accompany me, along with four constables."

"Which law are we seeking to enforce, sir?"

"I've already had a chat with the superintendent." The inspector pulled out a sheet of paper from a small pile on his desk. "Here we are...He wants to use the statute prohibiting the baiting of any bull, bear, badger, dog, cock, or any other kind of animal, whether of domestic or wild nature. That should cover it!"

"Very well, sir."

The six policemen duly attended the ratting contest on the appointed evening. They signalled the doorman to stand aside and, with Thurgut's guidance, they crossed the inner yard and entered the former cattle shed containing the boxing ring and the rat pits. Most of the cheering and excitement died immediately.

The inspector climbed up onto the canvas and ordered everyone to remain where they were. Thurgut took up a position at the side of the boxing ring. Two constables guarded the exits. The other two went to prearranged positions at each of the rat pits, from which the noise of dogs still killing rats emanated. Those surrounding the pits looked up to Wilfred Kimber for guidance.

The inspector spoke to him briefly with quiet authority. "Will the owners of the dogs please remove them immediately."

Murmurings and protests broke out.

"It's all right, everyone," Kimber announced. "Keep calm and do as you're instructed. This is only a police inspection. We don't want no trouble."

The two dogs were hooked out of their respective pits. One of them was badly cut around the mouth and was bleeding copiously.

Kimber spoke to the inspector in lowered tones. "What's this all about? There ain't no law against ratting!"

"It seems there is."

"What's the law I'm supposed to have broken?"

"The law covering the baiting of animals."

"Never 'eard of it!"

"Ignorance is no defence, I'm afraid, sir. You can argue your case before a magistrate."

"I will, you can be sure of that!"

Thurgut, meanwhile, had brought out his pocket book and, assisted by the two constables, began to gather names and addresses of those in attendance. He began with Wheeler, the scrutineer, and then the dogs' owners, along with descriptions of the condition of each dog. Then, much to his satisfaction and pleasure, he took details from the provider of the rats and his assistant, namely one Moses Jupp.

"Looks like we meet again, me and you. This should get you a ticket to Botany Bay if I have anything to do with it."

Moses did his best to look unconcerned. He'd assumed until then that Thurgut hadn't recognised him. Could he really get him transported?

Two wealthy-looking fellows stood at the back, each next to a closed wooden box with ventilation holes. They were fanciers and had brought their dogs along in order to participate. When Thurgut took their details, he noted that one was a marquis; the other had a prestigious address off Portman Square. He smirked to himself. There was nothing like catching out the gentry.

The inspector was particularly interested in the pile of betting tickets he spotted under the table. They'd been hastily hidden underfoot by Wheeler, but were revealed when he was requested to stand and provide his details. Here was proof that gambling was taking place on the premises, as well as the possible contravention of laws on animal cruelty. Both Wheeler and Kimber had large amounts of cash in their pockets. This was counted and the amounts recorded.

Once the police had all of the information they needed, the inspector announced the end of the evening and instructed the spectators and participants to leave in an orderly fashion. Before dismissing his officers, the inspector thanked them for their parts in the operation.

Thurgut left, feeling pleased with himself. Ever since he'd been robbed, his attitude to the Katherine Wheel and its patrons had been soured. He was looking forward to giving evidence in court as to what he'd witnessed. He would be a very important asset to the prosecution. It would be even more pleasurable if Kimber, and those involved in running the event, received custodial sentences.

Admittedly, a fine is more likely, but what if Moses Jupp is unable to pay?

He gloated as he imagined the magistrate condemning Moses Jupp to ten years' penal servitude.

Wilfred Kimber was summoned to appear on two counts before the Honourable Justice Porter, a magistrate of great experience: the first of baiting rats and the second of contravening The Betting Act 1853, by permitting unlawful gaming to take place in licensed premises. The case was heard without a jury at the local police court.

The prosecution, acting for the police commissioners, argued that Kimber kept a place for baiting rats. Sergeant Thurgut was called to give evidence. He explained how he had visited in plain clothes and seen the printed handbill announcing the forthcoming ratting.

"Who organised the printing of the handbill?" asked the magistrate.

Wilfred Kimber admitted that he had a customer who was a printer.

Thurgut then told of his second covert visit. He described the design of the rat pits and, in graphic detail, the scenes he had witnessed within, and the injuries sustained by the dogs.

The defence, led by a distinguished and well-connected solicitor, contended that the rats did not come within the Act of Parliament, prohibiting the baiting of any bull, bear, badger, dog, cock, or any other kind of animal, whether of domestic or wild nature.

In the public gallery, a number of gentlemen looked to one another with satisfaction. Their solicitor had begun well.

"Rats are vermin and the enemy of man. It could not be an offence to kill them," he went on to say.

The magistrate wanted to know who had supplied the rats. Edward Sabin and his assistant, Moses Jupp, rose to give their names.

"Which of you obtained the rats?"

"Me, your Honour. Moses 'ere just 'elps me on ratting evenings with the cages."

"From where do the rats come?"

"I have a contact what sends me healthy farm rats, your Honour, from the countryside. If they wasn't bein' killed by the dogs, they'd be eatin' up valuable grub on the farm."

The magistrate looked impressed with such an argument. He deliberated for a few moments before speaking again.

"Rats are not mentioned, nor specifically included within the Act and therefore could not have been intended for protection under the law. In this case, I am satisfied that they were not intended for fighting or baiting, but for killing. I therefore dismiss the first count!"

There was much jubilation in the public gallery. This was brought to order by the magistrate's gavel.

Thurgut looked shocked and visibly humiliated by the decision of the magistrate.

Proceedings were adjourned until after lunch, and the court resumed in the afternoon to consider the second count of permitting unlawful gaming.

The police inspector took the stand for the prosecution. He described how betting tickets were issued to customers by James Wheeler and Wilfred Kimber, on the length of time a dog took to despatch an agreed number of rats. Tickets removed from the Katherine Wheel were produced as evidence. They showed odds and the amounts wagered. Wheeler had seven pounds and four shillings in his possession. Kimber had twelve pounds, eight shillings and sixpence, both mainly in shillings and sixpences.

Wilfred Kimber and James Wheeler admitted the offence; however, great consternation occurred when Wheeler pointed to Sergeant Thurgut, who was seated on the prosecution's side and accused him of actively partaking in the gaming when in plain clothes. He further declared that the police officer had, on at least on one occasion, wagered five shillings at odds of 6–1 and that his winning bet had resulted in a payment to him of thirty shillings plus his stake.

There was a good deal of murmuring and sniggering from the gallery.

The Honourable Justice Porter called for order. He looked sternly over his half-glasses. He seemed to take a dim view of the policeman's conduct and asked if there were any other witnesses to support the accusation.

At this point Moses Jupp stood. He said that he had seen Sergeant Thurgut receive his winnings from Mr Wheeler and that he had put them into his inside coat pocket.

There were more murmurings and whispers from the gallery.

Still standing, Moses Jupp seemed emboldened. Now was his chance to deliver a well-deserved blow to his tormentor. "When I was in the Field Lane Shoeblack Brigade, he – Sergeant Thurgut – took part of my earnin's every week."

At this point there was uproar. The magistrate slammed down his gavel and called order again. The noise died down.

"These are serious allegations." He looked towards the inspector. "They are beyond consideration here today, but I would advise you to investigate them most thoroughly."

"Yes of course, your Honour."

The magistrate returned to the case in hand. "Wilfred

Kimber, I find you guilty of contravening The Betting Act 1853 and fine you fifteen pounds. For assisting you, I fine James Wheeler, ten pounds; Edward Sabin, five shillings; and Moses Jupp, one shilling."

The superintendent was notified by his inspector of the allegations against Sergeant Thurgut. Being most anxious to preserve the good character of the police, when any imputation was made against them, he always considered it important to investigate the matter thoroughly, for the sake of the public and the police force itself. An investigation therefore took place.

Thurgut denied that he had wagered any money when observing the ratting contest. However, one of his colleagues, who did not like the way Thurgut conducted himself as a policeman, told of how Thurgut had bemoaned the loss of nearly four pounds when he was robbed leaving the Katherine Wheel; the proceeds he said, of "a little bit of luck".

The trustees of the Field Lane Shoeblack Brigade were contacted. Thurgut was working at the police station near Seven Dials at the time and was responsible for supervising and allocating pitches to the boys. He denied any wrongdoing.

It was a matter of record that Moses Jupp had been expelled from the brigade in 1851, when he was found to have concealed some of his takings inside his sock. However, two other boys in the brigade had been dismissed that year for unsatisfactory conduct. The trustees looked into the records of disciplinary proceedings. One boy had been dismissed when he accused Thurgut of demanding a sum of money to give him a more favoured pitch. There was no evidence to support the allegation. In the other case, they found a simply written statement from the boy, claiming in defence that Thurgut had been "scimmin' off" some of his takings each week. However, the boy was not believed and was discharged from the brigade. Later that year, Thurgut had been transferred to other duties and there had been no subsequent allegations of a similar nature against any of the police officials involved in the scheme.

Thurgut's superiors decided that there was enough circumstantial evidence to suspect him of serious misconduct. He had also proved to be an unsuitable witness for the prosecution in the ratting case. The loss on the first count, in court, had caused the inspector and the superintendent considerable embarrassment. It was decided that the sergeant's conduct was not as it should have been and that he was not a fit person to continue in the Metropolitan Police.

Sergeant Thurgut, 6B of H division was no more. He left the police station for the last time as plain Harold Thurgut, single, looking for some means of employment and holding a grudge against Moses Jupp.

CHAPTER 19

LONDON, 1868

With his court appearance in the case of ratting long forgotten, Moses continued to work on the foreshore whenever the tide allowed. He took his interesting finds directly to Charles Blackett and did good business with him. It also gave him the chance to say hello to Bess, and steal a moment with her, if she answered the door.

He found that he was beginning to accumulate some cash. Rather than having to hide it against theft, he opened an account at the Post Office Savings Bank in Commercial Road. Whenever he sold items to Blackett, he deposited as much as he could spare into his savings account.

Work was taking place to enlarge and deepen Fontwell Dock. He'd heard a rumour that several items of interest had been recovered from the excavations. It was not really the sort of place in which he liked to search, but he went down to Fontwell to investigate. His luck was in. As he was about to take the stairs down to the muddy diggings, he stood back to allow an individual who was ascending to pass him. Like him, he was carrying a rake and a sieve. It was obvious he'd been searching in the mud.

"Any luck?" Moses asked.

"Nothin' really, 'cept this, an' I ain't got much 'ope for it."

The man, whom Moses had never seen before, showed him

a flat shield-shaped medallion, about two inches across and made of dark metal. Moses took it and examined it. It appeared to depict a bearded king in profile wearing a crown. It also had a suspension loop. It resembled those he'd seen in Blackett's window and the dealer had said he'd pay up to three shillings for one. He'd seen illustrations of similar examples regularly in *The Gentleman's Magazine*. They were definitely sought after by collectors because they came from the time of Richard the Lionheart and the crusades. He knew it was something Blackett would want to buy.

"What do you want for it?" asked Moses, as nonchalantly as he could manage.

The stranger weighed him up. "What would you be interested in it for?" He seemed suspicious.

"Look, I need to show somethin' when I go home. I'll give you sixpence for it."

The stranger knew it was generous offer. He'd expected about half that. "Call it a shilling, and you can have it."

"Nine pence," countered Moses.

"Done," said the stranger.

Moses paid the man and put the medallion in his pocket. He decided not to venture further into Fontwell Dock; he'd just had an amazing idea.

If there were collectors avidly seeking such objects, then what could be the harm in making a few copies and selling those too? They would be happy to add to their collections, and he could make some extra money. Everyone would be happy. The problem was that he did not have the skills or know-how to make copies.

On the way back to his lodgings, he tried to think of someone he knew whom he could trust to make an accurate copy. He discounted Foundry Tom. He was getting very old, and melting down metal was as far as he went. No, Moses needed to find someone who could make a die or mould from the object and use it to cast further examples.

Then he remembered Eddie Milner. Eddie was a couple of

years older, and taller, with strikingly blond hair. Like Moses, he was a Whitechapel lad who'd taken to mudlarking as a means to survive. They'd bumped into each other recently when Moses was on his way to the stall...

"Whatcha up to then?" Eddie had asked.

"Oh, still doing a bit a larkin'," Moses had replied nonchalantly. He didn't want to admit that he was making up his income by drawing the guts out of poultry. "What about you?" he asked quickly, hoping to divert the conversation. "Ain't seen you down on the river lately."

"Ah, well, I've moved on. I'm a metalworker now," Eddie had said proudly.

"Really? Where's that then?"

"You know Billy Nunn?"

"Yes, I know Billy...not seen him for a while. We were shoeblacks together."

"That's right, he was a shoeblack. Did well for himself out of it, did Billy. Got himself an apprenticeship with a metal founder and nowadays he's got his own workshop off Rosemary Lane."

Moses had been impressed, but couldn't help feel a pang of regret over the circumstances of his own dismissal from the Central Brigade.

Eddie had gone on to explain that Billy specialised in making small brass or pewter castings, and deck fittings for the many maritime shipbuilders situated along the river. Everything had to be of good quality to stand up to marine conditions.

At the first opportunity, Moses made some enquiries and found Billy Nunn's place of work. It was a yard with a small building attached. As he entered, Moses was struck by the pungent smell of hot coals and hot metal. The air was thick with acrid smoke, for Billy and Eddie were in the process of pouring the contents of a crucible into a line of moulds. The moulds were laid end to end on the floor of the yard. The heat was intense. They were using long handled tongs to grip a vessel full of white hot metal.

Moses waited patiently until they had finished. Billy came over to greet him, removing heavy leather gloves. They shook hands. Eddie joined them a few seconds later, using the break to light his pipe.

"Good to see you both," said Moses.

"And you too, Moses," they replied almost together.

"Any luck with the scavenging lately?" asked Eddie.

"Oh, could be better, but you know what it's like."

"Course I do, that's why I packed it in!"

"So what you doin' here then?" asked Billy. In contrast to Eddie, he was a dark swarthy character, more stocky and compact in build.

Moses showed them the medallion from Fontwell. "Do you think you could copy this and make more like it for me?" He handed it to Billy.

"Yes, I think we could." He passed it to Eddie who turned it over and examined it closely. "This is from the river, ain't it?"

"Yes it is," admitted Moses. He'd already decided it would be pointless to lie. Eddie would guess anyway.

"What you goin' to do with them if we make some copies?" asked Billy.

"I think I might be able to sell them."

"Really?" Billy considered for a moment. "Suppose it's no concern of mine what you do with them."

"How old is it?" asked Eddie.

"I'm not sure exactly...could be three hundred years." Moses knew that it was much older but, on that bit of detail, he doubted that Eddie would know otherwise.

"Problem is the look of it though," commented Billy. "If we made some, they'd look brand new."

"We could try treating them afterwards with chemicals to age them a bit or maybe rub in some traces of mud," added Eddie.

Moses smiled. Eddie was thinking along the right lines for his scheme to work.

"How many you wantin'?" asked Billy, "Only, we'll have to make a mould."

"I was thinkin' of having twenty to start with. Would that be worth your while?"

"I would have thought so," replied Billy. "Depends on the price, of course."

Moses left the workshop feeling pleased. The price he had negotiated with Billy Nunn would give him a nice profit, assuming he could sell them to Charles Blackett for a decent amount. He'd promised to return the following week to pick up the castings. He just hoped that they were of sufficient quality to make them attractive to Blackett and his collectors.

In the meantime, Moses revisited Fontwell Dock several times, in order to buy any other interesting artefacts, should they continue to be found. He hoped to time his arrival with navvies or mudlarks coming away from the dock. Unfortunately, the second time that he went to Fontwell, he encountered no one.

On his next visit though, he saw a gang of navvies at work. He asked their gaffer if any metal objects had turned up during the diggings. The man showed him a small lead pilgrim badge in the form of an ornate cross. He said, "Don't know what it is, but I reckon it's old an' worth sommat."

Moses bought it for sixpence. The man was delighted, for it would buy some beer that evening. He promised to look out for anything small, old, and made of metal, and to hold it for Moses to see.

On his fourth visit, the gaffer had something else for him. It was another medallion. It appeared to have a knight in armour on it and some unreadable marks around the rim. Moses was thrilled, but of course he disguised his interest. He paid sixpence, again, and left the dock well satisfied. Could he really have found a way to make some money? He now had more objects that could be copied, but before he got too confident, he decided to wait to see the quality of what Billy and Eddie produced.

As it turned out, he needn't have worried, for when he called at Nunn's workshop again, he was very pleased to be shown twenty very authentic looking medallions bearing the bearded face with a crown.

Billy explained how they'd used plaster of Paris to make a mould. "We poured in an alloy of two parts copper and one part lead, called cock-metal. We've aged them in acid. They look good, don't they?"

"They'll certainly do," beamed Moses.

Moses paid the sum agreed. He asked them to keep the mould for the moment, explaining that he hoped to be able to order more copies.

Moses' next task was to sell the medallions to Charles Blackett. He wasn't sure quite how to approach him. Blackett was no fool, but Moses knew he had an eye for a bargain and a ready supply of clients. As was usual, he called at the side door of the premises. Disappointingly, Bess was out on an errand and the door was opened by the cook. She called Mr Blackett, who invited Moses into his study.

"Got something interesting, I hope?" Blackett asked, rubbing his hands with excitement.

"Yes, Mr Blackett." Moses gave him the medallion. "What do you think?"

Blackett took the medallion over towards the window and pulled out his magnifier. He examined it closely. "I should say it's another Richard II medallion. Nice one too. I'll give you three shillings for it."

That was just what Moses wanted to hear. Not only had he offered sufficient money, but it was for one of his copies and it had passed close inspection!

"If I could provide some more like that, would you be interested?"

"Yes, yes of course I would."

"No, sir, I mean the very same…Just like that one, in fact?"

There was a pause while Blackett thought. "Identical, you mean?"

"Yes, sir, I do."

There was another pause while Blackett considered.

"I'm not sure. I'll need to think a little. One needs to be certain of the um...legal position. Can you come back the day after tomorrow?"

"Yes, sir."

"Good. I'll hold on to this one in the meantime. Bring any other examples with you. I'll give you my answer."

"Very well, sir."

With that, Moses was shown out.

When he returned two days later, Moses knocked at the side door to the shop feeling anxious. This passed when Bess welcomed him with a smile and a brief touch of the lips. She beckoned him in and called for Mr Blackett.

"Coming, coming," he called, his footsteps approaching. "Thank you, Bess. Back to your duties please."

Moses followed Blackett into the study, holding the medallions in a cloth bag.

"So, these are the others, are they?"

Moses nodded as he handed over the bag.

Blackett gently tipped the contents out onto his desk and moved them around slowly, carefully checking them. "And they're all the same?"

"Yes, sir."

"How many are there here?"

"Nineteen there, sir." Moses had decided to keep the original.

Blackett looked him in the eye. "I'm willing to buy them..."

Moses was delighted and relieved, but tried not to give anything away.

"...But I can't pay three shillings each."

Moses tried not to show any sign of disappointment. "So what would you offer?"

"Two shillings each, and I'll take the lot."

"That's not enough...half a crown each is my lowest."

Blackett looked at Moses closely. "Would you be able to supply more of these, if I required them?"

"Yes, and different ones too. If you liked these, then I was

142

hoping to bring in a different medallion and a nice lead pilgrim badge."

"You have different designs?"

"Yes."

Blackett turned to look out of the window while he considered. After a few moments, he turned back to Moses. "Very well, half a crown each it is. When can I see the other examples?"

"Give me a fortnight."

"Two weeks, eh?"

"Yes."

Blackett nodded. "Fine. Hold on here while I get your money."

Moses waited. *Two pounds and ten shillin's in total from Blackett*, he thought. *I only have to pay Billy Nunn ten shillin's. That's a tidy profit of two pounds! Can it really be this easy?* He tried to keep calm by concentrating on the sound of the clock ticking on the mantelpiece.

Blackett returned and paid Moses the money. "Here we are. Don't forget, if you come to me, I'll always give you fair prices."

"Yes, thank you."

After Moses left the shop, his first stop was at the Post Office to pay a pound into his savings account. Then he called at his lodgings to collect the second medallion, and the pilgrim badge he'd bought from the gaffer at Fontwell Dock. He then returned to see Billy Nunn and agreed terms on twenty of each, for collection in ten days' time.

He had the feeling that life was getting better for him. Perhaps he and Bess could have a future together.

Moses called to collect the second batch of medallions and the cross-shaped pilgrim badges from Billy Nunn. As agreed, Billy had aged the objects to give them an authentic look. Moses made sure that he was given back the originals although the copies were so convincing it hardly mattered.

"Do you think I could see one of the moulds?" Moses asked Billy.

"Course you can…Eddie, bring the medallion mould over."

Eddie picked up the two halves of the plaster of Paris mould and placed them on a bench in front of Moses and Billy.

Moses looked at the interiors closely. "Is that stuff fairly soft? I mean, could you cut designs into it if you had a sketch to follow? I'm thinkin' of addin' letters and symbols to a medallion, and maybe doin' a different pilgrim badge."

"Yes, easily," replied Billy. "We could add them to that mould or we could start with a new one. Wouldn't be a problem, would it Eddie?"

"Not for me. I like doing decorations an' such. I can use something pointed to cut them."

"Course, it would add to the price, but not too much," said Billy.

"Well that seems fair," acknowledged Moses. "I'll call in tomorrow with some designs and you can see what you think."

Billy nodded in agreement.

"And I need to settle up for these. Ten shillin's for each batch of twenty, correct?"

"That's right," confirmed Billy.

Moses gave Billy one pound. Billy helped to put the castings into a thick canvas bag, which Moses then slung on his shoulder, and then they shook hands.

"Nice doin' business with you, Moses. See you tomorrow," said Billy.

"Yes, see you tomorrow," replied Moses.

Charles Blackett bought all of the medallions and the pilgrim badges when Moses took them over to him. Out of interest, Moses had looked at the window display just before calling at the side door, and was a little disappointed not to see one of his medallions for sale. He mentioned it just before leaving.

"I'm keeping your items for my more discerning clients, Moses," Blackett explained, tapping the side of his nose with a finger. "Some of my collectors like things to be a little more discreet, if you know what I mean."

Moses got the message. Blackett could hardly sell a Richard II medallion to a collector who'd spotted it on display in the window, and have the same collector see an identical one on his next visit.

"I'll see you next time then, with further examples?"

"Yes, and they'll be different to what you've had," confirmed Moses.

"Excellent, excellent," and the dealer bade him goodbye.

Moses supplied Charles Blackett with a significant number of medallions and pilgrim badges, many of which Blackett then sold on to another dealer. The interest in antiquities was growing, with museums opening around the country and new publications catering for the collectors of such curiosities.

Just for pride, Moses took a strong basic belt buckle to the workshop and asked if one of his medallions could be attached permanently to it. Billy Nunn took on the challenge, and Moses was delighted with the result. The buckle had a decorative plate showing two knights in armour with swords raised in combat. He then took it to a saddler, who attached a belt made from high-quality leather. For Moses, it was the most extravagant thing he had ever owned and he had designed it himself.

He continued to create his own designs for the medallions and pilgrim badges, based on illustrations he found in *The Gentleman's Magazine*. He'd change things a little by adding his own flourish of mysterious symbols and marks. He also copied Arabic numerals from the dust cover of an edition of the *One Thousand and One Nights* and visited the British Museum as a source of ideas. Each of his designs was cut into a mould at Nunn's workshop. When finished, the items looked remarkably curious and authentic; suggesting in Moses' view that they did indeed come from the time of crusades and religious pilgrimages. His business was enjoying considerable success. Everyone involved in the creation and sale of the curios made money, and all was going well.

Soon, Moses had saved almost one hundred and twenty pounds. He knew that Bess earned about ten pounds a year. He was confident that if he proposed, she'd feel assured that he could provide for her. He could afford the rent on two nice rooms in nearby Stepney. Everything seemed to be fitting nicely into place.

CHAPTER 20

LONDON, 1870

Moses and Bess became officially engaged in September 1869, but only after she'd taken him to meet her parents one weekend. Moses was relieved to find that Mr and Mrs Doggett were kind country folk who welcomed him warmly into their home.

After they had made their introductions, any awkwardness soon disappeared and they settled into easy conversation.

"We've heard so much about you from Bess's letters," Mr Doggett commented.

"All good, I might add," Mrs Doggett chipped in. "Come, sit here both of you; I'll make us some tea."

During the evening, Mr Doggett invited Moses to join him in for a drink at the local public house. It was the opportunity that Moses had hoped for, as he wanted to ask Bess's father for her hand in marriage. As they supped their beer and chatted, the two men found they had similar views. Mr Doggett was a literate man; he enjoyed his daily newspaper and kept abreast of current affairs. Moses was impressed by his knowledge.

During a brief lull in conversation, Moses summoned up his courage. "Sir, as you know, I've been walkin' out with Bess for some time – about eight years, in fact."

Mr Doggett nodded, but said nothing.

Moses had the feeling that he sensed what was coming. "I would like to ask your permission to marry Bess." There, he'd done it!

"Would you, now."

It was more of a statement than a question. As Moses expected, Mr Doggett broached the subject of Moses' occupation.

"I hear you make a living from scavenging on the foreshore. Is that possible?"

"Very much, sir. I'm my own boss and I have a knack of findin' items of value, some of which I sell to Mr Blackett."

"Yes, I gather from Bess that it was you calling on her employer that first occasioned your acquaintance."

"That's right, sir."

"I know Mr Blackett only deals in valuable antiquities, but scavenging...can you depend upon it?"

"Well, I've almost become a dealer myself. I sometimes buy curiosities from other scavengers and sell them for a profit. But, at heart, I still consider myself a scavenger, like my father."

"There's nothing wrong with carrying on what your father did. I'm a firm believer in it. Look at me, fifth generation broom maker and proud of it."

"I agree, sir. I've managed to save up a tidy sum. I'm looking at rentin' rooms for Bess and myself in a decent street, if you give your consent, of course."

"So how much would these rooms cost?"

"About five shillin's a week."

Mr Doggett looked impressed. "And you could afford that?"

"Yes, sir."

Mr Doggett cupped his chin in his hand while he considered his answer. "I like you, Moses, and I know Bess loves you dearly. You've certainly known her long enough!" He paused, and then continued. "I think you'll make a good husband for my Bess. Yes, you have my blessing."

Moses was delighted. "Thank you, sir. I'll do my best to make her happy."

Moses and Bess married on the last Saturday in January 1870. The wedding took place in Theale. It was a quiet affair with a few friends and members of the Doggett family in attendance. Linus was best man, and Bess's sisters were bridesmaids.

When their details were entered in the marriage register, Moses' occupation was given as 'Scavenger'. He'd thought hard about what to call himself in the days leading up to the wedding. He could have used 'Dealer in curiosities' but something held him back. Scavenging was his trade. There was a possibility that his newfound prosperity might not last and that he might have to return to scavenging, but he realised that the foundation of the counterfeiting enterprise was built on collectors believing the curios to be genuine objects, found by him and other scavengers. He had to ensure that impression prevailed.

The two of them spent one night of honeymoon at a hotel in Pangbourne, situated on the Thames above Reading. On the Sunday, they moved into their rented rooms.

Mr Blackett had been invited to the wedding, but declined to attend due to a prior engagement. He indicated to Bess that, once married, she could stay on to do her former daytime duties only, and on a reduced weekly payment. If she found herself in the family way then she would be expected to leave.

Life for the newly married couple started well. Moses concentrated on designing his curios, as he called them, and passed fewer hours on the foreshore. He still helped Mrs R on the stall, but it was more out of loyalty than financial necessity.

CHAPTER 21

Eddie Milner had a jealous streak. He had wondered from the beginning where Moses was selling the items that he had helped to produce. He considered himself to be a vital part in the operation, because it was only he that had the skill to accurately cut the designs into the moulds. He believed that Billy and Moses were doing better out of the business than he was.

After Moses had left the yard, one morning, canvas bag slung on his shoulder, heavy with the latest output from the workshop, Eddie feigned illness and asked if he could be excused for a few hours. Billy was sympathetic, and Eddie left in order to follow Moses. He was in luck. He spotted Moses ahead of him and, even better, Moses went directly to Blackett's, albeit via the side door, but Eddie saw him being freely admitted.

He decided to wait out of sight, to watch when Moses left, and found somewhere that gave him a discreet view of the shop. He only had to wait about fifteen minutes. Moses came out of the side door holding the bag, but it was folded and empty. Eddie realised that Blackett had bought the entire contents. He smiled to himself.

So that's where you go with them, is it? Just as I thought. What do we need you for, Moses? I think I can persuade Billy that we should make our own arrangements with Mr Blackett.

Later, when Eddie explained to Billy that he had discovered where Moses was selling the 'Fontwells', as they now called them, Billy was initially reluctant to sell directly to the dealer. It seemed a bit disloyal to Moses and he wasn't entirely comfortable with the idea.

"Look, leave it to me," said Eddie. "Let me go to Blackett and see if I can agree a price for us to supply him directly. He might be paying twice as much for them as Moses pays us. Think how much more we could make."

The following day, Eddie Milner tidied himself up and called at the same entrance to the dealer's shop he'd seen Moses use. Bess answered and fetched her employer to see him. He was taken into the study.

"Thank you for seeing me, sir. My name's Edward Milner. Me and my business partner, Mr Nunn, operate a small foundry. We produce deck fittings and such, for local shipbuilders."

Eddie had decided to promote himself to partner, rather than mere employee. He hoped that Blackett would be more impressed. If he succeeded in cutting out Moses, he was going to insist on a partnership. After all, he was the one who had the skill to make the moulds.

"We've also been producing metal curios for Moses Jupp," Eddie continued, "I believe he sells them to you. Would you be interested in buying them directly from us, rather than through Mr Jupp?"

It was a straight question, and Charles Blackett was somewhat taken aback. However, it answered a question he'd had in mind ever since he'd started buying the copies from Moses: who was it that actually made them for him?

"Do you have any proof that you make objects that I may or may not buy from, um...Mr Jupp, did you say?" Blackett was cautious. He needed some evidence that Milner was as he claimed to be.

Eddie Milner had anticipated such a reaction. He opened the large bag he was carrying and brought out two examples of recent medallions made for Moses, along with the actual moulds from which they'd been cast. He also produced the sketched designs supplied by Moses.

"Mr Jupp comes up with the designs and I cut the moulds to produce the same. Here is a new sketch for a new medallion. We only received it this week and won't be casting until the mould's ready, but I can guarantee to you that you will see the finished product from Mr Jupp in the near future."

Blackett looked at the drawing and saw that the design was novel; one that he could see would fit nicely with its predecessors, and one that would be eagerly sought after by collectors.

"What makes you think that I buy objects like these from this Mr Jupp?"

"I followed him here the other day after he left our workshop with a bag full of them. When he came out of your side door, I saw the bag was empty."

Blackett considered what he'd just been told. Satisfied, he said, "I suppose I can't deny the logic of your reasoning, and you are correct. Do you know where Mr Jupp found the items that you copied, before he started doing sketches?"

"We made our own enquiries at the start and were told that the objects came from the excavations at Fontwell Dock. They've finished work there now, so he gives us sketches instead. I make the moulds from his sketches, but I know I could do my own designs, even better than Mr Jupp's."

"I suppose it all comes down to price. I'll need to be persuaded that you can indeed create such designs too. How much would you propose to charge me, let's say for a batch of twenty?"

"Our price would one shilling and sixpence each." Eddie had decided to aim high, for it was three times as much as they received from Moses.

"That's a little high," Blackett responded. "I think one shilling and three-pence would be as much as I could pay." Secretly, Blackett was thrilled. If he paid the price he had just countered with, it would mean that he would get the stock he wanted for half the price he was paying Moses.

"Yes, sir," replied Eddie Milner. "One shilling and three-pence each would be acceptable to us."

"Very well, but I will need to be convinced. First of all, I shall wait to see if Mr Jupp brings me a medallion that is the same as this novel design. Secondly, you will need to satisfy me that you too can produce castings of similar quality without his assistance. If I am satisfied on these two counts, then I shall place my business with you. For your part, you will have to treat me as your only purchaser. While we do business together, you must not supply them to any other dealer. Is that clear?"

"Yes, sir, we would be able to meet that requirement."

Blackett nodded in agreement. "Good, well, why don't you show me what you can do? Let me have some samples from you and we'll see if they're up to scratch."

"Yes, sir; I'll have them ready for you as soon as possible."

The two men shook hands and Eddie Milner left.

Back at the workshop, Eddie related his conversation with Charles Blackett to Billy.

The prospect of receiving two and a half times more than Moses was paying was enough to overcome Billy's hesitancy. He agreed to deal directly with Blackett. "But can you do the designs?" he asked Eddie.

"Course I can...Don't forget it's me that cuts them into the moulds. I know I can think up new shapes on my own, without Moses. The thing is, if I do, I think I should get a share in the business. I want to become a partner," demanded Eddie.

Billy pondered the request. "I'll tell you what: you make up some Fontwells in a new shape, as requested by Blackett. If they pass his inspection, then you can become a partner. I can't say fairer than that."

In the days that followed, Moses did indeed supply a new batch of medallions that matched exactly the design that Eddie Milner had shown to Charles Blackett.

Meanwhile, Eddie worked carefully and came up with three new medallion designs. If anything, they were a little more adventurous and flamboyant than before. Charles Blackett appreciated that Eddie had talent and could see no reason why his designs would not be acceptable to the growing collectors' market. He had showed them to his dealer, who was equally enthusiastic, although Blackett did not reveal that a new hand was responsible.

When Moses next called at the Rosemary Lane workshop with his latest sketch, Eddie looked at it closely, saw Billy approaching, and handed it back.

Billy apologised to Moses, saying that they had too much other work on and wouldn't be able to produce any more copies for him.

Moses looked surprised, then crestfallen. "But Billy, we've both been doin' well from this, haven't we?"

"Yes, but we've received a lot more work from our marine customers recently and we need to concentrate on them, I'm afraid. I'm sorry, Moses, but there it is."

Eddie Milner stifled a grin. He took pleasure in seeing Moses' disappointment. The truth was that they'd been neglecting some of their old customers, due to the work from Moses. Now, with the prospect of supplying Blackett at a price that would earn them some serious profit, they could drop even more of them and concentrate on producing the Fontwells.

After Moses left the yard, Eddie wrapped an arm around Billy's shoulders. "Come on partner, let's get to work and be earning some real money!"

CHAPTER 22

Moses was saddened when Billy and Eddie refused to make any further curios for him. He played it over in his mind as he walked away. He knew he'd been paying a fair price, so he couldn't understand why they didn't want to continue.

He decided he ought to warn Charles Blackett that there would be a delay before he could supply his next batch. He intended to find another smelter or foundry to make them for him. He called at the side door to the shop and was admitted by Bess. She had a duster and a tin of polish in one hand.

"What's up? You look worried."

"No, it's nothin'. Is he in?"

"I'll tell him you're here."

Charles Blackett came through and took Moses into his study.

"Mr Blackett, I'm afraid there might be a delay in the next batch of curios. I need to find a new smelter to make them for me."

Blackett didn't bat an eyelid, which surprised Moses.

"I'm glad you've come. It gives me the opportunity to let you know that I no longer wish to purchase from you, unless you can lower your price."

"What's happened? You like the designs and you're sellin' them aren't you?"

"Let's just say that I've found another supplier."

Moses was shocked. Who could it be? The dealer must be doing business directly with someone else, and Billy Nunn no longer wanted to manufacture for him either? Could it be a coincidence?

"How low?"

Blackett quoted a price that gave him no chance of profit.

"I'll see what I can do."

"Yes, you do that...Look at your prices." Blackett had opened the study door indicating that he had little else to say.

They shook hands awkwardly and Moses left.

That evening, Moses told Bess about what had happened.

"Will we be able to manage?"

"Yes of course," he assured her. "I've got plenty put by. I'll find someone else to make the curios. If Blackett won't buy them, then I'll find another dealer who will. Out of interest, has Blackett had any visitors recently?"

"There was a gentleman last week: tallish, fair hair, about our age, smelt of tobacco."

"Did he say his name was Milner?"

"Yes...I believe he did. Why?"

"I think I might know him, that's all."

So, Moses thought, *I've been well and truly shafted, and by Billy too, a fellow shoeblack. A dirty trick, and no doubt Eddie was the instigator. Then there's Blackett...he's ended our long business relationship so abruptly and he's profited well from it.*

Moses felt he'd been let down, but reasoned the dealer's treatment of him was not out of character. After all, Blackett was happy to dupe his customers by selling ancient objects that were actually of very recent manufacture.

Never one to be thwarted for long, Moses showed his designs to other smelters and founders in the vicinity, hoping to find a new manufacturer. Each time, the problem was the price. He couldn't get down to Blackett's price, not with the cost of making the medallions plus some profit for himself.

He continued to help out Mrs R on the stall and worked the foreshore at every opportunity. At low tide one day, he was pleased to find two late-medieval coins, but it was too much for his pride to offer them to Blackett, especially with Bess still working for him, so he found another dealer. Unfortunately the man had no shop. He only dealt in coins and obtained most of his stock from scavengers, which he sold on to more prestigious outlets in the West End. He was simply not interested in buying curios when Moses sounded him out.

By late summer, Moses had begun dipping into savings to pay the rent and other outgoings. He worried about where he and Bess might be in a year's time. His concerns were heightened when she told him in November that she was pregnant.

He put in as many hours as the tide would allow, but the rewards were meagre during that month. He hoped his luck would change; all scavengers went through lean patches. He maintained an air of confidence when at home, but at the back of his mind there was no evading the fact that his savings were dwindling.

In December, Bess had to give up her position when Blackett realised that she was expecting. He dismissed her with as little concern as he had shown for Moses. The weather in the metropolis was cold and damp, with light winds. Thousands of chimneys spewed out smoky fumes from coal fires, and a typical London fog established itself. It got worse as the days went by, becoming reddish-yellow and sulphurous. The air was thick and cloying. Dirty particles of soot stuck to everything.

Bess suffered badly from morning sickness. She went out to buy food and provisions whenever she felt able, but the visibility was so poor it became dangerous. Carts ran into one another, the shops put on their lighting at midday, and theatres played to houses where the audience could hear but barely see the performers. The fumes affected Bess's chest and she was laid low with a serious bronchial infection. She had to rest at home with the windows shut.

Down on the foreshore, Moses found that the cold seeped into his bones. He wore a scarf across his face to filter the air. The pickings from the river were slim. He couldn't believe the change in his circumstances. Less than a year before, he'd thought about calling himself a 'dealer in curiosities' on his marriage certificate, but now he was back to scavenging.

He worried about Bess's health. They were spending more than he earned. It was a miserable time for them both.

CHAPTER 23

LONDON, 1871

All was not well in the world of metal curiosities and artefacts from the time of the crusades. Rumours began to circulate that many of the recently acquired antiquaries in collections might not be as old as thought and could even be modern-day forgeries.

An eminent historian had presented a paper to the Archaeological Society about the present forgeries in lead. He claimed that the objects, reportedly from the Thames and called pilgrim badges, were being offered not only in London but also throughout the country, and so collectors should be on their guard in the purchase of them. He said that he had inspected several hundred and believed them to be of recent fabrication, though seeming to belong to the thirteenth or fourteenth centuries. He stated that these articles were entirely counterfeit and that the metal with which they were composed appeared to have been rubbed with something to give it the appearance of age, and that some had even been smeared with river mud. He expressed regret that there was no law in force to punish parties who were guilty of such disgraceful fraud.

A respectable journal called *Athenaeum* had covered the presentation of the paper. It reported a criticism, imputing to a dealer in curiosities, that certain of his wares were forgeries. That dealer, although not named, was Alfred Westbrook. He had a well-established and well-situated business, enjoying much

159

commercial success by supplying the collectors' market with the pilgrim badges and supposedly ancient medallions mostly purchased from Charles Blackett.

Westbrook had read the article and had taken exception to it. Ultimately, he sued *Athenaeum* for libel, claiming that the article was detrimental to his reputation and had affected his business.

A court case ensued. Various witnesses were called, arguing for and against the authenticity of the pilgrim badges, the associated curiosities, and the good character of Mr Westbrook. Among those who appeared in court was Charles Blackett, described as a supplier to Alfred Westbrook.

He explained that he had bought the items in good faith from scavengers. One, who he named as Moses Jupp, had found them during the excavations to extend the basin of Fontwell Dock. He further stated that he had been dealing in antiquities for twenty years and believed himself to be an expert judge of what was genuine and what was not. When he showed them to Mr Westbrook, he too was of the opinion that the items were authentic. However, Charles Blackett omitted to mention that he no longer dealt with Moses, nor that his source was actually a pair of metalworkers from Rosemary Lane.

After much legal argument, the judge decided that as *Athenaeum* had not specifically mentioned Westbrook by name, libel could not be claimed. He dismissed the case.

During the proceedings, several prominent and widely acknowledged experts had supported the authenticity of the curiosities and most collectors were happy to accept their opinions. In general, those who had built up large collections breathed a sigh of relief, in that they had not been fooled into buying modern forgeries.

One collector, named Titus Redding, could not shake his suspicion that Alfred Westbrook was either mistaken or crooked, and that the items Blackett had supplied were counterfeit. He had listened in court to the libel case and decided to seek out Moses Jupp, with the aim of interviewing him about the circumstances of the discovery of the pilgrim badges and crusades' medallions.

He visited Fontwell Dock, only to see that the work there was almost completed. Fortunately, he found a gang of navvies still busy. He managed to speak to the gaffer, who recalled selling a couple of metal objects.

"Do you know if the name of the man who bought them from you was a Moses Jupp?"

"No idea, but I've seen the same man helping out on a poultry stall near Spitalfields Market. It's the one that specialises in game...The name begins with R, I think. He does the mucky stuff: the drawing and plucking."

"Thank you," replied Redding. He handed his helpful informant a shilling.

"Thank you, guvnor," replied the man.

Redding took a hackney to Spitalfields and enquired about game dealers. One of the stall-holders suggested Rushtons'. He noted the location and thanked the man for his assistance. He stopped to buy some roasted chestnuts and stayed near the welcome heat of the brazier while he ate them. Refreshed, he soon found what he was looking for: a simple lock-up stall, open to the front only. Hares, rabbits, and partridges hung on each side. Above, a large banner announced 'Rushtons' – Poultry & Game Dealers'. On the stall itself, he could see skinned and plucked meat ready for sale. The only vendor was a woman who appeared to be in her late forties, well wrapped up against the cold; her cheeks flushed. He approached her.

"Fancy some nice fresh rabbit for your supper tonight, sir?" she asked.

Redding noted her friendly manner and country accent. "I think Cook's already planned dinner this evening, but I must say I'm rather partial to jugged hare. I'll take one of those please; Cook can prepare it for tomorrow evening."

The woman unhooked one of the hares, which she weighed and wrapped for the gentleman.

As Redding handed her the money, he decided to take a chance. "I was hoping to speak briefly to your assistant, Moses

Jupp. I was told that he worked here sometimes. My name is Redding, madam." He handed her his visiting card.

The woman studied it for a moment. "He's just gone down to the store to fetch some more birds. He'll be about twenty minutes."

Redding was delighted. His gamble had paid off. "And you are, madam?"

"Grace Rushton, sir."

"Could you pass him my card, please? I can return in a half-hour and would be grateful if you would allow me to speak with him briefly."

"Yes, I'll give this to him when he comes back. I don't mind if he speaks to you, but I can't say the same for him of course."

"Yes, quite…I understand. Just say that it might be to his advantage."

Moses reappeared at the stall with a barrow of pheasants. Mrs R handed the visiting card to him. "This gentleman, a Mr Redding, just came and asked to speak with you."

"Really?" said Moses. He flipped the card over, but the reverse was blank. "The name's a new one on me. What did he look like?"

"In his sixties, I would say; shortish, with a white moustache. He seemed quite a prosperous gentleman."

"Did he say what he wanted?"

"Not really, only that it might be to your advantage. He said he'd come back. You can speak to him if you want. I don't mind."

"Thanks, Mrs R. I suppose I might as well find out what he wants."

Presently, a gentleman matching the description came to the stall, and Moses went to greet him, wiping his hands on his apron before shaking Mr Redding's hand.

"Pleased to meet you, Mr Jupp," Redding said. "Could you spare a little time after your work here, to have a chat? We could go to one of the local taverns. I'm a collector of ancient curios."

Moses was instantly wary. "I'm not sure, sir. Why would you want to speak to me?"

"Your name was mentioned in the recent libel case involving Alfred Westbrook."

The libel case was news to Moses. He'd never heard of an Alfred Westbrook. "Was it? Are you sure?"

"Yes, absolutely, I was there. Charles Blackett, a witness, had said that you'd found a number of objects in Fontwell Dock."

Moses was reluctant to get involved, especially at the mention of Blackett's name, "I don't know about that, sir."

"Look, all I'm asking for is some information. They'll be no repercussions for you and I'll make it worth your while."

Moses thought hard. He desperately needed money. "Just information?"

"Just information," confirmed Redding.

"I finish at one o'clock. I could meet you in The Waggon and Horses soon after."

"Excellent. I'll be inside waiting for you."

Moses went back to his work. He tried to concentrate on what he was doing, but his mind kept going back to his conversation with Redding. What did the man want to know? Could Moses risk telling the whole story if Redding asked?

Why not? he thought. *Blackett, Eddie, and Billy have all done the dirty on me. I owe them nothing.*

When Moses entered The Waggon and Horses, he spotted Titus Redding seated at a small table by a window. The air was warm and thick with tobacco smoke. There was plenty of noise from market traders and those out shopping.

Redding beckoned him over. "Please, join me here, Mr Jupp. Tell me what you'd like to drink."

"Thank you, Mr Reddin'. I'll have a port, please."

Redding returned with a generous-sized measure and took his place at the table. He leaned closer to Moses in a conspiratorial fashion.

"Look, I won't beat about the bush," he said in a low voice. "I've bought a fair selection of lead pilgrim badges and a significant

163

number of medallions described as being of the fourteenth century, from Westbrook's, the big dealers in Haymarket. Have you heard of them?"

"No, sir, I haven't."

Redding looked disappointed. "What about Charles Blackett on Commercial Road?"

"Yes, sir, I have done business with Mr Blackett."

"You mean you've sold things to him?" Redding's tone grew a little excited.

"I might have."

"What sort of things?"

"I'd rather not say."

Redding reached into his jacket pocket. He pushed a folded five-pound note into Moses' palm and closed his hand around it.

Moses glimpsed the amount. He needed money, and it was easy to give information.

"Did you sell him coins?"

"Yes, sir."

"Did you sell him artefacts?"

"Yes sir."

"Did you sell him items you found in Fontwell Dock?"

"Not exactly."

"What do you mean?"

"Well, sir, they were things that came from Fontwell, but I didn't find them."

"Well, who did?" asked Redding, somewhat frustrated.

"The navvies, sir; in the course of their work."

"So you bought them from the navvies?"

"Yes, sir."

"Did you buy many items at Fontwell Dock?"

"Not really, only three."

"Really? As few as that?" Redding looked perplexed. "But there are hundreds of them on the market?"

Moses looked directly at Redding, and then glanced down to his hand. He rubbed his thumb back and forth against his forefinger. Redding understood the signal and reached inside his pocket and pushed another folded five-pound note into Moses' palm.

"I had them copied, sir," Moses said flatly.

There was a moment's pause from Redding. "Did you now?" he said in a satisfied tone. "How many would you say were copied?"

"Seven or eight hundred, I would think."

"But there are so many different designs, not just three."

"That's because I started to do my own sketches and they were used to make the copies."

"But you're a scavenger, aren't you, or you help out on the stall? You don't cast metal objects?"

"No, sir, but I found some people that would do that for me."

"Are you still doing it?"

"No, sir. They cut me out and now supply Charles Blackett directly."

Redding sat back, looking thoughtful. "I knew I was right." He leaned towards Moses and whispered in his ear, "So who is it that makes them?"

This for Moses was the critical moment. The port, heavy with alcohol, was having an effect. He felt more relaxed. He'd already decided, if asked, that he would tell the gentleman exactly who it was that made the copies. He thought of Bess; unwell, pregnant. He'd ten pounds in his hands, but he needed to get as much as he could.

"If I say, will you give me your word that you'll tell no one it was me who gave you the names?"

"Yes, yes," agreed Redding, impatiently.

Moses rubbed his thumb against his forefinger.

"You're going to bleed me dry," muttered Redding. He delved into his waistband and brought out a gold sovereign. "That's your lot, take it or leave it."

Moses took the coin and slid it into his pocket. "There's a little foundry workshop in Rosemary Lane, about halfway along, by the name of Nunn's Marine Castings. It's owned by Billy Nunn. He works with Eddie Milner—"

"So you're saying that this pair at Nunn's Marine Castings make the copies and sell them to Charles Blackett?"

"Correct."

"And are they still making them?"

"As far as I know, they are. They told me they'd got other work, but I know that was an excuse to fob me off."

Redding stood up. "Well, thank you, Mr Jupp. I need to be away now." He shook hands with Moses, picked up the parcel containing the hare, and left.

Moses sat by himself while he finished his drink. He had a decent sum in his pocket; Bess would be pleased when he got home. If he got a move on, he should have time to get down to the river. With luck, he might find something worthwhile.

CHAPTER 24

Titus Redding was an investor, and a canny one at that. He bought and sold stocks, and in recent years had enjoyed considerable prosperity. He hated to lose on an investment. He was interested in history, but his primary motive for amassing a collection of antiquities was a pecuniary one. He'd originally been attracted by the growing interest in the subject, especially among those able to afford the rising prices being sought for rare or unusual curiosities.

For most collectors, the recent libel case had largely laid to rest the doubts and uncertainties over the authenticity of the pilgrim badges and medallions. During the case, other equally eminent and knowledgeable individuals in their field had spoken of their certainty that the items were genuine.

When asked why so many objects could have originated from within Fontwell Dock, a well-respected authority and collector had expounded his theory that the ecclesiastical objects may have been aboard a vessel, which through some calamity had foundered and sunk in the vicinity. Other experts confirmed their certainty that the blue hue on the leaden objects could only be the result of lying in clay for centuries: the presence of alumina giving them the colour, and the clay preventing oxidation and promoting preservation.

The experts were very convincing and it was music to the ears of those who'd spent large amounts on building up a collection. In fact, during the weeks after the libel case, new impetus had been given to the interest in medieval religious souvenirs and crusades' medallions, with the result that prices were continuing to rise. It was against this background that Titus Redding decided to sell his own collection, before the truth of what he'd discovered became more widely known.

Titus believed Moses, but to be sure, he decided to pay a visit to Rosemary Lane to satisfy himself of the existence of Nunn's Marine Castings. Before he set out, he was careful to dress in less ostentatious clothes, fearing that he might otherwise attract the attention of the unpleasant characters and villains purported to inhabit the area.

He chose a day when the smog had cleared – the weather was fine, if cold – and timed his arrival for late morning when he hoped there would be plenty of people about. His first impression was as expected: that it was quite a comedown from where he lived. He had to mind his footing to avoid unsavoury detritus and rubbish. Frequent alleys and passages led off from the main thoroughfare, providing access, he was sure, to the overcrowded courts and slums, aptly named by the popular press as 'rookeries' of thieves and rogues. He had no intention of venturing down them to confirm such. Instead, he stuck to Rosemary Lane, hands firmly tucked into his pockets, and his coat well buttoned against pickpockets and the notorious locals. Avoiding invitations from females, whom he considered rather underdressed for such temperatures, and the outstretched palms of young urchins who scampered about intent on distracting him, he resolutely adhered to his purpose. He passed the point where Dock Street crossed Rosemary Lane to find the road widening a little. Buildings providing housing and shelter started to give way to those of more industrial nature. He noted this with relief, and hoped his chances of finding the foundry might be increasing.

Shortly after, on the right side of the lane, he stood before a pair of gates. A handwritten sign was fixed to one of them announcing the rather small and hemmed-in premises known as 'Nunn's Marine Castings' He was delighted to observe that the business was indeed real. Disappointingly, he couldn't see much. The gates were closed. Whatever went on inside took place behind a high brick wall. However, he could smell hot coals and see smoke rising so he had no doubt that metalwork of some kind was carried out within.

After Redding returned to his home, he changed into his normal attire. After lunch, he called at the premises of Alfred Westbrook in Haymarket.

"Ah, good afternoon, Mr Redding," gushed the dealer as he welcomed him.

"Good afternoon, Westbrook."

"So, what can I do for you today, sir? I've recently acquired some lovely examples that would certainly be of interest to someone as discerning as yourself."

"No thank you...I've decided to liquidate my entire collection."

Westbrook was incredulous. "What? Sell your collection, sir? But why would you wish to do that?"

"I wish to take advantage of an investment opportunity that has come to my notice. I've decided to dispose of the lot. Would you be interested in buying?"

Alfred Westbrook considered this request. His mind was whirring. He had some customers who would snap up Redding's collection, but he didn't want to appear too keen, for that might increase the amount he'd have to pay.

"Why yes, of course, sir, but I can't guarantee to give you what you paid for them. Is the sale urgent?"

Redding knew he was at a disadvantage; Westbrook was a wily character. "Not especially urgent, but you know how it is. Once one has made up one's mind, there is little point in procrastination."

"Quite, quite, sir. So, would you like me to call to assess and value your collection?"

"Indeed, I would...at your earliest convenience."

The following day, Alfred Westbrook called at the residence of Titus Redding.

How uncanny, Titus thought cynically. *As a buyer, the market according to Westbrook is likely to keep on rising. However, as a seller, well that's a different matter: the market is full of uncertainties and risk.*

After Westbrook had taken away the entire collection, Titus sat in his study staring at the vacant space previously occupied by a large glass-topped display case. The whole lot had come from Westbrook. He'd sold at a small loss, but that was the price he'd been willing to pay before – as he had predicted – the market for such items collapsed.

A devious thought entered his mind. What if he hastened the market's decline a little? What if he obtained evidence as to what was happening down in Rosemary Lane? Imagine if he could get hold of some moulds, and counterfeit items produced from them. Now, that would set the collecting world alight, and he, Titus Redding, would be able to glow in the glory of exposing the scandal. Of course, the other benefits would be that his decision to sell would be vindicated, and Alfred Westbrook would be exposed as a fraudster.

CHAPTER 25

Moses was drawing the guts from a partridge when he spotted the gentleman.

What does he want now? he thought.

"Good morning, Mrs Rushton. Might I have a brief word with Mr Jupp?" Moses heard him ask.

Mrs R turned to Moses. "I can spare you for a minute, if you want to talk to the gentleman."

"Thanks, Mrs R." He went round to the front of the stall to greet the man. "Mornin' Mr Reddin', I won't offer you my hand, not with what I'm doing at the moment."

"Perhaps not a good idea," chuckled Titus Redding. His tone turned serious. "Look, could you meet me in The Waggon and Horses?"

"I don't know, sir. What's it about?"

"I've a proposition for you...could be very worthwhile, you know."

"Proposition?" Moses considered for a moment. "Very well. Just after one o'clock, as before."

"Excellent. I'll see if I can get the same table."

When the time came, Moses found Titus Redding seated at the table in the window with a port already waiting for him.

"So what's this proposition you've got for me?" Moses asked.

"How would you like to earn yourself twenty pounds?"

Twenty pounds! thought Moses. *That's a lot of money, but...*"For more information? I've told you all I know."

"No, no; not information – evidence!"

"Evidence? What do you mean?"

"Could you get me some moulds and some newly cast items matching them?"

"What? You mean from the place where they're made?"

"Exactly."

"Oh, I don't know...That would be burglary, wouldn't it?"

"Well, perhaps, but this fraud needs to be exposed. Collectors are being duped. Nunn and Milner are making money from your idea. Blackett and Westbrook are too. Wouldn't you like to get revenge?"

Moses considered what Redding had just said. It certainly had its attractions and he could use the money, but what if he were caught? It would be prison, for sure, and not just for a short term. What would happen to Bess? Could he risk it?

"I'll tell you what," he said. "Let me think it over. I'll meet you here at the same time one week from today."

Titus Redding felt that Moses needed more persuading. "You'll be doing the world of antiquities a large favour, you know. As long as you don't get caught, I give you my word that I will never reveal how I obtained the evidence I need. If you are apprehended, then I also give you my word that I will pay to have you defended in court."

Can I trust him? Moses wondered. "As I said, Mr Reddin', meet me here in a week's time and I'll give you my answer."

It was after dark when Moses returned to Bess that evening. He was tired, cold, and hungry, but pleased to see a small fire burning in the grate. Bess was asleep in a chair. He tried not to wake her, noticing that her breathing seemed more even and less laboured. He placed the kettle on the grate, but a few minutes later the noise of the water boiling must have disturbed her and she woke.

"Oh Moses, you're back. Any luck today?"

"How are you feeling?" He went over to her and kissed her gently on the top of the head.

She raised a hand to caress the side of his face. "My chest

feels less congested today, definitely a little better. Since the fog cleared, it's really started to improve. That's what's caused it, I know it was."

"And what about the baby?"

She ran her hands over her apron. "Everything's all right, I think."

"Good, good; that's progress then."

"So, did you find anything worthwhile?"

"I did," Moses lied, "just below Blackfriars; a nice gold ring, for a change. I got three pounds for it."

Bess seemed relieved. "There's a pie under that cloth on the table and bread in the tin."

"Thanks, I'll make some tea as well. Do you want a cup?"

"Yes please, that would be nice."

After they'd gone to bed, and as Bess slept beside him, Moses thought about Redding's offer. He considered his own options. He certainly owed no favours to Billy Nunn or Eddie Milner. They were doing very nicely out of his idea. Not only that, they were using his contact, Blackett, as their buyer. Exposing the counterfeiting would be sweet revenge on all of them. But, a burglary? Could he really break in, and – more importantly – not get caught?

From his previous visits to the workshop, he could envisage the wall and the entrance to the yard through a pair of wooden gates, but they would surely be locked out of hours. Any burglary would have to take place late at night or in the early morning, and he'd have to climb over the gates or the wall. How dark was it in that part of Rosemary Lane? Were there people about who might spot him? How often did police patrols pass? He would need to carry out some night-time surveillance. Thinking back to his walk home that evening, he recalled that the moon between the scudding clouds was just a few days away from being full. He ought to take advantage of its light because a lantern would be too risky.

The following evening, just before midnight, and guided by the waxing full moon, Moses made his way to Billy Nunn's workshop. The sky was clear and the temperature was close to freezing. He was well wrapped up with a scarf, cap, and thick jacket. There was no one else about.

As he approached the junction of Dock Street with Rosemary Lane, he noted the gas lamp on the corner. He knew the workshop was little more than a hundred yards away, but a police patrol might pass soon. Given he hadn't yet spotted a constable, it was not worth taking the risk, so a few yards further on, he slipped left into the cover of an alley that he recalled passing on a previous daytime visit. Here, he waited, peering out warily, but as it was midweek, he didn't expect to see many souls at such an hour.

It was just as well, for moments later, Moses heard a man's cough coming from the direction of Dock Street. He peeped out of the alley. A policeman, equipped with a lantern, had paused under the gas lamp and was examining his pocket watch. Moses watched the constable replace it and then continue his patrol, heading right towards him! He quickly withdrew back into the alley, hoping that the constable wouldn't stop to examine it, but he'd already decided that if he was spotted, he'd pretend he was answering the call of nature. He heaved a sigh of relief when the policeman walked straight past without a glance and on in the direction of Nunn's workshop.

Moses let about a minute pass, and then turned away from the alley entrance, in order to shield the light from the match he struck. He noted the time on his own pocket watch, and then resumed his wait, although he wasn't sure how long that should be. Would the constable simply turn around and come back, or would he continue on as part of a larger circuit? Despite the cold weather, there was little choice but to wait, but for how long? He decided on half an hour. Any more than that and it was likely that the constable's route took him off in another direction entirely, in which case, Moses' question about the police patrol would be answered. He huddled into his coat, periodically flexing his toes and blowing on his hands against the cold…

Moses checked his pocket watch – just over twenty minutes had passed – when he heard two men laughing from the direction of Dock Street. Carefully, he peered out of the alley and noticed them standing underneath the gas lamp. One, obviously inebriated, was being supported by the other. Minutes later, the same policeman approached them from behind. Clearly, Moses realised, he took a circular route of about twenty to thirty minutes. There was a good-natured exchange and then the two men continued on their way along Dock Street. The policeman resumed his beat along Rosemary Lane once more, causing Moses to once again retreat into the alley. He'd wait a couple of minutes, and then make his way down to the workshop entrance. He'd have time to do that and study his surroundings before the constable returned.

He was about to leave the alley when he heard a man's voice and a woman's giggle nearby. Once again, he moved further back into the alley. To his exasperation, the couple stopped just inside the entrance. Moses crouched down to conceal himself as much as possible. His suspicion that the woman was a prostitute was confirmed when he heard her demanding a sum of money in a whispered voice. He heard the clink of coins as the man felt for some cash.

A match flared; enabling him to see the woman take what she wanted from her customer's outstretched palm. By the brief light, he could see that the man wore a sailors' hat. He looked to be in his mid-twenties. She was definitely older, by at least ten years, Moses guessed, with her cheeks heavily rouged. Their breath steamed in the cold. The match burned out.

"No, not 'ere," she said. "Come on, I've somewhere a bit warmer for us."

The couple left the alley and Moses heard their footsteps recede. He stood and then tip-toed to the entrance. He looked up and down Rosemary Lane. All appeared quiet, so he walked briskly until he reached the workshop entrance on the right. He checked to see if he could discern anyone in the moonlight and listened hard. Confident that no one was near or approaching, he pushed gently against the gates; they were locked as he'd expected. He'd have to somehow get over the wall and into the workshop, but not now; he would need to confirm how to do that in daylight.

Slipping into bed half an hour later, he was pleased to find Bess feeling much better.

"Did you sort out the business you said you needed to?"

"Yes, all done. You sound much better, my darlin'. You're not wheezin' at all."

"I know. It was the smoke, Moses. Couldn't we move away? I don't think it's good for me here."

"I can't promise, but I'm hopin' we might be able to move to somewhere in the country."

"Really? Do you mean that?

"I hope so, Bess."

"Oh, come here, Moses."

They made love for the first time in weeks. Afterwards, Moses lay awake, thinking. He knew that he needed to take Bess and their unborn child away from London; mainly in the hope that she could become completely well again. Her health and happiness were so important to him, but there were other reasons to leave.

He was tired of literally fighting the tide, getting muddy and cold, of scavenging in general. The prospect of fatherhood meant he had even more responsibility. He needed to find a more certain method of earning a living. With the river, it could be feast or famine. It was a fact that Moses was one of the best at what he did, but he could never rely, with absolute certainty, on what he'd earn from one week to another.

He cast his mind back to how things had been only a few months before, when he was designing and selling the leaden and copper-alloy curios to Charles Blackett. He was making good money until Billy and Eddie sidestepped him and cut him out. Now he was eating into his savings. He couldn't afford the rooms they were in and he couldn't bear to take Bess into lodgings, sharing the space with other boarders, some of whom were likely to be criminals and prostitutes.

Redding's proposal was tempting, but Moses wouldn't do it for less than forty pounds. It had to be enough to be worth the risk; enough to replenish his savings. He and Bess needed a financial cushion to make a new start, but where? It had to be in the countryside for her health, and the only place he'd ever heard of was Oxenhope!

Unable to sleep properly, Moses got up again several hours later. He'd been restless. He wanted to use the time before he was due at Mrs R's stall to reconnoitre Rosemary Lane once again, this time in daylight.

"You sleep on," he whispered to Bess. "I'm going down to the shed to sort some finds before the stall opens."

She murmured in response and he quietly left her to rest.

He walked to the workshop entrance with his collar upturned, a scarf across his mouth, and his hat pulled down. He wanted to avoid recognition in case he came across Billy or Eddie, but was relieved to see that the gates were still locked. All was quiet. He stopped to examine the brick wall on either side of the wooden gates. It was about seven-feet high, and screened off the yard from the lane. Each end of the wall butted up to the side of an adjacent industrial building. On the left stood a warehouse; on the right, a small two-storey factory. Where the water drained from the roof of the factory, a cast-iron pipe ran down the outside of the wall, just right of the workshop boundary. If Moses could shin up the pipe, he was confident he could stretch out his leg far enough to be able to stand on top of the wall, but this would depend on how securely the pipe was attached. He walked casually towards it, but was disturbed when he heard footsteps close by. Quickly, he knelt to pretend to tie his boot laces. A woman hurried by, but took no notice. Her footsteps receded.

When no one else was in sight, Moses stood and pulled against the downpipe. It was securely fixed; he had his means of

177

access. He'd have to get hold of some tools, but from what he'd learned so far, he thought he had a reasonable chance of getting away with the burglary.

Later that morning, in a lull between customers, Moses took his chance to speak with his landlady.

"Mrs R, I'm sorry to drop this on you, but if I were to leave do you think you could manage without me? Bess is much better since the fog cleared, but I really think we should move out of London and into the country somewhere."

Mrs R was silent for a moment. "I knew you'd go one day," she said, sadly. "I s'pose I've been lucky to keep you as long as I have. I shall have to get someone else, though. I need the help, you see."

"Yes I know, Mrs R. That's why I asked Jimmy if he was interested. He said he'd be glad to work for you, and he'll take over the rent on my storage shed. You won't be losing out."

"So, where you going to take Bess then, Moses?"

"Well, I was wonderin'…I was thinkin'…maybe we could go to Oxenhope. You've told me so much about it over the years and I've often thought I'd like to go there one day. What do you say? Would it be possible?"

"I s'pose it might be. In the last letter from my sister, she said a family had moved out at the farm. There might still be a cottage free, probably one near the yard. But what could you do? My brother will expect you to work there."

"Well, I've been thinkin' about that, and one thing I'm good at is diggin'. Surely there must be plenty of work like that."

Mrs R considered Moses' suggestion. "You know, Richard might have something for you. They're always out digging ditches or trenches to lay land drains, and I'm sure you'd be good at stone picking."

"Stone pickin'?" Moses looked a little alarmed. He associated that with convict labour.

"Nothing to be frightened of in stone picking. What happens is that the big flints gets pushed up during the winter when the ground is frozen. They can't be left out on the field cos of the damage they do to the plough and the harrow. We used to go out in the spring and collect them. They'd get carted away and either kept in a heap somewhere or sold off. They're used for building materials so come in handy."

"Oh, I'm sure I could do that," added Moses, feeling relieved. "I'm always leverin' up stones and bricks down near the river."

"Would you like me to write to my sister to ask if my brother needs anyone to help out on the farm?"

"Could you, really?"

"Yes, course I can. I owe her a letter as it happens. I'll write it this evening."

"Thanks, Mrs R. Do you think you might get a reply fairly soon?"

"Oh yes. Marion enjoys letter writing. She'll write back straight away, mark my words."

"I'll tell Jimmy that he can have my job if I go, right?"

"Yes, you can tell him that I'll take him on and that he can rent the lean-to after you've left."

"Thanks again, Mrs R. You know what, if we do move to Oxenhope, the only person I'll really miss around here is you."

"Oh, Moses, come here." Mrs R gave him a big hug. "I shall miss you too, you know. Perhaps I'll finally be able to persuade Mr R to take me back to the farm for a few days, then I'll be able to see how you and your family are getting on."

A customer spoke to Mrs R, so Moses returned to his grisly work. He thought over what she had said about the opportunity to move to her brother's farm. It sounded pretty hopeful. He decided he'd take a chance and proceed with the burglary, no matter what. If Mrs R's sister said there was nothing at Oxenhope, then they'd go temporarily to Theale, where Bess' parents lived. He had to get her out of London. The question was when to burgle the workshop. He'd need some tools and rope, which he'd ask Redding to get for him. He knew from his surveillance that Rosemary Lane was generally quiet midweek. If he chose a weekend, there was a likelihood of encountering more drunks and prostitutes, some no doubt with customers.

Tuesday or Wednesday the following week would fit in well. With a low tide around midnight, he could tell Bess that he was scavenging. He'd need an excuse to be out at that time; else she might wonder what he was doing. The moon would be on the wane but only by a day or two. Assuming little cloud, it should give enough light for his nocturnal adventure. He couldn't risk a lantern, but he could take matches.

Moses met Titus Redding as previously arranged. They found a table and with drinks in hand were soon deep in conversation.

Moses said, "I've been considerin' your proposition and I'm thinkin' that I might take you up on it."

Redding's expression registered faint surprise, followed by much delight. "Excellent, excellent...I hoped you would."

"But I've got some conditions."

"Oh?"

"Yes, first of all, I want fifty pounds, not twenty."

"Go on," said Redding.

"Secondly, I want you to provide a crow-bar, a long screwdriver, a large carpet bag, and seven yards of decking rope."

"Yes, I'm happy to provide those, but thirty pounds is my best offer."

"Look, you can't expect me to risk bein' transported or imprisoned for life for thirty pounds. I've got a wife, and we've a child on the way. Forty-five pounds, that's as low as I'll go."

Redding sat back and considered his options. He could walk away and forget the whole thing, but he kept thinking of the pleasure he'd get from bringing down Westbrook and Blackett, and all those gullible collectors who'd been fooled. He was a wealthy man; he could afford it. "I'll tell you what, I'll increase my offer to forty pounds, but that's it."

Forty pounds was what Moses was angling for. He put out his hand and they shook on the deal.

"Right, so when is this happening?" Redding asked eagerly.

Moses ignored the question. "Can you bring me the things I've asked for by Monday?"

"Yes, of course. Where do I deliver them? I don't want to bring them in here."

"Finish your drink and follow me."

Moses took Redding to his wooden lean-to behind the meat store. "I'll be here on Monday afternoon. I'll be cleanin' my equipment and sortin' out some finds. I'll want twenty pounds up front and the other twenty pounds when I deliver."

"Very well, I'll return on Monday afternoon."

They shook hands and Redding left.

CHAPTER 26

On Monday afternoon, Titus Redding arrived at the lean-to with a large carpet bag containing all that Moses had requested. He'd taken a hackney cab and had asked the driver to wait for him at the main thoroughfare.

Moses checked the contents.

"When are you going to do it?" Redding asked.

"Can't say exactly, but it will be durin' the next two days."

"Good."

"And I'll need an address so that I can deliver the goods."

Redding took out a visiting card and wrote his address on the reverse before handing it to Moses, who noted it as being in Bedford Place; close to the British Museum and an affluent area.

"I'll aim to bring the goods on Wednesday afternoon," Moses said. "I'll have twenty pounds now and the rest on delivery."

Redding nodded and handed him four five-pound notes, which Moses tucked away out of sight. They shook hands.

"Good luck," Redding said, and then turned and left.

Once he was alone, Moses examined the items in the bag. He pulled out the rope. It was new, pliable, and strong, but light-coloured so possibly visible at night. He dropped it into a bucket of water stained black with soot and left it to soak. Later, he dried it. All was prepared.

On Tuesday afternoon, after spending a fruitless morning on the foreshore, Moses called in at Mrs R's boarding house. He found her having a rest in the kitchen.

He wanted to tell her that he was intending to finish at the stall the next day. He'd decided that after the burglary he and Bess would go to Theale.

"Hello Moses," Mrs R said warmly. "Any good this morning?"

"Nah, nothin' much," he said with a sigh.

"Well, I might have some good news for you." She pulled out a letter from her apron pocket. "Came this morning. Marion's written back and Richard's happy to have you at Oxenhope. He's got an empty cottage. Room enough for you, Bess, and the baby when it arrives. At the moment, there's plenty of shovel-work going on. They're deepening the ditches around Long Lay. Later on, they'll be planting new hedging. He's sure that if he finds you useful then he'll have no problem in keeping you on."

Moses beamed with delight. This was great news. He wouldn't need to ask for help from Bess' parents.

"So what d'ya say? That sound all right?"

"Mrs R, you're a diamond, a regular diamond. It's just what me and Bess need. When can we go?"

"Well, reading this, it says you'll be welcome anytime. It's up to you, Moses."

"Look, I know it's sudden, but could my last day with you be tomorrow?"

"Tomorrow?"

"Yes, I'll bring Jimmy along. He'll have no trouble pickin' up the routine, but it would mean we could leave for Oxenhope on Thursday."

Mrs R pondered for a moment. "Well, yes, I s'pose that should be all right, long as you think Jimmy'll be up to it."

"He'll be fine, don't you worry."

Just after midnight on Wednesday, Moses waited in the same dark alley off Rosemary Lane with the carpet bag of tools and rope. It wasn't long before a policeman walked under the gas lamp and continued on past him. Moses knew he had less than thirty minutes to get inside the workshop before the policeman returned again, so he counted up to two hundred before he stepped out and followed the policeman's route towards Nunn's Marine Castings. The sky was scattered with light cloud, but the waning full moon provided enough illumination to help him. When he reached the neighbouring factory building, he felt his way along the brickwork until he touched the cold iron of the drainpipe.

He looked up and down the lane, but couldn't see or hear anyone. He took the rope out of the bag and tied one end to the bag's handles. He tied the other end into a noose and put his arm through it. He gripped the drainpipe and pulled himself up until his feet were level with the top of the workshop wall. He stretched out his left leg and placed his foot on the wall's surface; it felt substantial, wider than his boot, but then came a crunching noise and what sounded like small pieces of glass falling into the yard.

To deter burglars, Moses realised too late.

Should he carry on? He had to. He must. He held his breath for a few moments to concentrate on listening. Everything was fine.

He gingerly put his full weight onto the first foot, and then brought the other onto the wall so that he now stood on top of it. He pulled up the carpet bag and lowered it gently over the other side and down into the yard. The crow-bar and the screwdriver were wrapped in cloth to deaden any sound. The bag landed silently, fortunately avoiding anything fragile or unstable on the workshop side. Moses undid the noose, tied the free end of the rope around the drainpipe, and secured it firmly. Carefully, he lowered himself into the yard until his feet touched solid ground, relieved not to have landed on something that might cause injury.

Across the yard, to his left, he could identify the roof of the workshop. He untied the rope from the bag's handles, picked up the bag, and crept slowly and softly towards the building, trying to remember it as he saw it last. He made his way to where he thought the window was, feeling along the wall until his fingers found the opening and frame.

He then placed the carpet bag on the ground and leaned

back against the building for a few seconds before peering around the edge of the window into the workshop. He ducked back. There was a fire in the grate! Someone must still be in there! Panic started to rise until he realised it was no domestic fireplace, just some hot coals left in the brazier. He calmed himself and looked in again, confirming that he was right. Usefully, the coals gave off a small amount of extra light.

Kneeling down, Moses opened the carpet bag and carefully felt around inside for the large screwdriver and the crow-bar, which he removed. He unwrapped them both and positioned himself at the centre of the window. The lower catch was about chest height. He carefully worked the screwdriver into the gap between the bottom frame and sill, levering it up and down until he managed to gain enough room for the crow-bar, which he then inserted. With the crow-bar clamped between the frame and the sill, he retrieved the screwdriver and placed it on the ground. He placed both hands onto the crow-bar and pulled down hard. *Crack!* The catch gave, as the strain ripped out the screws securing it.

Close by, a dog barked. Moses held his breath and listened. *Surely, someone must have heard the noise.*

"Be quiet, you daft hound!" a man shouted from somewhere nearby. The dog whimpered and stopped. "Get in here!" The dog yelped and a door slammed shut. All was silent again.

Moses removed the crow-bar and quietly laid it beside the screwdriver. Then, standing in front of the window, he pulled it up until he had a sufficient opening. The frame stayed in position, held by the sash cords. He picked up the empty carpet bag, put an arm through the handles, and hauled himself over the sill and headfirst through the gap and into the workshop.

Feeling for somewhere to place his hands below the window, he was thankful to touch the flat surface of a workbench. He dragged his legs through and squatted on top of the bench to get his bearings. His first impression was that the interior was very warm. He could see the glowing coals in the brazier, and could vaguely make out the shapes of several moulds set out on another bench opposite.

He unhooked the bag from his arm and placed it next to him. Then he dropped to the floor and reached into his pocket to retrieve a box of matches. He struck one and crossed the workshop. He had just enough time to examine the mould closest to him before the match burned out. He discarded it and lit another so that he could examine the inside of the plaster mould. It was for a crusades' medallion. Its form had been created by cutting into the plaster of Paris with a small knife or a sharp nail. It was very similar to ones he'd designed. He struck a further match and moved along to the next mould. It was for a heart-shaped medallion. Even looking at it in reverse, Moses was able to envisage what it would look like. He could make out a horizontal sword above a full-bearded face, above which sat a crown with four long radial spikes. The medallion was bordered with dots and intricate swirls, all topped by a suspension loop. It was a little more flamboyant than he might have done, but still essentially similar.

It angered Moses that Eddie was still using his designs as a basis, but he put the thought out of his mind and returned to his task. He retrieved the carpet bag and carefully laid both moulds into it. Then he looked around for any finished castings. Further along the bench, he could make out several piles. He struck another match and was delighted to see several examples produced from each of the moulds he'd taken. He put some into the bag and lifted it to check the weight. It wasn't too heavy, so he scooped up a couple more handfuls of finished castings and placed them into the bag. He wouldn't risk carrying any more.

A malicious thought occurred to him. *Why not put a match to the whole place? No,* he reasoned, *that would be more than revenge, and anyway, a fire would draw attention and prevent my escape.*

He struck one last match to check the time on his pocket watch. He calculated that the policeman would pass the gates to the yard again in about seven minutes' time. Before the light from the match faded, he noticed a thick leather apron draped over a chair. He took that as well; he could use it to cover the pieces of glass on top of the wall.

Crossing back to the open window, Moses placed the carpet bag onto the sill. He then climbed up onto the workbench, dropped the apron out of the window and, feet first, manoeuvred through the opening, carefully lowering himself to the ground. He then lifted the bag and placed it at his feet. He left the screwdriver and the crow-bar where they were, but put their wrapping cloths back into the bag, aware that he needed to deaden any metallic clinking noises as much as possible. He picked up the bag and the apron, and tip-toed across the yard to the corner where the end of the rope lay. When he reached it, he sat down quietly, hoping that his research from a week earlier would confirm the timings of the policeman's circular route past the workshop.

He waited patiently, ears straining for any sounds, and debated with himself whether to risk lighting another match to check the time, but the decision was averted when he heard the heavy regular footsteps of a solitary constable on the beat. Moses held his breath as the footsteps came closer, passed by a few yards, and then stopped. His heart thumped wildly, fearing that the policeman would notice the rope looped around the drainpipe, but he then heard a trickling noise followed by the sound of breaking wind. He smiled to himself.

Eventually, the footsteps continued along Rosemary Lane and receded. Moses counted to two hundred again. Once satisfied that all was quiet, he threw the leather apron up onto the top of the wall. He tied the trailing end of the rope to the handles of the carpet bag, and once again used the rope to climb up to the top of the wall. He sat on the apron. From up here, he had a good vantage point. Nothing moved, so he hoisted the bag up and lowered it softly over the other side.

Moments later, he'd kicked the apron back into the yard, lowered himself down the drainpipe, and stood in the lane. After untying the rope from the carpet bag's handles, he threw it over the wall. He picked up the bag and, cradling it gently in both arms to avoid any noise, made his way cautiously back to the lean-to where he concealed his booty.

Before the day was out, Moses would sort out a few castings to keep for himself and deliver the remainder to Titus Redding.

CHAPTER 27

Moses was shown into Titus Redding's study when he called in with the spoils of his nocturnal activity. A servant announced his name as he entered.

Redding was seated behind a large oak desk. He rose and came over to shake hands with Moses. "Good afternoon to you, Mr Jupp. A successful outcome, I trust."

"Good afternoon to you, Mr Reddin'. Yes, very successful."

Redding rubbed his hands with glee. The carpet bag he'd delivered two days earlier looked bulky. He could hardly contain his excitement. "Here, open it up on here," he said helpfully, pointing to the nearby desk.

Moses rested it down carefully, which only seemed to increased Redding's anticipation and excitement. "There you are, take a look for yourself."

Redding opened the bag as wide as it would go and took in the contents. Two moulds were immediately apparent. He lifted out the first and placed it on the desk.

Moses could see that he was unfamiliar with such things. "Look, you pull it apart here," he demonstrated, opening the mould and laying the two parts side by side. The interior and design were revealed.

"Wonderful, wonderful," Redding said, "and I have to envisage this design in reverse to imagine the finished article, yes?"

"That's correct, but you don't need to imagine too hard..."

Moses reached into the bag, "for here it is." He placed the matching heart-shaped medallion into the mould. It fitted exactly.

"And what about this one?" Redding asked excitedly.

"Different design, but same principle."

Redding pulled out the second mould and this time he split it himself. Then he rummaged in the bag and pulled out a handful of medallions, finding one that fitted into the mould's cavity perfectly. "Excellent, excellent, this is just what I need. So, how many castings have you brought me?"

"You've got eight for each of the two moulds here and another twelve that belong to three other moulds, four from each. I couldn't carry any more, but I'm sure that's enough for you."

"More than enough, more than enough," he said excitedly. "So, did anyone see you?"

"No, sir."

"Good, good, and does anyone suspect you?"

"I don't know, but they've got no proof if that's the case."

"Quite, quite. Well, look, I'll uphold my end of our bargain. I'll never reveal how I came by these little beauties."

"Thank you. Nor will I ever admit to any involvement."

Redding pulled some notes from his inside pocket and counted them out. "There we are, that makes forty pounds as agreed."

"Thank you, sir." Moses took the money and placed it in his own jacket pocket.

Redding went over to the fireplace and pulled a cord. A few moments later, the study door opened. "Ah, Peterson, would you see Mr Jupp out?"

"Of course, sir."

Redding held out his hand to Moses once more and they shook. "Good day, Mr Jupp."

"Good day to you, sir."

Moses left by the front door and descended the three steps to the pavement. He was overjoyed. He'd earned forty pounds and Nunn, Milner, and Blackett were going to get what they deserved. Everything was falling into place. He just needed to check the train timetable. He'd worked his last morning on the stall so he wouldn't be drawing the guts out of rabbits and partridges anymore.

When Moses arrived back in Whitechapel, he went directly to his lean-to. Jimmy was already there.

"You happy with everythin' at the stall, and the rent for takin' on this place?" Moses asked him.

"Yes, Mrs R's great to work for."

"Good. Well, I'll just take this old cloth bag here." It contained eight surplus castings. Moses was proud of his idea and wanted to keep them, even if they weren't actually his design. He was sure he could always sell them if he was desperate for money. "As far as I'm concerned, you can have everythin' else."

"What? All the tools?"

Moses nodded. "You can have the lot. I shan't be comin' back."

"Thank you, Moses, although I'm sad you're leavin'. It won't be the same round 'ere without you."

"Come on, Jimmy, you'll be all right." He hugged his friend briefly. "And remember, not a word to anyone about where I've gone."

"Don't worry, my lips are sealed."

Bess was busy with a dusting-brush when Moses arrived home. She saw him come into the room with a grin on his face. "What's up with you? You look like the cat that's found the cream!"

Moses laughed and put down the bag of castings. "I have! We're leavin' London! We're movin' to the countryside!"

Bess dropped the brush in order to embrace her husband. He wrapped his arms around her and kissed her gently.

Bess nuzzled his neck. "Where are we going? Where are we going?"

"Oxenhope!"

She drew away from him. "What? That place Mrs R was always telling you about?"

"That's the place. I've got work lined up and somewhere for us to live too."

"Oh Moses, I'm so happy, I can't wait!"

"You won't have to, we're going tomorrow!"

"Tomorrow! But I'll have to let my parents know."

"Just send 'em a quick note, and then you can write later with the address and everythin'."

"Yes of course, that won't take long. So how are we getting there? It's in Wiltshire, isn't it?

"That's right. We're taking the train from Paddington, just before noon. Can you get packed?"

"Just watch me!"

"Oh, that makes me so happy, Bess, to see you excited again. Look, I just need to see Mrs R about some final details. Make a start on packin', but don't tire yourself out. Take it easy and I'll finish everythin' when I get back. I won't be long."

Moses kissed her again and put the bag behind the curtains, making a mental note not to leave it behind. He left Bess, who was already looking for writing paper. He went straight to Mrs R's lodgings. She'd be resting after the morning's work.

"Hello Moses, you back already?" she said when he arrived.

He laughed. "Mrs R, could I have a quiet word?" His left arm was hidden behind his back.

"Of course, come through here," she said, and took him into the parlour.

"These are for you, Mrs R," Moses presented her with a bunch of daffodils. She was thrilled. "Bess and I are catching the train to Swindon tomorrow."

"Oh, that's wonderful, Moses."

"How long does it take to get to Oxenhope."

"What time's your train?"

"About midday."

"Well, let me think. You'll arrive in the afternoon. The market'll be over by then, so they'll have already gone back up to the farm. There aren't any hackneys, you know! There's a carrier that goes up that way most days, and there's nearly always someone who comes down from the farm to the market. You'd be best stopping over at the Railway Hotel. It's right by the station. Just ask there about getting out to the farm. They'll know."

"Could I ask you one last favour, Mrs R?"

"Course you can. Go on, ask away."

"If anyone comes wonderin' where we've gone, could you keep it under your hat? Jimmy and Linus know, but they're sworn to secrecy. I don't suppose anyone will ask, but if they do, could you say you've no idea?"

"For you, Moses, yes, I will. I don't know what it's about of course – I don't want to know either – but I won't tell, not if you don't want me to. It's just between us – oh, and your two friends, I s'pose!"

"Thanks again, Mrs R. You're a gem, you are." Moses squeezed her hand.

Mrs R pulled him close to hug him. "Take care, my lad. You look after that wife of yours, and the baby when it comes."

Moses could see a tear trickling down her face. "Will do, Mrs R. Let's hope you and Mr R can come and visit us some time."

"Yes, let's hope for that," she said, wiping her eyes. "Let's hope for that."

CHAPTER 28

It was Billy Nunn who first arrived at the workshop on that Wednesday morning. He was not feeling particularly well. He'd developed a persistent cough that seemed to be getting worse.

After unlocking the gates, he entered the yard. Looking about, he noticed a leather apron lying on the ground in the corner. Frowning, he went to investigate and spotted the decking rope. He pulled on it and found that it was attached to something firm and unyielding on the other side of the wall. He walked slowly out of the yard – moving quickly exhausted him – and looked towards the factory. He could see that the rope was fixed to the downpipe.

"Damn!" he muttered to himself, "Looks like we've had some uninvited visitors here."

He approached the workshop and was relieved to find the door intact. However, looking around the corner, he spotted the open window and a screwdriver and crow-bar left on the ground below it.

Eddie arrived soon after, puffing on his pipe as usual, and entered the workshop.

"We've been done over, Eddie!" Billy told him, pausing to cough. "I think some tealeaf's had some moulds and castin's. Do you remember what was here?"

Eddie looked around to see if anything was different. "You're right, Billy. There's two complete ones missing from the end of the bench over there, and a lot of the castings have gone from here."

"But who'd want to take them? Could you keep that smoke away from me?" He was irritated and coughed again. "Unless someone else is goin' to use them to make castin's, they're useless. We know everyone around here in our business. I can't see anyone on this manor doin' it."

Eddie took his pipe from his mouth and tamped the bowl. He left it on a bench in the corner. "No, that's good thinking," he agreed. "It's got to be some other reason. What if someone wanted to get hold of some moulds to make their own Fontwells or even prove how we make them?"

"Really? You think that's a possibility?"

"It might put us out of business."

"But who'd want to do that?"

"One name comes to mind for me!"

Billy thought for a moment. "You're right! And me!"

"Moses Jupp!" they said in unison.

They decided not to mention the burglary to the police. It might mean they'd have to answer difficult questions. They had some of their own questions for Moses Jupp, though, but first they had to find him.

The search for Moses proved to be difficult. Eddie asked down at the foreshore, and even at Fontwell Dock, but got nowhere. Moses seemed to have disappeared.

CHAPTER 29

The Great Western Railway express pulled into Swindon station just after half-past two in the afternoon. About a dozen passengers alighted from the train. Most seemed familiar with the station and made their way directly to the street outside.

The weather for March was typical: periods of sunshine interspersed with heavy showers and a cold gusty wind.

Moses helped Bess down onto the platform and found her a seat under the station canopy. He looked around for a porter and spotted a young man wearing a uniform approach him.

"Need any help with baggage, sir?"

"Yes please. We've two large trunks and two cases in the guard's van."

"What's the name, sir?"

"Jupp."

"Right, sir. I'll just go and fetch them."

A few late passengers arrived and hastily climbed on board, slamming doors behind them. The guard looked up and down the platform, blew his whistle, and waved his flag. The train rolled forward, slowly gathered pace, and left the station on its journey to Bristol.

"Is anyone coming to collect you, sir?" the porter asked, on his return with Moses' luggage.

"No. We've got to get out to Oxenhope, but I think we're probably too late for someone to take us today; at least that's what I've been told."

"Yes, you're right about that, sir. Mercer, the carrier, comes in every morning to meet the half-eleven from Paddington. He makes the collections and deliveries for the villages up towards Oxenhope. He's usually happy to take a passenger or two if he has the room. His timetable is outside on the station notice board.

"Thank you, we're going to stay overnight at the Railway Hotel."

"Very good, sir. It's not far away but, if you like, it might be easier to store the trunks here in the baggage office overnight."

"Yes please, that's a good idea."

"I can wheel the cases down to the hotel if you wish."

"Thank you, that would be very helpful."

Moses walked with Bess as they followed the porter the short distance to the hotel. Fortunately, the rain had stopped, but the footpath was wet and slippery and they had to be careful. When they reached the hotel, the young man placed their luggage just inside the door. Moses slipped him some change and then sought out the hotel keeper to arrange their stay and have the cases delivered to their room.

They settled in and unpacked a few clothes and necessities. Bess felt tired, even though they'd spent most of the time seated, watching the countryside from the train's window.

"I think I'll have a nap if you don't mind, Moses. Maybe it's the change of air, but I think half an hour will do me good."

"You do that, love. I'll go and investigate and see what's what. I'll find out if we can have somethin' to eat here later. Is there anythin' you need?"

"No, I'm fine, just a little tired...and Moses, thank you. It's such a relief to have left London."

Moses decided to go for a stroll, leaving Bess to have her nap. It was only the third time he'd been out of London. He was quite surprised to find how civilised it was. All the shops and businesses he was used to seeing in London were here, but there were differences. He'd never before seen a Corn Exchange and he was quite surprised to see a photographer's. But then of course, he reasoned, Swindon – apart from being a market-town – was

197

the place Brunel had chosen to build locomotives for his Great Western Railway. The local works produced some of the finest and most advanced engines in the world, so the town was used to the latest inventions.

It occurred to him that if they found themselves unhappy at Oxenhope, he could always fall back on obtaining work in Swindon. He was certain he would have no trouble in finding a job.

The following morning, Moses left the hotel and walked back to the station. It was just after ten and he found the carrier's notice on the station board. It told him that Mr Mercer left daily at noon, serving the villages of Wyke, Beech Upton, and surrounding areas. The road outside the station was quite busy, with carts and wagons parked everywhere. Moses saw the young porter again and asked if the carrier had arrived.

"Over there, Mr Jupp; the blue wagon."

Moses wandered over to take a closer look. It was a four-wheeled affair, open to the elements, with a pair of horses munching from their nose bags contentedly. The carrier, he presumed, was busy elsewhere.

Presently, a short swarthy man wearing a leather apron appeared and patted one of the horses. He smoked a clay pipe.

"Are you Mr Mercer, please?"

"Aye, that be me," he answered in a country brogue.

Moses realised the man spoke a bit like Mrs R, but his accent seemed much stronger. "Would you be able to take me and my wife out to Oxenhope today? I was told it's on your route."

"I shoulda' thought so. It's after Wyke. You just visitin' or you gonna be livin' out there?"

"Livin'…we hope. We've got two big trunks and a pair of suitcases, so we can move in."

"Should have room for everythin', if I plans my load correct. You'll both have to sit up front with me, though."

Moses had already considered that. "How long does it take to get there?"

"Couple of hours or so."

"She's expectin' but she should be all right."

"I'll find an extra cushion for her if you like. Be a bit more comfortable then."

"Thank you, that's kind."

Moses confirmed the departure time and agreed the cost with the carrier.

Well before noon, Moses and Bess stood beside the wagon with all of their baggage.

"Hope it doesn't rain or we might get wet," laughed Bess.

Moses noticed that her spirits were improving all the time. It made him feel much happier.

When Mr Mercer appeared, Moses helped to load their possessions onto the wagon. There was just enough room to fit everything on, and the single bench seat at the front easily accommodated all three of them.

"You comfortable, Mrs Jupp, with that second cushion?" asked the carrier.

"Yes thank you, Mr Mercer."

"Right then, we'd best get goin'."

The carrier flicked the whip and the pair of horses set off at a gentle pace.

The rain held off during the journey to Oxenhope and spells of sunshine illuminated the downland scenery. Moses and Bess were treated to the sight of some glorious countryside. Moses found it delightful and invigorating. Bess, too, inhaled and exhaled deeply with pleasure.

Mr Mercer talked throughout the entire journey, happy to share little titbits of gossip or indicate something of interest; his pipe either clamped between his teeth or serving as a pointer. Fortunately, he didn't attempt to light it. His knowledge of nature and the farming year was encyclopaedic. Mercer gave the impression he knew every field and hedgerow. He asked his passengers about their life in London.

"Never been to London," he said. "Heard there's several

million what lives there, not like round 'ere. Don't think I'd like that. I knows everyone 'ere, I do."

"You're right about there being lots of people in London, Mr Mercer," replied Bess. "It's nothing like this." She indicated the steep grassy hills they were approaching. They were dotted with sheep.

The horses hauled the wagon to the top of a sharp incline and then the road flattened out for a while. Despite the sunshine, the gusting wind was strong and Bess needed to keep one hand on her bonnet to avoid losing it.

After a while, they descended into Wyke. Once down in the valley, it was noticeably calmer.

Mercer pulled up his wagon near to a small church and public house. "Just got some deliveries for the village shop – won't be a minute," he said as he jumped down. He shuffled some boxes and packages around to find what he wanted

Moses looked at their surroundings. "I think that must be the church where Mr and Mrs R got married. Mrs R said they spent their honeymoon night over there at The Fox. This is so excitin', to see the places she talks about. It's such a shame that she hasn't been back. I know she'd like to."

"I can understand why she misses it all so much," said Bess.

The carrier returned and climbed back up onto the seat. "Right-oh…" and with another gentle flick of the whip, they set off once more.

"Are we near to Oxenhope?" asked Bess.

"Not far now, 'bout twenty minutes."

Moses could see that Bess was becoming uncomfortable. Despite what Mercer had said, it looked as if the journey would take almost three hours.

They climbed the slope at the far end of the village. When they reached the top, the wind had become even gustier. They were fully exposed to it, but it also meant that the air was clear. The views were breathtaking.

"That's the county of Oxford behind us, and that's the county of Berkshire over yonder," indicated Mercer. "You can see more than twenty-five miles in any direction today."

The road continued straight ahead, with a steep drop on one side, perfect for the grazing sheep. A tall hedge of hawthorn and blackthorn fronted the thick woodland on the other.

"This used to be a Roman road," the carrier explained, "goes to Cirencester eventually."

They came to a wide break in the hedge and Mercer turned left onto a muddy track that entered some tall trees.

"Right, hang on as we go down...bit steep in places, but the horses 'ere, they're used to it. They always gets a drink and somethin' to eat when we gets there."

Bess and Moses grabbed the edge of the bench seat to steady themselves, but they needn't have worried. Mercer skilfully controlled the wagon, keeping to the track as it descended sharply through a wooded hillside. The bare trunks of the trees that loomed above them were a few weeks from coming into leaf. Looking straight ahead through the sparse canopy, they glimpsed a field below containing several labourers at work. The woodland ended as they came down to level ground and they got their first real sight of Oxenhope.

The carrier halted the horses and one of the labourers straightened up and waved. Mercer waved back. "There's the farm, and the cottages are at the far end," he explained to Moses and Bess. "Lovely spot down 'ere. Notice how calm it is. It's like another world on days like today."

Moses and Bess carefully stood up, so that they could take it all in.

Mercer was right, Bess thought. It was calm and so very different to the windy conditions up on the road. She hoped it was metaphor for how their life might be from now on.

Moses felt much the same, but he also cast a professional eye over what he could see of the fields, wondering if there were any more Roman gold coins just waiting to be found.

CHAPTER 30

At the fortnightly afternoon meeting of the London & Wessex Society of Antiquities, Titus Redding was the principal speaker. His paper was entitled, *The Fontwell Fakes*.

In a side room to the main hall, he had set up a display of the moulds and the counterfeit castings. As he didn't want to risk anything happening to them, he had arranged that his servant, Peterson, remained on guard near the exhibits while he delivered his speech.

"Good evening, dear members," he began. "What I am about to tell you, I do so in the interests of archaeology and from no personal feeling. Given the facts that I have uncovered, I could do no less."

The room was packed with academics of ancient history and collectors of historic artefacts.

Redding briefly described how the market had become flooded of late with thousands of supposedly ancient leaden badges and medallions. How could so many have originated in one place, namely Fontwell Dock?

"Because a ship's cargo of such articles was lying there in the mud," shouted a heckler.

The comment received murmurs of support from one faction and laughs of derision from another.

Redding raised his hands. "Look, we all know that certain eminent historians support their authenticity, but a number doubt it. Apart from that, the popularity and mystique surrounding these objects has fuelled a commercial market, from which a number of prominent dealers have made significant profit."

Again a murmur rose from the audience at the mention of dealers. Everyone was aware of the court case in which Alfred Westbrook sought damages from *Athenaeum* for libel. Redding was on dangerous ground and risking another similar action from Westbrook or his like.

"Yes, I'm well aware of what you're thinking and the risk to me personally. However, I am willing to state here and now that the vast majority of these so-called antiquities found in Fontwell are fakes!"

There was uproar in the hall.

"Furthermore, I intend to expose these imitations, for that is what they are. I have proof! Proof that I can reveal to you at this very meeting!"

The chairman intervened at this point. "Order! Order! I will not have behaviour of this nature in here. Quiet please!"

The noise subsided.

"Mr Redding, if you have evidence of fakery then kindly explain to the members as to how and where they may be able to view such."

"Of course, Mr Chairman. My proof is on display and available for inspection in the side room over there." He pointed to a closed door. "What you will see are two moulds that have been used to produce counterfeit articles. You will also see a number of castings that match the moulds, obviously made from them. I have also displayed four identical examples of three other recently moulded designs. They came not from Fontwell Dock, but from a small foundry workshop in Whitechapel. I have witnesses to support my assertion that the fakes from Nunn's Marine Castings, as the foundry is called, were supplied to Charles Blackett, and in turn to Alfred Westbrook. Of course, I am not saying that Mr Blackett or Mr Westbrook sold them knowing them to be fakes. You must draw your own conclusions on that."

Once more, the noise in the room grew louder. Redding's

mention of witnesses was actually a bluff, but he was sure that neither Westbrook nor Blackett would dare refute his revelations.

"Mr Chairman, if you would care to accompany me next door, you can be first to see the evidence. I suggest the rest of you form an orderly queue behind."

In small groups, the members gathered around the display table. The general agreement was that although the castings on show were slightly novel, they were too similar not to be from the same manufacturer. It was obvious to Titus that those who'd believed in the authenticity of these items had indeed been fooled and swindled by some very clever forgers. Some voiced their anger, saying that they would go to the police. Others just looked downcast and bitterly disappointed. Many had invested heavily in the fakes, having been swept up in the excitement of acquiring more examples.

A contributor to *Athenaeum* was in attendance. He left the meeting afterwards and went directly to the editor with a report of the proceedings. It was decided that an article on Titus Redding's exposure of the fakes, and the implications for the antiquaries market, was worthy of halting the presses to ensure it was included in the next edition. It would vindicate the magazine's reputation with regard to the libel case. The 'extended special' edition went on sale and was distributed to subscribers within forty-eight hours. It sold out in record time.

CHAPTER 31

Two days after Titus Redding's revelation, a pair of police constables came into Billy Nunn's workshop early in the morning. Billy and Eddie were both there and, fortunately for them, had not started the day's production of Fontwells. Since the burglary, they'd been cautious; ensuring that the special moulds and finished castings were kept hidden until work on them took place. They didn't want to risk any more being pinched.

They were questioned by the policemen, who had learned that some moulds may have been stolen from the workshop. The moulds had then been used as evidence to expose a counterfeiting operation in fake archaeological artefacts. Several wealthy collectors had contacted the Metropolitan Police and asked that they investigate.

Billy and Eddie denied all knowledge of any counterfeiting, but were taken into custody to assist the police in their enquiries. They took advantage of a brief opportunity to speak to each other and decided to change their story and to stick with a new version. When interviewed independently, they both said that a burglary had occurred; however, they claimed they were victims of the break-in and had suffered criminal damage.

"Who might have carried out this so-called burglary? Which, by the way, you didn't report," asked a detective.

They both named Moses Jupp.

"Do you have any witnesses or evidence to support this allegation?"

Both were reluctantly forced to admit that they hadn't.

They were pleased to be released within a few hours. The police, having taken legal advice, decided that no law had been contravened, there being nothing specific to forging historical artefacts.

After their release, Eddie went straight to Charles Blackett's shop. He needed to find out if it was true that the stolen moulds had been used to prove the fraud. He found a 'Closed' sign on the shop front. He knocked frantically at the side door and eventually Blackett opened it. He looked haggard and appeared worse for wear from drink.

"What are you doing here?" he slurred.

"We've had the police at the yard," explained Eddie. "It seems someone's got evidence that the Fontwells are forged. I want to know if you still want our stock."

Blackett threw Eddie a stern look. He swayed slightly and then shouted, "I'm ruined! Can't you see? It's over…finished. Now clear off and don't come back here again!"

He slammed the door in Eddie's face.

Eddie turned away and headed back to the workshop. He felt sick. He and Billy had dropped most of their former customers to concentrate on the Fontwells. Now, the rent was overdue and all they could make were castings that nobody wanted. They needed to get back some of their old customers, and quickly. In the meantime, he would have to try to sell the Fontwells they had. Billy was not at all well, but he might be able to call on local boat yards to drum up business. Eddie wondered whether he might go farther afield to hawk the forgeries. It had to be worth a try.

♦

Eddie Milner stepped off a train at Windsor. Being a lovely Berkshire town with its castle and royal associations, he thought it an ideal place to fool the locals into buying some of his forgeries. He was about twenty-five miles from Whitechapel; hopefully far enough from the capital.

He had dressed as a labouring man and carried a bag containing a selection of Fontwells: mainly medallions, a few pilgrim badges, some recently concocted Saxon rings – one of which he wore – and several dozen coins that had been an experiment, but had turned out well; surely good enough to dupe an unwitting buyer.

He walked around the town for a while, familiarising himself with the area. He found a public house in a side street and ordered a jug of ale. He lit his pipe before starting up a conversation with the publican, playing casually with the ring on his finger as he supped his drink and chatted.

"That's a most curious ring you're wearing," observed the publican.

"Yes, it got dug up the other day along with some coins. I've no idea if it's valuable, nor the coins."

"Could I look at the ring and the coins?"

Eddie removed it from his finger and produced a couple of coins from a pocket. He passed them to the man who examined them closely.

"Where did these come from?"

"You know those excavations going on behind Victoria Street?"

"Oh yes."

"We've been knocking down an old storehouse and digging out some new foundations."

The man seemed quite taken with the items. "The ring and the coins obviously have some age; clearly green from lying in the soil. What do you want for them?"

"You want to buy the lot?"

The man nodded.

"Seven shillings."

"Were any more found?"

"Only two other coins, but I sold them yesterday."

"I'd be willing to pay five shillings."

"Sorry, it's got to be seven. I was persuaded to sell the others too cheaply."

The man pondered for a while. "All right," he said, and he

paid Eddie seven shillings.

Eddie left the premises delighted with his performance. He sauntered along the high street and came across another public house. He thought he'd try his luck again, so he entered and ordered another beer.

The barman seemed an affable fellow and they soon fell into a discussion of how often Her Majesty stayed at the castle or whether she preferred Buckingham Palace.

"Are you interested in history?" Eddie asked the man.

"Oh yes, very much so. That's why I like all the pageantry and the royal comings and goings."

When Eddie ordered another drink, he counted out the coins to pay; making sure the barman got a clear look at all of the coins in his palm.

"What are those coins you've got there?"

"What, these green ones?"

"Yes."

"No idea; they came from some excavations."

Eddie passed the five in his hand to the barman who took them and looked at them with interest. He turned each over in his hand, his expression giving nothing away.

"Have they any value?"

Eddie shrugged, "No idea. You interested in buying them?"

"I might be; it depends on what you want."

"Twelve shillings."

"As much as that? It's more than I can afford."

"I'll tell you what," Eddie said, "you can have them for eight."

The barman turned them over and then handed them back. "No, sorry, it's more than I can afford."

"Oh well, never mind," said Eddie, finishing his drink.

He said goodbye and left. He'd gone twenty yards down the street when he heard the barman call out and run up to him.

"Here you are, eight shillings."

Eddie took the money and handed over the five coins. *That's the rent paid this month*, he thought with glee. *Billy'll be pleased.*

Windsor was proving to be a lucrative market for the Fontwells. Growing in confidence, Eddie thought he would try to fool a more educated individual. He spotted Welburn's Chemist Shop, entered, and boldly walked up to the counter. He assumed the man behind the counter to be Mr Welburn.

"Any idea what these are?" Eddie asked, showing him two medallions.

"Why are you asking me?"

"Well, you must know about science and chemicals. I thought you might be able to tell me if they're old."

The chemist took the medallions and studied them. "Where did they come from?"

"From the excavations in Victoria Street."

"Really? Was anything else found?"

Eddie showed him two coins.

A customer standing behind Eddie looked over with interest. "They could be worth ten pounds or nothing."

Eddie could see that the chemist was tempted. *He's probably thinking he can get some valuable artefacts at a knock-down price from an ignorant labourer. More's the fool*, he thought.

"How much do you want for them?"

"Fifteen shillings."

"I'd be careful, Mr Welburn, if I was you," warned the customer behind Eddie.

Wish you'd go away, thought Eddie.

The chemist ignored the customer. He looked more closely at the medallions and then briefly rubbed the green patina on the coins with the tail of his overall. "Very well," he said, and gave Eddie fifteen shillings from the cash drawer.

Eddie decided he'd done enough for the day. He said goodbye, left the shop, and found a small hotel for the night.

Leonard Welburn, excited with his bargain purchases, went to see his friend, the Reverend John Rowley, after work. He also happened to be a well-known antiquarian collector who resided in Windsor.

"Have a look at these, John, would you? I bought this pair of ancient medallions and two very old coins from a labourer today. I'm sure they're Greek or Roman. Just look at the medallions. They must date back to the crusades!" Welburn was so excited.

The Reverend Rowley looked at the objects through a magnifier. He tried to find meaningful inscriptions on the coins and medallions, but failed to do so. He didn't want to disappoint his friend, but he couldn't lie. He put down the magnifier.

"I'm sorry, Leonard, but I believe these coins to be forgeries, and the medallions too. You may not be aware that a scandal has broken out recently in the world of antiquities. Hundreds of medallions and religious badges thought to date, as you rightly said, from the crusades have been circulating in London. Rather than centuries old, they are in fact of recent manufacture."

Welburn was stunned. "You mean that I've been had?"

"I'm afraid so. Where are they supposed to have come from?"

"Excavations in Victoria Street."

"Well, why don't you and I go down there first thing tomorrow and find out if things like these really have been unearthed."

Having organised an assistant to open his premises, at nine o'clock the following morning, the chemist and the clergyman stepped gingerly across the disturbed mud and rubble of the building site in order to speak to the gaffer.

"Good morning, sir," Reverend Rowley, wearing his clerical collar, addressed the workman.

"Good day, vicar. What can I do for you?"

"My friend here, Mr Welburn, and I were wondering if any ancient coins or artefacts may have come to light recently during the works here."

The man seemed surprised. "What, here?"

"Well, that's the rumour…Medallions and coins, possibly Roman or Greek?"

"First I've heard and I would know. The only coin that's turned up was a sixpence. It was about fifty years old, no more. I found it, as it happens; nothing else though."

"Oh dear, we've obviously been misinformed. Thank you for

your time. Good day to you, sir."

"Good day, gentlemen."

The two friends walked to the high street, lamenting the fact that Welburn had indeed been deceived and wondering whether there was anything they could do about it.

"Look! Look!" Welburn grabbed the Reverend's arm and brought him to a halt. "Look over there; that man outside Jones' Book Shop."

"Yes, I see him, Leonard."

"That's him: the man who sold me the forgeries! Look, he's going in. Let's find a policeman, quickly!" Welburn had become quite agitated.

"Good idea. You go that way and I'll go this way," ordered the clergyman.

The two men set off in opposite directions.

Inside the bookshop, Eddie Milner browsed the shelves.

"Can I help you, sir?" asked the proprietor.

"I was looking for history books. I dug this up recently and wanted to find out about it." Eddie held out a leaden pilgrim badge depicting two monks at a shrine.

"Well, let me think. Yes, we do have a book that might help." He went to fetch some library steps, which he placed nearby, and mounted them. "Yes, here we are. *Pilgrim Badges* by Thomas Hughes," he announced triumphantly. "Would you like to inspect it?"

"How recent is it?"

"Erm, let me see…printed three years ago."

"Yes please, I'd like to look."

The bookseller descended the steps and took the book to the counter. "Could I have a look at what you've found?"

"Yes, of course," said Eddie. He was happy to let the bookseller take over the research. The man examined the badge carefully and then studied the book's index before turning to a specific page.

"Here it is! Or at least one very similar. Says it dates from the fourteenth century."

"Really? Does it say if it might have any value?"

"It describes it as a rarely seen example being from the shrine at Canterbury." The bookseller was becoming quite enthusiastic. "Would you consider selling it?"

"Oh, I don't think so. I mean, if it's rare, it's probably worth hanging on to."

"I'll give you ten shillings for it."

"I'd like a bit more, really."

"How much more?"

Eddie pretended to consider. "You can have it for twelve."

"Done," replied the bookseller. "I suppose you won't be requiring this book now?"

"No, not now, thank you."

Eddie pocketed the money and turned to leave the shop. At that moment, a police constable opened the door, accompanied by the chemist Eddie had duped the day before.

"That's him! That's him!" shouted Welburn, pointing at Eddie. "Arrest him! Arrest him!"

There was no escape for Eddie. The policeman marched up to him and grabbed him by the arm.

"What's going on?" asked the bookseller. "I like to engender a quiet atmosphere in my establishment."

"Er, sorry, Mr Jones. Excuse me, but allegations have been made that this man has been fraudulently selling ancient artefacts and coins of recent fabrication."

At this point, Reverend Rowley, who was somewhat portly in stature, also entered the bookshop, accompanied by another policeman. The race to the bookshop had left him extremely red in the face and gasping for breath. Fortunately, he didn't have to answer any questions. He found a chair and sat down, where he could observe events while he recovered.

The first policeman kept a firm grip on Eddie's arm. "Mr Welburn, do you recognise this man as the one who sold you fake antiques?"

"Yes, constable, I do. That is definitely him!"

"Why, he's just sold me a pilgrim badge," said the bookseller.

"It must be a fake. I want my money back!"

"Is that true?" the policeman asked Eddie.

"Look, he wanted to buy it. I only came in here to find a book about them. He can have his money back if he wants. Can I put my hand in my pocket, please?"

The policeman relaxed his grip slightly allowing Eddie to retrieve the bookseller's money, which he placed on the counter.

"I'll take that lead object, Mr Jones, if you don't mind," said the first policeman. "We may need it for evidence. You can give your statement to my colleague, Constable Hackney; you too, Mr Welburn." He pulled out some handcuffs and snapped them around Eddie's wrists. Then he looked inside the bag that Eddie had been carrying. "Looks like a regular museum in here. I think you'd better come along with me, and we'll see what you've got to say to the sergeant."

A week later, Eddie Milner appeared at the Slough sessions charged with obtaining money under false pretences by the sale of fabricated and factitious antiquities. The prosecution argued that he had induced persons to become purchasers, inferring that the objects had been found during excavations in Windsor. The defence contended that Milner had at no point offered the objects for sale, but merely shown them. At no time had he claimed that they were ancient and at no time had he said they were of value. Rather, it was the purchasers who had decided that the objects were valuable and had sought to obtain them from him at the lowest price possible. The witnesses, namely the chemist, the bookseller, the publican, and the barman all had similar stories. In each case, they admitted that the accused had not offered the objects for sale.

The jury concluded that the purchasers knew tolerably well what they were buying and it could not be proved that Milner had induced them to make a purchase. He was found not guilty.

Immediately on his release, Eddie Milner bolted back to Whitechapel, leaving his bag of Fontwell Fakes in the hands of the police.

CHAPTER 32

Two men sat huddled in the corner of a coffee house, located just off The Strand. It was their regular meeting place. One was a seller, the other a buyer. Information was the commodity traded.

"Heard a little whisper about somebody the other day. Somebody who you'd be interested in, I reckon."

"Really? And who would that be? Not that bloke Heatherton who's been seeing the wife of one of my clients on the side. He's proving to be a right slippery character to track down."

"No, no, not him…Someone who put one over on you once, someone I know you've said you'd like get even with."

The buyer's expression changed. "It wouldn't be my old friend Moses Jupp would it?"

"Right first time."

"Go on then, George, tell me all. What's he been up to then?" He rubbed his hands with anticipation.

"Well, Harry, it seems our friend Moses might have taken up house-breaking, or more specifically, workshop-breaking."

"Really? How come?"

"Have you read in the papers recently about the Fontwell Fakes?"

"What, those counterfeit collector things?"

"That's the ones."

"Yes, I did see something, but what's the connection to Jupp?"

"I heard some gossip at the station, the other day. It seems your man Jupp was suspected of stealing some moulds and castings

214

from a workshop. They later turned up in the hands of a collector. The collector showed them to a history society as evidence that the things were modern forgeries and not ancient at all."

"So who suspected him?" Harry Thurgut got out his pocket book and pencil.

"Couple of rogues called Billy Nunn and Eddie Milner. They've got a small smelting foundry in Rosemary Lane. Not sure of the name, but it'd be easy to find it."

Thurgut wrote down the details. The name Billy Nunn vaguely rang a bell, but he didn't think he'd heard of Milner before. "Who was the collector?"

"That I don't know…some wealthy investor. He said they were delivered to him anonymously."

"What about Nunn and Milner? Are they reliable?"

"No, not really. They were definitely making forgeries. It's all been exposed. They might even be out of business, I don't know. It seems they hadn't actually broken the law though and it was only their word that Jupp was involved in the burglary. There was no evidence, so the whole thing was dropped. It might be worth your while paying them a call. You could see if they're still there and maybe have a sniff around."

"Yes, I will. Thanks for that, George." He put his pocket book away. "See you in a fortnight then, at the usual time?"

"Yes, that's fine."

Thurgut discreetly slid two half-crowns across the table. George slipped them into his pocket.

The two men got up, shook hands and left, going their separate ways.

Thurgut found the foundry easily enough. The gates were open and he walked into the workshop, where he saw two men deep in discussion. He got the impression that there was little smelting going on; the place was cold.

"Excuse me…my name's Harold Thurgut. I'm looking for Mr Nunn and Mr Milner."

The two men stopped their discourse and turned towards him.

He offered his card, on which was written 'Private Investigator'. One of them took it and then passed it to his colleague. Thurgut watched the shorter of the two examine the card carefully. Clearly, he was just about to say something when he turned away and coughed long and hard.

The other man looked apologetic at his colleague's reaction. "I'm Eddie Milner and this is Billy Nunn," he said helpfully, as Billy tried to recover his composure.

Finally, Billy croaked, "You used to be a police sergeant, didn't you? I was in the Central Shoeblack Brigade."

"Of course, I thought I'd heard the name before." Thurgut replied. He then thought, *My God, you look terrible. I'd never have recognised you.* "So how are you?" he asked Billy, before looking around. "I can see you've done well for yourself."

"Oh, not too bad…Got a bit of a cough at the moment, though. Have you got somethin' you want us to make," he asked hopefully.

"As it happens, no, but I was hoping you might be able to help me with something I'm working on."

Both men looked at him suspiciously.

"I understand that you were recently burgled, and that you think Moses Jupp was responsible."

At the mention of the name, the two looked interested.

"About time someone followed up on what we told the police," said Eddie.

"Yes, 'bout time," agreed Billy.

This was just what Thurgut wanted to hear. "What makes you think that Moses Jupp did it?"

"A few things," answered Eddie, as Billy started to cough again. "First of all, he had a motive."

"A motive?"

"Definitely. We took over his customer and started doing designs ourselves. He didn't like that."

"You mean these Fontwell things?"

"That's right. We had a good business going. He was jealous, that's what he was."

Billy cleared his throat. "And he wanted to put one over on

Blackett too," he croaked.

"Who's Blackett?"

"Charles Blackett," Billy continued. "He's a dealer. He was sellin' the Fontwells to his customers. He dropped Moses to buy directly from us. Look, sorry, but I need to sit down." Billy groaned.

"Mind if I make some notes?" said Thurgut.

"Fine, go ahead," said Eddie. He turned to Billy, thinking, *He really doesn't look well.* "Sit down over there and have a rest. I'll do the talking and you can chip in if you want."

Billy sat down gratefully.

Thurgut turned to Eddie, "So, do you have any evidence it was Jupp who did the burglary?"

"Not exactly, but we know it was him, cos he took the moulds to a collector."

"Which collector?"

"Don't know his name, something like Redman. It was in the press, I believe."

"But do you have any actual proof that Jupp broke in?"

"The crow-bar and screwdriver he used are over there."

"Yes, but can you prove they were his?"

"Well no, but I'll tell you something: he and his wife have disappeared since the burglary; vanished, they have. I've been round all of his old haunts, asking. No one seems to know where they've gone."

"And what were his haunts? The foreshore I know, but were there any others?"

"I later found out he used to work on a stall sometimes, down at Spitalfields Market – Rushtons' – but they said he'd moved on when I went there, nothing more."

"All right, leave this with me; I'll see if I can track him down."

"Tell you what", said Eddie, "if you find out where he is, let me know. Meanwhile, I'm going to keep on looking for him myself. I said to Billy, didn't I Billy?" Billy nodded. "I said I'm going to give him what for. He's ruined us, he has. We might be thrown out anytime unless we can get some new business. We can't sell the Fontwells we've made – I've tried that – so we'll have to melt them down. Billy's got a wife and child to support. All our problems are down to Jupp. He's really got it coming to him."

Thurgut turned to go. "I'll do my best," he promised. With that, he left.

PART THREE

CHAPTER 33

Peter had given Norman Coles a ring and was pleased to hear that he was welcome to do some detecting the following day. This was to be his fourth time out on the field and he hoped to equal the success he'd had on his first outing. Unfortunately, his last two sessions had been disappointing and he hadn't found much to get excited about.

That was typical of his luck. He'd once been offered a new site to search and within the first hour had found a beautiful Queen Elizabeth I silver sixpence dated 1569. He'd shown it to the landowner who'd said she'd like to keep it. Peter could hardly refuse, and he was confident that he would find more. But, despite going back many times and spending nearly forty hours searching diligently, he never did find another, nor did he find anything else of particular note. He hoped that scenario would not be repeated at Oxenhope.

It was mid-August. Peter had seen nearly all four seasons down in the valley. He'd not been allowed on the field during the pheasant shooting in the heart of the winter, but had managed two days of detecting once the field was dressed and seeded in early spring. After that, he'd had to be patient. Now that the crops had been harvested, Norman was happy for him to try the stubble, which fortunately was quite patchy. The farmer had explained that he intended to start ploughing the following week, but if Peter wanted to wait, conditions would be much better once the soil was turned over. Peter, though, was desperate to do some searching, having waited several months. Stubble or not, he was keen to give it a go.

The following day, Peter parked his car near the corner of the field named on the tithe map as Oak Meadow. It was just within sight of the farmhouse. He was confident that Norman would recognise the vehicle, should he see it. As usual, he'd come well prepared. In his backpack, he carried some cold drinks and sandwiches. His plan was to start straight away, stop for a drink mid-morning, and then continue until lunchtime when he'd find a good spot to enjoy his picnic. After that, he might return to any 'hot' areas, had he found any. If not, then he'd move on to another part of the field.

His visit to the county archives had enabled him to copy the tithe map and to superimpose it over the present-day arrangement of one big field. Oak Meadow was where the Roman gold had been found, but the exact find-spot was unknown.

After passing an hour in the general area without success, Peter decided to try searching the part of the field where a former hedgerow divided Oak Meadow from its neighbour, Long Lay. Old field boundaries were sometimes good places to search, for they would have seen more foot traffic and therefore sustained more losses from individuals skirting the edge of a field, rather than walking directly over a crop; although, the theory only tended to hold for losses made within the last three or four hundred years. It was difficult to predict where boundaries may have existed in truly ancient times.

Non-detecting friends often asked him why agricultural land produced finds at all. They were puzzled; until he explained that prior to the Industrial Revolution the fields were where the majority of the population worked. They dropped and lost things. Not only that, straw was used to cover the bare earth floors in dwellings and stalls. Objects like buckles, buttons, coins, and rings fell into it and were lost. When the straw was renewed, the old material was pitched onto a wagon and then spread on the fields to improve the soil. The lost objects were unwittingly distributed on the land, waiting for the day when someone like Peter came along with his metal detector.

He consulted the map he'd produced to see where the old hedgerow would have been. He turned it to orientate himself and when happy made his way to a starting point at the edge of the field. Scanning along the line where he estimated the boundary to be, he looked for any humps or bumps, but nothing attracted his attention. The only thing of interest was an oak tree that was roughly at the end of where he thought the hedgerow would have run. He switched on his detector and, aiming for the tree, made his way slowly across the field.

It took him nearly an hour to reach the far side. Signals were few and far between. Pieces of lead and shotgun caps were all that he found. He sat down on the bank, near the oak tree, and took a long drink from a bottle of water. The covering of cloud which had obscured the sun earlier that morning was starting to burn off. He could see himself removing a layer of clothing by lunchtime.

Refreshed, Peter headed back towards his starting point, but this time he took a parallel line about ten yards inside the previous one. Occasionally, the stubble was quite stiff and he had the option of swiping it to bend it over, or skimming the head of the detector above it. The latter method was easier, but it meant that he couldn't pick up signals from deeper objects. It was a compromise, so he did a bit of both. On reaching the other side, he had at least managed to find two coins but disappointingly they were worn copper discs with no detail remaining.

He turned around and set off once more towards the side of the field with the oak tree. He wondered about it. Had it been notable enough to have given Oak Meadow its name? Would more than one be required to name such a meadow? Perhaps it was a remnant of several that had once stood at that end of the valley.

With nothing interesting found, Peter started to feel frustrated, so rather than maintaining a slow steady line, he decided to deviate and zig-zag for a while. Suddenly, he heard a whisper of a pleasing signal in his headphones and paused to see if he could isolate it from the background chatter. He retraced a few steps and swept the head of the detector from side to side.

Yes! he thought. *There it is, nice and clear now. I must have caught the object's edge before.*

He judged the target's centre, and then used his shovel to lever out a square section of stubble. He checked the hole, but the signal had gone. Then he checked the clod clinging to the stubble, and there was the signal. Out came his pinpointer. He switched it on and prodded the clod of earth. The pinpointer beeped. He pulled the clod apart and continued to divide it until he held a small lump of damp earth in his hand, which according to the pinpointer contained the object. With care, he crumbled it apart and felt the edge of something cold and thin. He rubbed off the soil sticking to it and saw with delight, and relief, that his patience and perseverance had paid off. He'd found another silver coin – not medieval, but later. It had the distinctive double shield of The Commonwealth, and Peter identified it as a silver half-groat, struck during the time of Oliver Cromwell in the mid-seventeenth century. He was elated, even though he hadn't found a stray coin from the hoard of Roman gold – but then he hadn't really expected to. He carefully placed the coin into his finds box, and then refilled the hole he'd made. He checked the immediate vicinity to see if there were any more signals but, regrettably, there were none.

By now, it was almost lunchtime, so Peter left a yellow plastic tent peg to mark where he'd got to. He carried his machine towards the oak tree in order to enjoy some lunch. The sun now shone strongly and it had become quite hot. A warm smell of straw filled his nostrils, and the stubble shimmered in the heat haze, brightly reflecting the light. Peter wished he'd brought some sunglasses. When he reached the tree, which was substantial and clearly several hundred years old, he was relieved to find a shady area at the base, among its roots. He set down the detector and shovel, removed his headphones, and then his backpack. He looked around and selected a comfortable place to sit on the cool earth.

The moment his backside touched the ground, the peace was broken by the beeping of his pinpointer. Although it was in its belt holster, the tapered sensitive end had made contact with the soil. Peter realised that he must have forgotten to switch it off. He pulled it out and did so.

Probably caused by another buried shotgun cap, he thought.

Out came his sandwiches and the bottle of water. He settled down, with his back partly leaning against the tree's trunk, and gazed contentedly across the field. It had become even hotter, but thankfully an occasional light breeze cooled the sweat on his brow. He decided that after lunch he'd return to the marker where he'd retrieved the silver coin, but if it got much warmer, and he failed to find anything else, then he'd pack up about mid-afternoon.

He ate his lunch and enjoyed the beautiful country scene before him. The sky was clear and deep blue. A red kite, whose presence above him he'd been aware of during the morning, continued to cast its shadow some thirty feet above the stubble. It was searching for carrion, supported by what little breeze there was. On the far side of the field, he spotted three deer as they broke cover. They stepped cautiously into the open, sniffed, and stared in his direction before turning and slipping back into the cool dark woodland from which they'd emerged.

Sitting at ground level, in the shade, the heat haze across the open stubble was even more perceptible. Peter's thoughts wandered. He recalled old black and white movies he'd seen where a weak and thirsty survivor staggered towards the shimmering oasis on the horizon. Through his wavering view, he thought he could see two Victorian labourers in the distance, waist-deep in a trench, swinging their pickaxes. A mirage, he realised, but perhaps there really were more gold coins out there.

The rattle of a magpie's call disturbed his nap, making him realise that he'd dozed off. He looked up and saw a pair of the birds on a branch high above him.

How does the rhyme go? One for silver, two for gold. No that's wrong. It's five for silver and six for gold! If only it could be true. Come on, he told himself, *another hour out there and I'll call it a day.*

He packed away his lunch, got up, and strapped on his backpack before checking that he'd not left anything on the ground. All was tidy; nothing indicated that he'd even been there, and then he remembered the beep from his pinpointer when he'd first sat down. He thought it would probably be a waste of time, but he removed the device from the holster and switched it on. He traced its end across the dirt where he'd been sitting. It beeped. He could tell from the signal that it wasn't a coin or a shotgun cap. It was bigger and definitely not circular in shape.

It's probably a large piece of silver foil, or a crisp packet discarded by some former picnicker. Shall I bother investigating? Trouble is, if I ignore it, it'll bug me. I might have missed something good and then I won't be able to concentrate properly out on the field.

Peter pulled out a small trowel and dug a shallow hole at the centre of where he thought the target lay. The pinpointer only penetrated a depth of about two inches so he knew it was near the surface. He removed some soil. About an inch down, he checked the signal with the pinpointer once more. The target was still there. He used one of his plastic tent pegs to gently scrape a little deeper. If the object was something interesting, he didn't want to scratch or damage it with a metal trowel. The tent peg touched something smooth and flat. He blew away some loose soil and leaf mould, revealing a small part of whatever it was. It was a dull matt brown and probably made of brass. Still using the tent peg, he carefully prodded and scraped away more soil. He discovered that the object was rectangular in shape, about two inches by three inches. A tin, perhaps?

Once he found the edge, he dug carefully at one side and saw that the object was quite thin, no more than about half an inch thick. He removed more of the soil around it, and then pushed the tent peg under one end and levered it up. He was right. It looked like a small brass tin, with what appeared to be a hinged lid.

He picked it up and studied it for a while before rubbing a small part of the lid's surface. It had some sort of design impressed in it. Gently, he turned it over, but the underside appeared plain.

Something inside shifted. He turned it back over, and felt the contents move once more. Gingerly, he attempted to open the lid. It moved slightly, but the hinge was stiff so he gradually worked it open until the gap was wide enough to peer inside. He gasped with excitement and tipped the contents onto his palm.

In his hand, Peter held three coins. They were Roman, bright and clean, and unmistakably gold! He stood up and looked about. The scene in the field in front of him may not have changed, but, for him, detecting would never be the same again. He'd found his first hoard of gold coins. He jumped up, clenched a fist, punched the air, spun around, and let out whoops of joy. He couldn't believe his luck.

I guess this is what detectorists call the gold dance, he thought. *Yippee!*

CHAPTER 34

OXENHOPE, APRIL 1871

Moses and Bess had settled in well at Oxenhope. Their accommodation consisted of a terraced cottage, one of four simply called 'The Row'. It was close to the farmhouse, just behind the stables and animal stalls. The cottage was small, with two rooms upstairs and two rooms downstairs, but it was dry and as much as they needed. It had a cast-iron range for heating and cooking. The previous occupants had left a bed and a kitchen table. Most of all, it was their first proper home.

Bess's pregnancy proceeded without complications. She felt she'd made a good impression with Marion, Mrs R's sister, and had been introduced to two other expectant mothers whose husbands worked for Mr Turnbull and who lived in the valley.

A wagon ride into Swindon market to buy some additional furniture and more bedding had given her a chance to chat with several other 'Oxenhopers', as they liked to call themselves.

She found that her days passed quickly. Washing, cleaning, laying the fire, and cooking seemed to take up a fair amount of time. The smoky London fog of winter, and the stink from the Thames in summer, were in the past. The air here was fresh and clean. She decided that she liked life in the valley.

The neighbours in the other three cottages were friendly and had made her and Moses welcome. On one side, a widow named Florence lived on her own. Her husband used to be the shepherd and she was ever grateful to the Turnbulls for allowing her to stay on. She helped out at the farmhouse whenever she could. Next door to Florence lived Mr and Mrs Rutherford. They were in their fifties and had two sons in their thirties. Both Mr Rutherford and his sons worked on the farm. Bess assumed the boys must still share a bedroom.

The cottage on the other side to Bess and Moses was occupied by Archie, a bachelor, who was one of the most senior and experienced workers whom Mr Turnbull employed. Bess had the impression that Archie had an eye for her. She was careful how she spoke to him and made sure that she did nothing that might encourage him. She assumed that he knew she was expecting; if not, then he would soon find out. She was definitely getting bigger.

Moses was becoming more confident that their new life would be a success. His first few days after their arrival had been spent with the gang, employed on hedge planting. Moses was in his element, helping to dig out old diseased parts of a hawthorn and hazel hedge, and replanting with new. The gang had managed to do a fair stretch and Mr Turnbull was pleased with their progress.

However, Moses worried that Titus Redding might implicate him in the robbery at Billy Nunn's, despite giving his word that he wouldn't, and so he decided to take precautions. He'd hide the bag of castings he'd brought with him, just in case the police ever turned up and searched the cottage. He'd held on to them as he hoped they might still have value; something he could sell if money got tight. He'd looked for a suitable place where they could be hidden and retrieved easily and chose one corner of the granary, behind some sacks of corn. To conceal them, he used the pretext of going out to the privy when he knew most of the neighbours would be inside their homes eating supper, but it took two evenings: the first to loosen the bricks and the second to remove some soil, conceal the castings, and replace the bricks.

The following week, Moses found the work more demanding. He was unaccustomed to looking after animals, and Mr Turnbull had explained that as he was temporarily short of a fogger, he would need Moses to take on that role until he could find a permanent replacement. One of the Rutherford boys showed him the ropes and within a few days, he was feeding, milking, and tending a couple of dairy cows, as well as collecting slops and peelings for the pigs and chickens. A bonus was that he was very near to Bess, so nipping back to the cottage at lunchtime had its compensations.

When the census enumerator called at the cottage on the night of 2 April, he insisted that he had to enter an occupation for Moses.

Moses looked blank.

"Well what are you doing at the moment?"

"I'm the fogger."

"That'll do."

In mid-April, Moses was out in a field helping to spread basic slag fertilizer – a black cement-like powder – that improved the ground to produce strong and healthy crops. They were working in Oak Meadow. Moses was one of six men, each equipped with a wheelbarrow and shovel.

A wagon loaded with a large heap of slag had been parked in the middle of the field. Each man returned to it to refill his barrow before spreading the fertilizer on the section he'd been allocated. It was a dirty job. Every time a gust of wind caught the powder as it was being distributed, it blew back towards the spreader. Moses, however, didn't mind too much. He was outside in the open, which he preferred, and using a shovel was second nature to him.

The ground was almost bare after a long winter; with little new growth so far that year. The rain had constantly spattered the earth, flattening it, and exposing small stones and pebbles. These had become washed clean and were visible on the surface. Moses noticed small pieces of brick, almost orange against the dark soil. He also spotted broken pieces of pottery and small fragments of black glass. He wished he'd brought all of his books with him, rather than the few he had. They would have given him some idea of the pottery's age.

On the second day, he was absorbed in the rhythm of shovelling and broadcasting the slag, when he glimpsed something shiny and gold-coloured on the patch of bare earth he was just about to cover. He stopped, laid down his shovel, and knelt to look closer. It appeared to be a gold coin. Moses looked up and around. The closest man was forty yards away and wheeling his barrow in the opposite direction. Moses casually picked up the coin, rubbed off the mud and put it into his mouth. He was ecstatic; feeling the familiar thrill of finding something valuable in the ground. Whether it was in mud, shingle, sand, gravel, or in the middle of a field, the feeling of excitement was the same. This time, however, it was heightened, because he'd found gold!

He went to relieve himself behind a large oak tree at the side of the field. There, he noticed a flint sticking out of the bank, so when he'd finished, he sat next to it, pretending to tighten his boot laces. He took the coin out of his mouth and pushed it into the soil, just under one side of the flint. Tomorrow, he'd bring his faithful brass tin, put the coin inside it, and hide it somewhere. It was always possible he might find some more coins and he didn't want to risk leaving them in the cottage.

CHAPTER 35

Peter calmed down. He realised that his first duty was to let Norman know about the hoard. He searched around in his backpack and was relieved to find his mobile phone, and with sixty per cent of its power left. He was always forgetting to charge it. He tried to make a call, but, annoyingly, due to the geography of that part of the valley, his phone had no signal at the time. He did, however, manage to take a few photographs with it.

For the record, he placed the small brass tin back into its hole and photographed it in place. Then he remembered some sheets of kitchen towel in his backpack, kept for cleaning his hands. He laid out a sheet and took some close-ups of the tin's contents. He knew his detecting friends would be really impressed when they saw pictures of the coins, and the tin in which they'd been found.

After retrieving the tin and placing the coins back inside, Peter gathered up his gear and made his way back to his car, hardly noticing the walk because he was so preoccupied with his discovery. He placed everything into the rear, apart from the tin, which he placed gently in the passenger footwell so that he could keep an eye on it.

On his arrival at the farmhouse, Peter jumped out of the car and shouted for Norman. Almost immediately, two excited dogs came tearing around the corner of the house towards him. Norman came ambling around a few moments later.

"Hello Pete, what's the panic then? Nothing wrong, I hope?"

"No, not at all. Quite the opposite, in fact. I've got something amazing to show you."

"Really? What? Something you've found?"

"Could be!" Peter had hidden the tin behind his back. The dogs were sniffing and licking his hands, hoping he was concealing a tasty treat for them. "Have a look at this…" He revealed the tin and passed it to Norman, who peered at it closely. "See there, it has a hinged lid; it opens, but be careful."

Norman followed Peter's instruction and warily levered back the lid. "Good grief!" he exclaimed when he saw the contents. "Where on earth did you find this?"

"You know that big oak tree at the far end, just before the track goes up into the wood?"

"Yes, I know the one…oldest tree in the valley, according to my father. D'you find this near it then?"

"In among the roots, actually!"

"Really, how amazing…So what about the coins? I can see they're gold, but how old are they?"

"The coins are Roman. They could be anything up to two thousand years old!"

"Blimey," mumbled Norman in astonishment. "And what about this tin? Is that some marking on the lid?"

"Yes, there is something on it; let's see."

Norman passed the tin back to Peter who spat on his own thumb and started rubbing away the remains of any dirt. He fished in his pocket for the sheet of kitchen paper he'd used earlier and wiped the lid's surface with it.

"What is it? Does it say anything?" asked Norman.

Peter passed the tin back to him. Although the brass was dull, it was possible to make out the impression of a sailing ship.

"An old ship, eh? How old do you think the tin is?"

"Judging by the ship's design – which looks like a clipper to me – I'd guess the tin's probably about two hundred years old."

"Gosh, so it's much more recent."

"Yes, which means that these coins were placed in the tin for safekeeping, and it was either mislaid or deliberately buried during, I'd guess, Victorian times. Using a spot near a marker –

like a large tree – is fairly common practice. It was a few inches down, so more likely that it was buried rather than dropped."

"Do you think these are the same type of coins as the others?"

"I'll need to look them up to be sure, but it wouldn't surprise me. I've only looked briefly, but I think they show the Emperor Trajan. If that's the case, then they probably came from the same hoard I told you about from my research at the county archives; the one found by the two labourers back in 1842. Perhaps someone found more of those same coins later, or maybe the labourers hid a few themselves so that they didn't have to give all of them up for treasure trove."

"But these wouldn't be treasure trove too, would they? They were found on my land, so surely whatever's found here should belong to me?"

Peter explained. "It's not that simple, unfortunately. The law has changed a bit, but even so, two or more gold or silver coins found in the same place constitute a hoard. We're legally obliged to declare it. Because of the Treasure Act, the Crown can claim such things and has been doing so for hundreds of years."

Norman looked crestfallen. "So the blighters who make our laws could take these away from me. That's bloody typical!"

"We have to report the find to either the local coroner or the Finds Liaison Officer – an archaeologist appointed to deal with potential treasure items. I happen to know the local FLO; she sometimes comes to our detecting club to record finds. We'll have to tell her, you know, otherwise we'll be breaking the law."

"So if this hoard is declared treasure, will I ever see these coins again?"

"That depends on whether a museum wants to keep them or not. They'll be valued and that's what they'll pay out if they're not going to be returned."

Peter was starting to feel uncomfortable. He had the impression that Norman was far from keen on reporting the find. Failure to do so would make both of them criminals in the eyes of the law. He also didn't like to mention their verbal agreement to split anything of value fifty-fifty. He knew that he was entitled to half because he was the finder, but he didn't like to labour the point at that particular time.

Norman seemed to be considering what Peter had told him. "Is there any time limit for telling the authorities?"

"Two weeks, I think. I can check when I get home."

"All right, you do that and let me know. In the meantime, I'd like to hold on to these, if you don't mind. It's not every day that something like this turns up. I'd like to think about what I want to do."

"Of course," replied Peter, but actually thought, *What else can I say at the moment? With luck, once Norman gets over his shock and excitement, he'll realise that if he wants to stay on the right side of the law, the find must be declared.*

As soon as Peter got home, he showed Felicity his photographs. For once, she was actually impressed.

"So where's the tin with the coins then?" she asked excitedly.

"Ah, well Norman seemed a bit reluctant about reporting it as treasure and asked if he could hang on to them for the moment. I said that was fine, but frankly, what else could I have said? I wanted to bring them home, but I found the tin on his farm and I couldn't insist. I felt a bit awkward actually."

"So he'll be reporting it then?"

"I hope so. I'm going to look up the details of the law. There's a time limit in which to report a find, but if he doesn't want to hand it in after that, I'm not too sure. It might put me in a difficult position. I could be breaking the law too!"

At his computer, Peter read through the details of the 1996 Treasure Act. It was as he had thought: both he and Norman had fourteen days in which to inform the coroner, and the easiest way to do so was through a FLO. Once declared, the tin and its contents would be expertly examined. A coroner's inquest would make the final decision. If the find fell within the definition of treasure, it would either be returned or valued if a museum wanted it. In which case, he and Norman would receive fifty per cent each as finder and landowner. Valuations were made by a panel of experts at the British Museum in London. The whole process could take up to eighteen months.

All that was fine on paper, but Peter wondered if such valuations were based on market value. He phoned Norman to explain what he'd learned.

Norman remained unconvinced. "So it all has to go to court then? To an inquest?"

"Yes, that's how it's done. It gives everyone involved a chance to have their say and then it's up to the coroner to decide whether a find counts as treasure. There's no jury. The coroner usually acts on the report and advice of the experts at the British Museum."

"I don't like this valuation business. Can we trust them to come up with the true value?"

"Unfortunately, we don't have much choice, although you can appoint your own valuer to give an opinion, if you prefer. Trouble is, they'd have to go to the British Museum to examine the coins and you'd have to pay their expenses. What I have heard is that the valuation committee might reduce the value if there's a delay in reporting, or if they suspect that the number of coins declared is less than the number found."

"How are they going to prove that? I trust you, Pete, I'm happy that you only found three, but what if they think there were ten?"

"I took some photos when I uncovered the tin. We might have to swear an affidavit or something, but I'm sure if we do everything properly, they'll be more likely to believe us. I don't know all the answers though; this is all new to me as well."

"Look, I'm sorry, Pete, but I need to think about the implications. I don't want archaeologists tramping all over my fields. I've got ploughing to get on with next week, you know. Leave it with me and I'll get back to you in a day or two." Norman ended the call.

Peter's concern that he might become an accessory to a crime had not eased. He hoped that the farmer would see sense, but would just have to wait to see what happened. He'd give it ten days before he really started to sweat. What he'd do after that, he wasn't sure. In the meantime, he decided to research the Treasure Act more closely. He wanted to be absolutely sure of their legal position. If there was a loophole, then he was determined to find it.

CHAPTER 36

OXENHOPE

Moses' mind was elsewhere as he pulled at the teats of the cow. She'd been bellowing with discomfort because she was late for her afternoon milking: the reason being that everyone had been called to help extinguish a burning hayrick that had somehow caught fire. Now though, she was content, munching on the fodder he'd placed in her manger.

With Moses being made temporary fogger again, he now sat on a milking stool, his cheek against the animal's warm side, his body between her and the confines of the stall. The milk spurted rhythmically into the bucket. It was another skill he'd recently mastered.

He couldn't help but think excitedly about the three gold coins he'd found in Oak Meadow. There could be more out in that field. What was he going to do with the ones he'd found? He'd have to go into Swindon to see if he could find a dealer who'd buy them. Otherwise, it would mean a trip back up to London; somewhere he was reluctant to go.

The cow shifted to turn her head and look towards Moses. Realising that she had sensed something, he paused to glance down behind him, noticing the man's boots on the straw.

"Well, well, what have we got here then?"

Moses slowly looked up, right into the face of someone he thought he'd left behind. He tried to rise, but a firm hand pushed down on his shoulder and gripped the back of his neck like a vice, forcing his head back towards the cow.

"Regular dairymaid now, eh?" the man hissed into Moses' ear, spraying tobacco-laced spittle as he did so. "I've been savouring this moment, I have…savouring it. Thought you'd got away with it, didn't you? Hiding out here in the middle of nowhere. Well I know it was you that did it. Someone spotted you climbing out the back of the workshop with what you'd nicked and it seems an awfully odd coincidence that you and your wife disappeared a day or two after."

Moses was confused. Had Titus Redding said something? No one had seen him, he was certain. It was dark, the middle of the night. Was this a bluff, trying to get him to admit he'd done it? *No, no, don't be fooled, don't admit anythin'.* He needed to think. How to get out of this position? He was at a disadvantage, with his head forced down and his view restricted. He cast his eyes around, hoping to spot some means of defending himself.

"Ruined everything, you did," the man continued. "I said I'd get revenge though…said I wouldn't rest till you paid for it."

"How'd you find me?" asked Moses, grimacing with discomfort.

"Some discreet enquiries here and there. Not much progress early on, but your old landlord gave me the clue. Shame for you that he likes his beer so much. A few pints was all it took, with him telling me all about how he'd met his good lady all those years ago. Country girl, he told me, and from a little place called Oxenhope."

"Yes, but how did you know I was actually here?" Moses was playing for time, trying to think of some way out of his predicament.

"Not difficult really…A few questions at the village pub. There's not many folks with your accent in this part of the world. Course, my little side-show gave me the chance to watch and confirm your whereabouts."

"What? The rick? You set it on fire?"

"Like I say, out came everyone to help and there you were,

just like I hoped. It was easy to see where you went afterwards."

Moses tried to rise again, but was still being restrained. His assailant was tall and strong. He didn't want to shout for help, for that might cause a commotion, and it would mean explanations.

"You had it comin', you know," Moses said, while searching for a means to distract the man. "I was gettin' on in life, makin' my way, earnin' good money, buildin' my savin's, but you messed it up!"

Then, he had an idea.

Sorry old girl, I hope this doesn't hurt too much. He pinched and yanked two of the cow's teats. She instinctively raised a hind leg and kicked back. Moses heard a bone crack. At the same time, the grip on his neck was released, and he was able to turn his head.

The man, who had been standing behind the cow, had taken the full force of the kick on his right shin. He growled in pain and hopped about on his good leg, but soon lost balance. He fell backwards and struck his head hard on a wooden post supporting the roof of the cowshed, but rather than sliding to the hay-covered floor, Moses noticed that he seemed to be suspended at the point where his head had made contact with the post. His arms and legs twitched for a few seconds before they went limp, and then he remained motionless against the post.

Moses was suspicious, unsure of whether the man was unconscious or not. He got up stiffly from the milking stool and moved around to the side of the post, keeping out of arms' length. Then he noticed that the man's skull had been pierced by one of the four-inch iron spikes fixed at intervals to the post for hanging up harnesses and tools. It was as if the back of the head were hung on a hook. The neck seemed slightly longer than normal, due to it being stretched by the weight of the body.

"Oh God, what have I done?" breathed Moses. He began to panic, unsure of what to do and who to tell. He tentatively prodded the abdomen, and thought he heard something before the man's tongue flopped out of his mouth and dripped spittle. There was a short gurgle, and then all remained still.

He's still alive, Moses thought with relief. He tried to lift the man's head from where it was impaled, but the body hung limp and gave him no help.

He placed his arms around the torso and, using all his strength, bear-hugged the body as he pushed upwards. This caused a groaning sound as air was expelled from the man's lungs. Moses managed to lift the body enough to unhook it, and then he let it slide down the post, where it ended up lying sideways on the straw.

CHAPTER 37

"Ah Pete, you're at home…I thought it wouldn't be you."

It was late evening and the phone had rung.

"What do you mean, Norman? It wouldn't be me?"

"There's something going on out in my field, near where you found that tin with the coins. Obviously it's not you. I noticed a faint light just as I was drawing the curtains. It came on and went off, as though someone was trying not to show it. Do you think it could be someone metal-detecting? My first thought was poachers, but they tend to stick to the trees and not in the open like that."

"It could be illegal detectorists. The actual detectors don't have lights, but pinpoint probes have a light that comes on when you use them. The light may appear to be going on and off if someone is digging a hole and then poking the pointer down into hole to find the target. Can you hear any beeping sounds, or perhaps voices? There may be more than one, you know. I've heard that these nighthawks, as they're known, often hunt in twos or threes."

"I've got the window open, but I can't hear anything. It's quite a way over there from here. The dogs don't seem to have heard anything either. Nighthawks? Is that what they call them?"

"Yes, have you not heard of nighthawking? I would have thought some of your farmer friends might have been victims."

"No, but come to think of it, there was something – a little while back – about detecting without permission, and at night, in one of the farming magazines. Do you reckon I should call the police?"

"Yes. I would."

"I could scare them off myself, you know. I've got several shotguns."

"Don't even think about it, Norman! What happens if you shoot one of them, eh? It'll be you they lock up."

"I'd better call the police then."

"Yes, I would. I read recently they've got a campaign to tackle rural crime. Apparently, too few farmers report it and they want to change that."

"I'm sure I could sort them out myself!"

"No, don't go out there on your own, even with the dogs. I've heard of cases of violence. They'll be carrying shovels. Dial 999 and wait for the police to arrive. Would you like me to come over?"

"Yes please, Pete…that might be a help."

"OK, I'll leave now. Just don't do anything you might regret."

"How long will you be?"

"About half an hour; although, I'll stop up on the road and ring you before I come down through the wood. You can tell me if the police have arrived or not. I don't want to spook the nighthawks. If anyone's going to do that, it should be the police."

"Yes OK, I'll call them now."

"Do that, and I'll be there as quickly as I can."

"Who's died?" called out Felicity.

Peter went back into the sitting room and explained to Felicity about the call. They'd been watching the late evening news on television. She looked worried when he said he was going over to Oxenhope.

"It's a bit late surely?"

"Don't worry; I won't go down there before the police, I promise. You go to bed. I'll let you know what's going on when I get there." As he spoke, Peter gathered up what he thought he might need. "I'll take two torches with me, and before you ask, yes, I've got my mobile!"

"But is it charged and is it switched on?"

Peter jumped into the little Fiat and set off towards the farm. One thing he kept thinking about was how had the nighthawks, if that's what they turned out to be, found out about his hoard and where it was found? It couldn't be coincidence that they were searching near to the find-spot. Suddenly, he was shaken from his thoughts. Driving along a single-track road, he noticed fast approaching headlights in his rear-view mirror. He knew that there was a passing place just up ahead, so not wishing to delay whoever it was, he accelerated briefly and pulled in when he reached it. He expected the vehicle to race past, but it slowed and came to a stop alongside. It was a police car. He lowered his window in case he needed to explain where he was going.

"Good evening, sir, would you mind telling us what you're doing out here?"

"No, of course not. My friend, Norman Coles the farmer, rang me. He said he thought there might be someone metal-detecting illegally in his field at Oxenhope. Is that where you're going, because I told him to ring the police?"

"What's your name, sir?"

"Peter Sefton."

The officer turned to his colleague who nodded back to him: they'd obviously checked out his number plate.

"You're right; we're responding to a call from Oxenhope Farm. You can follow, but don't get in the way. It could be poachers. We don't know what's going on yet."

The police car accelerated away and soon disappeared around a bend in the road ahead. Peter set off too in hot pursuit, all 1200cc of power in his car's engine straining in protest. The whole encounter with the police had lasted less than a minute, but his heart was beating fast. He understood why they'd questioned him. Obviously, he could have been an accomplice to whoever was in Norman's field and they were perfectly reasonable to ask what he was doing out there so late in the evening.

This is all quite exciting, Peter thought, *as long as Norman comes to no harm.*

He'd reached the turn-off to the track, hoping the police hadn't driven past it. Country roads were notorious for people getting lost. He pulled in again to ring Norman.

There was no reply, so he rang Felicity. "I'm up at the top and just about to go down into Oxenhope," he told her.

She came back with a hundred reasons why he shouldn't do so.

"Look, don't worry. I've seen the police. They said I could follow them, but I'm not to get in their way. It should be all right."

"Be careful, that's all!"

"Yes, I will. I'll let you know what's happening when I get down there."

Peter started his descent of the steep, narrow, winding track. He debated whether to turn his headlights off, but decided that might be a little too clandestine and he might be confused for a nighthawk himself. He was about halfway down when he realised that headlights were coming straight up towards him. He blasted his horn and slammed on his brakes. The brake pedal vibrated under his foot as the wheels sought some grip on the gravelly slope. He came to a halt, and got ready to reverse.

The vehicle coming up the track swerved to avoid him and went off the track into the undergrowth. It stopped violently when it struck a tree. One of its headlights shattered, and steam started to escape from the grill.

Peter locked his doors and engaged reverse gear, but he needn't have worried. Two men jumped out of the respective sides of their crashed vehicle and ran into the woods. The driver came around the front, crossing the track in clear view of Peter's car headlights. Peter could see that the man wore camouflage leggings and jacket. He was in a panic and paid no attention to Peter at all.

Peter picked up his mobile phone. The signal looked weak, but it held long enough to call Norman. This time he answered, but before Norman could say anything, Peter told him to listen, and then explained what had happened.

"So you've blocked them on the track, have you?" Norman shouted.

Peter could hear murmuring in the background.

"Well done! The police are here with me now. They missed them somehow, but if you've stopped them getting back up onto the road, then there's a chance to catch them. Hang on; a police officer wants to talk to you…"

"How far down are you?" he asked Peter.

"About three-quarters of the way, I think."

"Are you in your car?"

"Yes."

"Good. Stay there and keep the doors locked. We'll be up in a minute."

Peter double-checked the central locking. He breathed a sigh of relief when, not long after, he saw the police car coming up towards him, blue lights bouncing off the trees, headlights blazing. The vehicle stopped and both officers climbed out.

The passenger examined the abandoned car; the driver came over to speak to Peter. "Did you see the occupants?" he asked, indicating the stricken car.

"Yes, two. They both ran off into the woods, it seemed in slightly different directions." Peter indicated the direction. "They were in a bit of a panic."

"Did you get a look at them?"

"Only a quick glimpse of the driver. I'd say he was about thirty, average height, and wearing army camouflage jacket and trousers."

"What about a hat?"

"No, he had short fair hair, I think."

The second police officer joined his colleague next to Peter's window. "There's some metal detectors and shovels in the back. Definitely illegal detecting."

"Right, this is what we'll do," said the driver. "There's no room to turn around so we're going to reverse down to the bottom. You follow. When we get down there, park your car out of the way. We've called for backup and we'll need to keep the access clear."

Peter did as instructed. Afterwards, he was invited to sit in the back of the patrol car where he was soon joined by Norman.

"Norman! You OK?"

"Yes thanks, Pete. How many are there?"

"I saw two, and they legged it off into the wood."

"I'd dearly like to see these boys catch those blighters."

As one of the officers used their radio, Peter and Norman listened to what was being said.

"We ran the registration number and came up with a blank… currently unregistered, and uninsured. I think we need extra resources and the dog unit. What's the chance of some aerial assistance? They should be able to find them using night vision."

"Pretty slim, but you might be lucky," came the response. "They're not too far away…dealing with a traffic incident. I think they're just about finished. I'll call them up and see if I can get them over to you."

Peter and Norman exchanged glances. Were the police really going to use a helicopter? The radio went quiet and they waited patiently. It seemed an age, but was probably no more than a minute.

The controller's voice cut in again. "Aerial support just been authorised…be with you in about eight minutes."

Presently, another police car and a dog van came down the track to meet them. The handler immediately brought out what Peter considered to be an extremely ferocious-looking dog, but then, Peter wasn't very confident around dogs. The officers got out of their vehicle and went to speak to their colleagues.

"Come on, let's get out and see what's going on," suggested Norman to Peter.

"Good idea, we don't want to miss all of the fun."

A quick discussion took place among the officers, and it was decided that they would go back up to the crashed car and see if the dog could pick up any scent. One officer was ordered to stay in the patrol car, and to leave the blue lights flashing, to help the helicopter pilot locate the farm.

With the car's window open, both Peter and Norman could hear the radio. They strained their ears to hear what was happening up near the abandoned car.

"I wonder why the police didn't see the nighthawk's car

when they came down to the bottom of the track and out into the open?" Peter said.

"I was wondering that too, but there's a large beech tree, over there, with room to park behind. It's certainly out of sight from the farmhouse."

"I wonder if they left anything lying around. Shall we have a quick look? I've got a torch on me," Peter suggested.

They wandered the twenty yards over to the tree, and Peter shone his torch on the ground. There were wheel tracks leading back to the track but nothing more. Just then, some furious barking up within the wood caught their attention. They heard several shouts followed by a cry of anguish and a howl of pain.

"I reckon that dog just got his teeth into one of them," chuckled Norman. "Let's get back over to the patrol car. We might be able to hear some more stuff over the radio."

In the distance, they heard the faint sound of a helicopter approaching. The sound got stronger; thirty seconds later, it was overhead. A searchlight was switched on from under its nose; the beam illuminating the tops of the trees, and scanning the far end of the valley where the farmhouse lay.

"I guess they might have spotted him with a thermal image camera," explained Peter. "It picks out body heat. If he's got as far as that then he must be quite a fit bloke. He's obviously trying to put as much distance as he can between himself and the police."

The beam danced about on the tree tops, moving steadily away from them towards the ruins behind the farmhouse.

Norman poked his head inside the police officer's car. "I think he might be heading towards the gap in the trees where I had a muck heap tipped recently," he explained to the driver. "I was leaving it for a few days before spreading it. He'll either have to cross it or go around it, but it should slow him down a bit; might even confuse him in the dark." Norman rubbed his hands with excitement. "Should make him smell nice too, which I'm sure your dog will appreciate!"

From inside the helicopter, the co-pilot spoke over the radio to the pursuing officers down in the trees. The policeman in the car turned up the volume on the radio, so all three could hear the exchanges.

"The canopy's pretty thick, so we can only get glimpses, but he seems to be heading towards a hot patch. It's glowing bright on the infra-red, probably some sort of manure heap, I guess. It's the right shape. It's much warmer than the surrounding ground. If he gets onto that we might not be able to pick him out."

"OK, we're following as quickly as we can," came the gasping reply from the ground. "Maybe you'll get him in the searchlight if he breaks cover."

Down on the ground, the remaining nighthawk had emerged from the trees and had paused to catch his breath. He extinguished the pocket torch he was holding. He knew the police had a dog, as well as a helicopter. *Seems a bit of a fuss for some illegal metal-detecting*, he thought, but unfortunately that wasn't his only misdemeanour. He was pretty sure his mate had been arrested, but he could be relied on not to blab too much. Still, he'd rather not get caught if he could help it. He looked up. The helicopter was almost overhead; its rotors making an incredible racket, but behind him he could still hear the barking of the dog. It was getting nearer. He decided to run across what appeared to be open ground. He could just about discern a hump in the field with the dark outline of another wood beyond it.

He sprinted into the open and reached the side of a mound about four feet high. He leaped onto it and found his boots sank down about six inches. He clenched his feet so as not to lose his footwear. His progress slowed markedly. Each step was a big effort, but he managed to reach the top. From the smell, he realised that he was on some sort of dung heap. He was panting with exertion, and it crossed his mind that he should give himself up.

As the beam of the helicopter's searchlight swept across the mound, the nighthawk did his best to dodge it. *Must be my cammos…They can't see me…That should give me a chance*, he thought.

Back at the patrol car, Peter and Norman listened intently to the exchange between the helicopter and the police team on the ground.

"We've lost him! He's somewhere on the dung heap, but we can't see him until he moves away from it. His body temp is about the same as the shit. He's invisible to us...Can't pick him up with the searchlight either."

"Roger...we're nearly through the trees now. The dog's got his scent, dying to get him."

Above the nighthawk, the clatter from the helicopter was even louder making it impossible to hear the dog, but he knew it couldn't be far behind. The thought of being brought down by it reinvigorated him and any nagging thought of capitulation and surrender went out of his mind. He managed to stumble across the remaining part of the heap, slipping down the slope on the other side. He was on firm grass once more. He ran as fast as he could in order to reach the cover of the trees. He made it and looked up. The helicopter had obviously spotted him again and had swung to face his new position. He also saw three torches flashing on the heap. He turned about and using his pocket torch as carefully as he could, set off once more, threading his way through the trees with as much haste as he could manage.

He stumbled his way uphill into sloping woodland, trying to avoid low branches, hoping he wouldn't trip on a root or a fallen branch. He was wheezing and gasping and had to pause for breath. He turned around to catch sight of his pursuers, but his torch picked out a glimpse of a dog's white teeth about thirty feet away. There seemed no sign of a handler. The dog would seize him within seconds! He looked down with his torch for a weapon or something with which to defend himself, and spotted a piece of broken branch. The dog was almost upon him. As he stepped towards the branch to pick it up, the ground beneath him gave way. With a cry of surprise, he felt himself falling feet first into some kind of hole. His shoulder struck and grazed something hard and he dropped his torch, but it wasn't long until he hit the bottom. His legs buckled and he found himself on his knees, wedged against a wall. Groaning in pain, he reached down and picked up his still illuminated torch. He aimed it up and saw that he was in a narrow brick-lined shaft. Above him, the dog was looking down, barking madly, still hoping to get hold of him. It dislodged some earth and small stones, which rained down on him. He was trapped with nowhere to run and with stinking manure on his boots.

On the surface, the dog handler, accompanied by the other police officers caught up with the dog. He pulled it back from the edge of the opening and reattached its leash and muzzle. The officers peered cautiously over the rim of the hole. "Must be an old well or something," said one of them, shining his torch down at the same time. "You OK down there?"

"Think so," came the defeated and disconsolate reply. "Might have sprained my ankle."

"Good! Well you're not going anywhere! We've cuffed your mate. How many of you were in the car?"

"Just me and him."

The dog handler made reassuring noises to the agitated dog and it quietened down. One of the officers radioed the helicopter to confirm capture of the fugitive suspect.

"He says there were only two of them. If you've seen no other suspects then you can call it a day. We'll finish up here. He's fallen down an old well or something. He's not badly injured, but he'll have to wait until we get some ropes to pull him out."

The helicopter pilot acknowledged the information. He turned away, gained height, and set off towards base.

Back inside the police car, Norman looked at Peter and grinned with pleasure. "Well done, there," he said to the officer in the car. "Bloody well done!"

CHAPTER 38

When the sound of the helicopter had faded into the distance, Peter and Norman wondered what to do. They decided to wait as instructed and fortunately they didn't have to wait too long. They spotted a police officer holding a torch emerging from the trees quite near them.

"It's OK," he said. "We've got 'em both. What a nightmare though, tramping through that lot in the dark." He brushed his trousers with his hand to remove thorns and burrs. Thick undergrowth was not something he liked. "Lucky for you that the Chief Constable is an archaeology nut."

"What do you mean?" asked Norman.

"He's into all that English Heritage stuff...protecting archaeological sites from illegal metal-detecting. Operation Artefact it's called...some recent initiative. We caught a gang down near Stonehenge the other week. He's happy to chuck resources at it, but it's not the same with every force. Like I say, you were lucky we could respond with air support; only because it was close by, I expect."

"Can we go back to the house now?" asked Norman. "Did they catch the other one up at the far end?"

"Yes they did. He fell down a well or something. He's stuck in it for the moment. Any chance of a cuppa for us and have you got some rope to pull him out?"

"I'm not sure about rope. How far down is he? Some of those old wells go down quite a long way."

"Don't think he's too deep. They can see him, and apparently he's in one piece."

"Bloody lucky then." Norman turned to Peter. "Can you run me back, and I'll stick the kettle on."

"Course, no problem."

They climbed into Peter's car and drove back to the farmhouse. Peter stayed outside. The signal on his mobile phone was just about strong enough. He rang Felicity with an update while Norman went inside.

"I'm going to hang on here for a while with Norman. They've arrested one of the nighthawks and the other's trapped down a well...No, he's not going anywhere!...Yes, I'll be careful, don't worry."

Norman came outside. "Kettle's on," he said to Peter. "Come on, let's go and see what's going on. I can't be bothered looking for rope at this time of night. He can rot down there for all I care. I've left the dogs inside...don't want them getting into a tangle with that police dog!"

A little way up into the wood, just behind the pheasant pens, they could see torchlights and hear voices. Peter and Norman made their way over to where the police officers were gathered.

"Ah, there you are, Mr Coles. We've got one cuffed in the car back there and the other's down here." He shone his torch down the open shaft.

Norman noted that it was beautifully lined with evenly laid red bricks.

"Careful if you want to look, sir. We don't want anyone else falling down it."

Norman knelt by the opening and peered down. At the bottom, he could see the nighthawk leaning dejectedly against the wall of the narrow shaft. It was about twenty feet deep and too small for him to stretch out.

The man looked up. "Who are you?" he asked.

"I'm the landowner, the man whose land you were in the act of bloody pillaging!"

"Now, now sir, calm down," said one of the police officers.

"Nothing's been proved yet."

Norman was encouraged to stand and step to one side. It was Peter's turn to take a peak. He shone his torch down and noted the narrowness of the shaft and the sullen figure stuck at the bottom. He also noticed something else. His kept his torch on the spot and invited one of the officers to look where his torch was pointing.

"See there," he said, "by his left foot...right at the edge where the bricks first become visible?"

"Yes," replied the policeman.

"There's a rounded shape just showing above the surface with part of a hole on the side; the rest of it appears to be buried..."

"Yes," the policeman said again, but with no hint that he recognised anything.

"Well, I might be wrong, but I think that's bone and it looks skull-shaped."

There was a pause while the officer weighed up what he was seeing. "Blimey, you could be right!"

The trapped nighthawk looked down to where the beam of the torch had been directed, and rocked the object with his smelly boot. It moved slightly. He nudged it again and loosened it. Then he dug the toe of his boot into the dirt and levered it out. It rolled over. He recoiled in fear and let out a cry of anguish. "For Christ's sake, get me out of here!"

◆

A plastic bottle of water and some food was dropped down to sustain the trapped individual. He was forced to stay where he was until a cave rescue team arrived. Working under police supervision, one of them was lowered to the bottom. He took down with him a spare harness and a caving helmet. It was cramped, but the rescuer managed to attach a harness to the nighthawk and tighten the chin strap on his helmet. Both were hauled to the surface, the nighthawk first, who was freed from the harness and then handcuffed. It was

254

three in the morning when he found himself on his way to Swindon police station in the back of a police van.

The finding of human remains meant that a forensic police investigation would have to take place. During the rescue, the police at the scene were aware that evidence could be spoiled and asked that as little as possible be disturbed at the bottom of the well. The immediate area on the surface was taped off to prevent unauthorised access.

By mid-morning, a forensic team had arrived, one of them equipped with climbing gear. A tent was erected over the well opening. Due to the confined space, only one investigator was able to work at the bottom. She was lowered to the floor along with a container which was also attached by rope to the surface. The first items brought up in the container were the plastic bottle and some food wrappings discarded by the nighthawk. She then began photographing and painstakingly removing layers of material to see if there were further human remains. More bones were exposed. The position of each one was recorded before it was removed. It was a slow and meticulous procedure. Numerous photographs were taken. Everything had to be bagged and labelled.

By the end of the second day, the forensic team were confident they were dealing with a complete skeleton.

The excavation continued over three days. Eventually, the team was sure that they had recovered and labelled all of the human remains, along with objects thought to have belonged to the deceased. The scene was cleared of forensic equipment and the well closed off with a heavy steel plate.

CHAPTER 39

OXENHOPE

Moses still believed that the man was alive – after all, he'd groaned – but he could see no signs of breathing. He offered the back of his hand to the man's open mouth, but felt nothing. He noticed the blood all around the man's neck; his collar was soaked. There was blood on the straw too; the contrast was stark and terrifying. He rolled the body onto its back and put his ear to the chest…nothing. He tried the wrist to find a pulse… still nothing.

"What the blazes? You can't be dead…Hell, what am I goin' to do?" muttered Moses. He stood up and looked down at the body. He had to think quickly. Outside, it was still a lovely, early summer evening, and wouldn't be dark for several hours. He'd have to wait until then to do anything more with the body.

Hide it, that's the answer…No one will believe me if I tell them…I'll be facin' the gallows…What about Bess?…and the baby?…No, I can't tell anyone.

Moses lifted both of the man's arms and dragged the body into an empty stall. He was surprised by the weight. He stuffed any visible blood-stained straw into the man's pockets and covered the body with more of it.

Try to act normally…No, don't look in the stall. It's fine, no one will notice. Right, finish milkin' and take the bucket over to the scullery.

Moses tapped on the back door of the farmhouse. It was answered by Florence, the widow who lived next door to them in The Row.

"Evening Moses, just in time you are; we've nearly run out."

"Sorry Florence, but with the fire and everythin'."

"That's no problem, not your fault Moses. You all right, you looks a bit pale?"

"Yes fine. I felt a bit sick just now, might have been all the smoke I breathed in."

"Yeah, could 'ave been that. You get off now and get your supper."

"Thanks Florence, I will."

That night, Moses couldn't sleep. He lay next to Bess who slept soundly. He was worried sick, but fortunately, she didn't seem to have noticed at supper or during the evening. When he judged that it was as dark as it was likely to be, he crept downstairs and slipped on the pair of old black trousers and the dark shirt he'd changed into after returning from the cowshed. He felt about for the matches and placed them in his trouser pocket.

Peering through the window, he could see that the sky was cloudy and the moon barely discernible. The only excuse he could think of, if Bess woke, was that he needed to check some rabbit snares he'd set with the younger Rutherford boy. They were up in the wood behind the cottages. The week before, he'd found that a fox had stolen a rabbit from one of them, leaving behind a grotesque head with its bucked teeth looking abnormally large.

After pulling on his boots, he left the cottage, closing the door as quietly as he could. He waited for a while for his eyes to adjust to the light. There was just enough to make out the outlines of the buildings and the trees. He crept across the yard to the cow stalls. He'd already made a plan. Inside, was a strong wooden sack truck for wheeling heavy bags of grain; it would be perfect.

Once inside the cowshed, he felt just inside the door for the small glass jar that contained a short stub of candle and lit it with a match. Cupping his hands around the jar to shield the brightness, he located the truck and trundled it quietly along to the stall where the body was hidden. He lay the trolley down, and placed the lit jar in a roughly hewn niche in the wall at the back. The corpse was still there.

Moses knelt down to feel the body; it was noticeably cooler to the touch and neither was it as flexible as it had been. He realised with horror that rigor mortis must have started to set in. With great effort, he dragged the body and then rolled it onto the truck. Loose change jingled and something crunched in the corpse's waistcoat pocket as he heaved it on. He used a rope halter to bind the body to it. He found the experience awful. He'd never touched a corpse before. He struggled to lift the trolley upright and, while doing so, the body started to slide off.

Damn! Moses thought. He lay the truck down again and rewrapped the halter around the legs of the corpse. He looked around for more rope, but none was visible and so he improvised by taking off his leather belt, the one with the Fontwell buckle, and used it to strap the upper part of the body onto the truck. It just fitted around the man's chest on the last hole.

With one huge exertion, Moses employed all of his strength to right the truck. He held it in position with one hand while he reached out to collect the candle in the jar. The body flopped forward a little, but remained in place. He blew out the candle and stuffed the jar into his trouser pocket. Then, he grabbed and pulled the truck slowly backwards out of the stalls and across the yard to the cover of the trees.

He paused in the darkness to recover his breath. An owl hooted from somewhere close by. Apart from that, everything remained quiet. He glanced behind him, trying to make out the gently sloping path that he needed to follow up to the wood. He couldn't see anything. He checked the upright truck for balance. It seemed firm and stable, so he removed his hands and pulled out the candle in the jar from his pocket. He relit it. He could see that the truck was on a short flat piece of ground, so he risked leaving it and quickly walked ten yards farther up the path where he set the lighted candle down. Having fixed his bearings, he returned to the truck. Looking over his shoulder, he dragged it backwards up the path as far as the candle. He repeated this procedure about six times, each time having to satisfy himself that the truck would remain upright.

Now where is it? He asked himself, taking a much-needed breather. He was looking for a thin track to the right, one apparently created and used by deer. *Ah, there it is. It's just wide enough. I'm nearly there.*

As before, Moses planted the candle ahead of him, and by a series of stages managed to drag the truck along the game track. At one point, he nearly tripped on a tree root, but managed to save the truck from rolling over. A short distance along would be the old well, hidden in the undergrowth. The Rutherford boy had pointed it out when they were setting the snares. It had been covered with wooden boards. He stopped when he arrived at the right place, and managed once again to rest the truck upright.

Leaving the sack truck where it stood, Moses picked up the candle jar and walked into the undergrowth next to him, hoping to feel a wooden board under his boots, rather than the softer ground. A few yards in, he stepped onto a solid surface. He dropped to his knees and tapped with his knuckles. Yes, this was the right place. He set the candle down beside him.

The boards, Moses noticed, were about nine inches wide and five-feet long, but brambles and weeds had grown over and around them. He set about clearing two boards on one side, carefully scuffing away the greenery and dirt with his boots, trying not to disturb the scene more than necessary. He then squeezed his fingers under the end of one board to lift it up. He flipped it carefully to one side and then did the same with the second one before returning to the truck.

He wheeled the truck carefully to its destination and, with a hard shove, managed to push it up onto the boards, parallel to the gap. Slowly, he laid the truck down, and kneeling next to it, he undid the halter, releasing the legs. Unfortunately, he couldn't easily reach the belt buckle, so he tipped the trolley onto its side. He began to undo the belt and had just released the tension when he felt a bramble thorn penetrate the flesh of his knee. In shifting his position to stop the pain, Moses accidentally kicked over the jar behind him, extinguishing the candle, and he began to panic.

Just get him down the well! He told himself while he fumbled with the buckle in the blackness.

The dead weight of the stiffening corpse and the release of the restraint around the upper part of the body was enough to give it enough momentum to slide off the truck, feet first. Before Moses could grab his favourite leather belt, it was gone. There was an echoing splash as the body disappeared into a watery grave several feet below.

Damn! Damn! Moses cursed.

Frantically, he relit the candle before replacing the two boards; trying to rearrange the vegetation to disguise any visible evidence of disturbance. Satisfied, he held the candle in one hand, using the other to guide the truck, which now felt as light as a feather, and set off as quickly as he dared back down the track to the yard.

CHAPTER 40

The phone next to Peter's computer rang. It was Norman.

"Just got off the phone from the police...You'll never believe it, they've only let those robbing thieves go, with no charge!"

"What?" Peter was astonished. "But they were caught in the act, surely?"

"Well, it seems not. When they were searched, they didn't have anything on them that could be proved to have been found here, and certainly not anything of value."

"But they were detecting on your land...they had metal detectors in the car."

"That's not enough, apparently. It seems they hadn't found anything valuable or of historic interest. If they had, the police would be looking at confiscating their equipment, and a fine, but it seems that's not the case. I went down there this morning with a policeman to have a look at where they were searching. There are holes in the stubble all over the place, and discarded bits of metal junk, too...crap they'd obviously unearthed, but he said criminal damage is the only charge they could make."

"Well, that'll do, won't it?"

"That's what I said, but he reckoned that as it was stubble and I was going to be ploughing it anyway, they'd have a job to make the charge stick. Problem is, you couldn't really call it damage."

"What about the car then? It damaged one of your trees, didn't it?"

"That's another problem. Seems the car wasn't insured. They're going to do the driver for that, apparently, but that's all. The only good news is that the police will remove it. But I'll tell you what...letting these blighters off really makes me sick. I mean, what do I pay my taxes for? Anyway, there's a bit more..."

"Really?"

"When the two men were questioned, one of them let slip about a hoard of gold coins being found down here recently, but he said it was just coincidence that they were on my land!"

Peter's mind was racing. This news put a whole different perspective on the growing concern he'd been feeling over whether or not Norman would declare the find. If the police knew about the hoard, then Norman had no option now but to report it. How had the nighthawks heard about it in the first place?

"Listen Norman, apart from mentioning it to my wife, and she wouldn't tell anyone, I've spoken to no one, absolutely no one about the gold coins. So who told them?"

"Well, I'm sorry, Pete, but I might have mentioned something up at the pub, the other night. I mean, I only spoke to Barry the landlord, but thinking about it, some strangers were in there that evening and maybe one of them overheard and tipped off someone they knew who owned a metal detector."

"You think that's what might have happened?"

"Maybe," he replied sheepishly.

"You know what this means don't you, Norman?"

"Yes, I know. We've got to report the coins."

"Exactly! So what did you say to the police officer?"

"I told him I'd allowed a friend do some detecting and that he'd found something that might be treasure. I told him that you had it and that you were going to show it to the FLO at your detector club. He asked what a FLO was, but I must admit I couldn't remember. I said she was an archaeologist you knew."

"And did he seem satisfied with that?"

"Yeah, he said it'd be fine as long as we declare them."

"Right, well listen…I found the tin with the coins nine days ago, so I'll ring Rosie today. There's a detector club meeting tomorrow evening and I think she's due to attend. If she's going to be there then we've no problem, because she'll record them within the fourteen-day deadline."

"OK Pete, it'll be best if you could handle it. Sorry, I know I shouldn't have told anyone, but it was just so exciting."

"Yeah, well don't worry. At least now we can do the right thing. I, for one, will be relieved when she takes over responsibility. I'll pop over tomorrow afternoon and collect the tin and the contents."

"Yeah, OK Pete…I'm not going anywhere."

Peter found Norman in his office when he called at the farm the following afternoon. The dogs were obviously getting used to him, because they didn't even bother to get up off the floor when he entered.

"Hello Norman, how you doing?"

"Oh not too bad," he said in a slightly subdued manner.

"You OK? You seem a bit down."

"Well, parting with these little beauties is hard," Norman was looking at the gold coins in the brass tin, "and all that aggro with those bloody nighthawks. I still can't get over the police letting them go."

"Look, don't let it get you down. That's how the world's changed, I'm afraid."

"Too bloody true it has. Do think I'll get these back?"

"I don't know. Rosie will record the details and probably take them away until it's decided if they're treasure or not. I've been reading up on the Treasure Act. If we could prove who it was that hid those coins, then any descendants would be the rightful owners and they wouldn't count as treasure."

"Really?"

"Yes, but it is a long shot…You wouldn't have any ideas would you? Old family tales, something like that?"

"Can't think of anything…I mean, you told me about

the Turnbulls and the old pork. I don't know much about my family either."

"Never mind, Norman, don't worry about it. By the way, I hope you don't mind me asking, but did you ever have any luck cleaning up those things we found under the granary floor?"

This was a question that Peter had been waiting for months to ask. He hoped his timing was good. Norman was a busy man, with concerns like running the farm on his mind. By now, he might have even thrown the items away. The relationship between a detectorist and a landowner could be tricky. Permission to detect was a privilege and Peter was always mindful of the need to tread carefully; he didn't want to embarrass or irritate the farmer.

"Not yet, Pete."

"Do you think I could have a go at them?"

"Yes, of course...Got to recall where I put them, though." Norman got up from his desk. "They're soaking in a bucket, if I remember."

Peter followed the farmer outside and across the yard, relieved at the reaction to his query. He was led to a patch of concrete used to hose down modern farm machinery and the beloved vintage tractors. A hose-pipe trailed across it.

"Ah, there it is." Norman pointed to a bucket with grass growing around it. It was almost brimming with dirty, green water. He tipped it out carefully onto the ground. "Here they are, Pete."

Peter looked at the eight metal objects. Soaking them for several months hadn't improved their appearance. He was still unsure what they were. He picked one up and rubbed it. "I could try using electrolysis to get the corrosion off."

"Yes, you go ahead."

It was clear that Norman's enthusiasm at the time of their discovery had waned. Peter could tell that he wasn't really interested. He picked up the bucket. "I'll just use this to get them as far as the car."

"Yes, of course."

Back in the office, Norman picked up the brass tin containing the gold coins from his desk. He stared sadly at the contents for a few seconds, and then handed it to Peter.

"Have you got any photos of them, Norman?"

"Never thought of that."

"I took some when I found them, but I could get a shot of you holding the coins in your hand, if you want?"

"Oh yes, at least I'd have some photos," he said more brightly. He displayed the three coins in his palm.

Peter took a photograph with his mobile phone, and afterwards passed it to Norman so he could see the result.

"Great pictures, thanks."

"Have you got email, Norman?"

"Yes, but my computer's slow and there's no widthband, or whatever they call it, down here."

"Don't worry; rather than email them, I'll get some printed off for you."

"That'd be great, thanks."

CHAPTER 41

As soon as Peter got home, he showed Felicity the brass tin with the gold coins. She was genuinely impressed.

"For once, you've actually found something recognisable and valuable too!"

He didn't bother to show her the metal objects which had been soaking in Norman's bucket. Instead, he took them out to his workshop and gave them a scrub with an old toothbrush, but it barely shifted the corrosion. He could see enough to confirm that they were castings of some sort and two were particularly interesting in that they were heart shaped.

Thinking that he could try cleaning one of them so that he could take it to his club meeting for any suggestions as to what it was, he set up his mini, homemade, electrolysis tank. He used an alligator clip to make the connection and then immersed the casting in the electrolyte. He switched on the power. It was from a small charger for a handheld, rechargeable vacuum cleaner. Fortunately, Felicity hadn't missed it.

Almost immediately, the object started to bubble gently. He left it for thirty minutes and then switched off the power to examine it. A good hard rub with a cloth removed some of the black corrosion. He gave it another fifteen minutes of electrolysis before inspecting it again. This time it was much easier to rub off. A soft wire brush completed the restoration. Peter found himself holding an unusual heart-shaped medallion. He'd never seen anything quite like it before. In the centre was a bearded face with a spikey crown and around the edge were some unfamiliar markings, which he couldn't decipher.

He was running short of time to clean any more, so he wrapped it up in a clean piece of rag and took it back indoors to show Felicity. It was fair to say that this time her reaction was more what he was used to, somewhat lukewarm in fact.

There was a good turnout, that evening. It was the 'Find of the Month' competition and some very impressive finds were on display. Peter inspected the various entries and then voted for his favourite. The result would be announced later.

Up to that point, he hadn't shown the gold coins to anyone at the meeting. He kept glancing over to Rosie, the FLO, who was seated in the corner at a table with her laptop and briefcase. She had a queue of 'customers' declaring finds and giving her the information she needed to record the details.

When he saw that she was finally free, he went over and opened the tin to reveal its contents.

"Wow, it's not every day I see a group of coins like that! Were they found together?"

"Yes." Peter could sense her excitement.

Rosie picked up one of the coins. She used a magnifying glass to read the inscriptions. "Emperor Trajan…Are all three the same?"

"Yes."

"And are there any more?"

"No, that's how I found them: three in that tin."

The archaeologist took the coins out and examined the tin.

"Not terribly old…For snuff or maybe tobacco I'd say. That impressed ship design looks mid-Victorian."

"That's what I think."

"They must have been hidden some time since the 1860s, at a guess. Right, let me take some details. They'll have to be reported to the coroner as potential treasure, you know."

"Yes, I assumed that would be the case. I took some photographs at the time I found them. Do you want to see?"

"Oh yes, let's have a look."

Peter passed over his phone and Rosie quickly flicked through the images.

"Can you email these to me? They might be helpful."

"Yes, no problem."

Someone passing the table had noticed what Rosie was recording. Soon after, most of the members gathered around, excitedly speculating on where the coins had come from and their value. Rosie shooed them away. The find-spot had to be kept confidential. After order had been restored, she passed an official form to Peter and he filled in the details. He gave her a map reference. She noted Peter as the finder and Norman as the landowner. They exchanged email addresses. Boxes were ticked and Peter signed the declaration. The form acted as a receipt too. He was given a copy to retain to confirm submission. When he left Rosie's table, he was immediately surrounded by everyone wanting to know the details. All he could do was to show the photographs he'd taken.

After getting himself a drink, he joined a group of friends. He told them as much as was allowed, choosing not to mention the nighthawks – that might give the location of the farm away. Eventually, the conversation moved on to what others had been finding. He decided to show them the strange medallion badge he'd cleaned up. It was passed around and most agreed that it looked old and interesting. Guesses on age put it as most likely medieval. Trevor, who'd been detecting about thirty years, thought he'd seen something like it before, but couldn't think where.

Peter showed it to Darren, who inspected it and carefully turned it over.

"I don't think those marks mean anything, really," Darren said. "They're just to give it more authenticity."

"You mean it is some sort of replica?"

"Not exactly...I think it might be what is termed a 'Fontwell fake'."

"A Fontwell fake?"

"Yes, I've seen some in the Museum of London. They've got a collection. They were made in Victorian times by two crafty metal smiths from the East End of London. They turned out hundreds and fooled the collectors of the time. I don't know the details, but I'm sure you could find out more online."

"That's great, Darren...I'll do that. Thanks."

"Show it to Jim; he might have an idea on it."

Jim examined the item carefully. "Yes, I agree with Darren. It's very like the Fontwell medallions. Could I photograph it?"

"Yes, please do," said Peter.

Jim was the club's photography expert. He used a special frame to present and light the object from the granary to its best advantage. Peter watched with interest as he took a series of shots and then reviewed them.

"I think that's the best one. What do you think of that?"

To Peter, it looked amazing. Jim had magnified it, and the lighting had caught the small scratches and indentations in a way that he hadn't noticed before. "Do these have any value, Jim?"

"I think they do, but you'd need to do some research. Museums have them. Some collectors specialise in them. They sometimes come up on auction sites. I've seen them advertised for five or six hundred pounds."

"Really? Even though they're forged?"

"Oh yes. Of course, I don't know what people actually pay for them."

When he got home that evening, Peter searched for information on the Fontwell Fakes. There were several hits. Looking at the images, and reading the story behind them, it didn't take him long to conclude that both Darren and Jim had been correct. The heart-shaped medallion clearly came from the same family, but he couldn't find one exactly the same. He was amazed by the number of different designs.

Felicity went to bed and was fast asleep when Peter finally slipped in beside her. It was difficult to close down his mind and he lay there for a while going over what he'd discovered.

There was plenty of information from previous researchers about the Fontwell Fakes. It had enabled him to quickly get a grasp of what Billy Nunn and Eddie Milner had been up to back in Victorian London.

In one article on the forgers, Peter came across the name of a coin dealer called Charles Blackett. He was said to have been involved in the illicit trade. He was sure he'd heard the name before. As he mulled it over before he fell asleep, he realised where: Charles Blackett was head of the household on the 1861 Census in which Elizabeth Jupp, formerly Doggett, was employed as a parlourmaid. It was too coincidental for there not to be some relationship between him and Moses.

Some other research mentioned that Billy Nunn died of tuberculosis at the age of thirty-two, in April 1871. Eddie Milner was recorded on the census of that year, but afterwards nothing further was known of him. He apparently seemed to disappear from records

Peter resolved to get on the hunt the following day, to find out as much as he could from newspaper reports and also from genealogy records. Surely he'd be able to trace Edward Milner in later life.

Peter was up and about early the following morning. His first job was to clean the other medallions. He rigged up two electrolysis tanks and by midday they'd all been stripped of corrosion to reveal themselves as remarkably nice objects. They certainly looked old.

While they were bubbling away, he had searched online again for contemporary newspaper reports that concerned the Fontwell Fakes. He found several stories in the press covering a libel hearing, in which Charles Blackett had appeared as a witness. He had given evidence in support of the plaintiff, Alfred Westbrook, and had told the court that he had obtained the artefacts, which he believed to be genuine, from a scavenger named Moses Jupp!

So, there it was, in black and white! Peter could hardly believe it.

Moses Jupp supplied Charles Blackett with Fontwell fakes. Moses must have brought the eight Fontwells with him and buried them in the granary. His cottage was within fifty yards! How else could they have got there? Peter's imagination went wild.

Blackett was a dealer in ancient coins. What if Blackett had got to know Moses by purchasing coins from him before he came to Oxenhope? Moses was a scavenger. His eyes would have been accustomed to spotting coins and artefacts on the foreshore or in the sewers. Such items are still being turned up by modern-day mudlarks who just search for pleasure. Was it stretching imagination and coincidence too far to link the discovery of the tobacco tin, hidden during the last hundred and fifty years, to Moses Jupp? Could Moses have found the gold coins while working on the farm and stashed them among the tree roots?

The problem was lack of evidence. If only Moses had scratched his initials on the tin; that would have helped, but really, anybody on the farm could have concealed it.

Peter switched his research to genealogy, hoping to trace Edward Milner after 1871, but drew a blank. He looked at earlier census returns, and the births, deaths, and marriages indices for clues, but got nowhere. Part of the problem was that although Milner was shown on the 1871 Census in Whitechapel, it was only as an unmarried lodger in a boarding house. Peter could see no relationship between Milner and any of the other lodgers.

He looked on the 1881 Census and found a record of an Edward Milner married to a Rosemary Milner, living in Whitehaven in the Lake District. They were a childless couple and were both born in Whitehaven, so Peter discounted them.

He also investigated Billy Nunn, in case he and Eddie had some earlier connection. Nothing transpired, until he looked at the 1851 Census. It wasn't a link between Billy and Eddie he found, but a link between Billy and Moses.

In 1851, William Nunn was a ragged scholar and an inmate at the address of Thomas Chambers. His name was listed on the same page as Moses. *There it is!* thought Peter. *They slept at the same address and knew each other from the ragged school!*

Peter returned to one of the newspaper articles covering the exposure of the fraud. It was dated 25 March, 1871. A wealthy collector named Titus Redding, suspicious that he'd been duped by Alfred Westbrook, bribed a mudlark to break into the smelters' workshop. The mudlark stole some moulds and castings. These were delivered to the collector and the fraud was exposed.

'Mudlark', 'scavenger', these terms are easily interchangeable. What if the mudlark who carried out the theft was Moses Jupp? Peter thought excitedly.

He continued researching, and found a provincial newspaper report of Edward Milner appearing at court in Slough on 10 April, 1871. He was charged with obtaining money under false pretences by the sale of fabricated and factitious antiquities in Windsor. *Surely, he could only have been accused if the antiquities were known by that date to have been recently fabricated?*

Peter looked at the timescale. Titus Redding had uncovered the swindle towards the end of March. By early April, according to the census, Moses and his wife were at Oxenhope. *It all fits. It could well have been Moses who burgled the workshop, took payment from Titus Redding, and left Whitechapel for a new life in the country.*

However, as much as Peter felt convinced that Moses Jupp had supplied the evidence to Titus Redding, and as much as it seemed to account for him leaving London, there was no actual proof; similarly, with his idea that Moses Jupp may have found and hidden the gold coins. He had to admit to himself that his conjecture was based on circumstance and coincidence, nothing more.

CHAPTER 42

Peter went to see Norman the following week. He found him in the barn that garaged the farmer's most prized tractors. His head was bent under a cowling while he tinkered with one of them.

"Hello Norman, sorry to bother you."

The dogs barked half-heartedly and Norman extricated himself from his position.

"That's OK, Pete – shut up, you two!"

They quietened down and sniffed Peter in a friendly way. He stroked both of them. "Have you been asked to attend the inquest on the body in the well?"

"Yes, I have…End of the month. You too, then?"

"Yes, me too. I can give you a lift if you want."

"That'd be handy, thanks Pete."

"Thought I'd let you see those things we found under the granary floor. I've cleaned them up and found out what they are." He patted the lid of a small cardboard box he was carrying.

"Really? Horse brasses, I bet."

"No, much more unusual…Fontwell Fakes!"

"Never heard of 'em."

Peter removed the lid and handed the box to Norman, who picked over the contents. Peter explained how someone at his detecting club had solved the mystery. He told him about the counterfeiting and how it had been exposed.

"You think Moses Jupp had something to do with stealing the moulds then?"

"It's possible. He seemed to know those involved and it might explain why he ended up here, and why those were in your granary."

Norman looked closely at one of the castings, but Peter could see he wasn't particularly impressed with it.

"Do you want to keep them, Norman?"

"No, you hang on to them," he replied as he passed the box back. "I would if they were gold."

"Thing is, these might have some value."

Norman looked surprised. "You've got to be joking!"

"No, I'm not. They could be worth about five hundred pounds each."

"What? Four grand for these old things!"

"Could be. You OK if I test the market and see if anyone's interested in them?"

"Yeah fine, Pete, you go ahead."

"The other reason for calling is to see if you've received one of these?" Peter removed an envelope from his pocket.

"What's that then?" Norman wiped his greasy hands on a rag.

"It's a letter from the British Museum...came today. You should be getting one too."

"Ah, well the post's a bit slow out here. I expect it'll turn up in a day or two. What does it say?"

"The British Museum has written to confirm receipt of the gold coins. They are responsible for assessing items that might be treasure."

"Of course they're treasure!"

"No, they mean 'treasure' within the provisions of the Treasure Act."

"What provisions?"

"Two or more coins made of precious metal and more than three hundred years old."

"There's no doubt then, they must be treasure."

"Well, it does seem that way."

"So, what do you think of the old Allis?" asked Norman, changing the subject and resting one hand affectionately on the radiator cap.

"Ah, so this is the famous Allis-Chalmers." Peter was genuinely impressed. "Looks amazing, just like new. What year?"

"1934…One of the early ones brought over from the States."

"And this was your grandfather's?"

"Yes, the one that was missing the spanner from its toolkit."

Peter walked around the tractor. Its colour was somewhere between bright red and orange. The paintwork gleamed. It was in showroom condition. "I see there's a starting handle."

"Yes, I'd start her up for you if I could, but I'm halfway through making some adjustments."

"That's OK, don't worry."

"Come over here, for a minute, and I can show you some photos of her working in the field."

Norman led Peter to a table and chair positioned next to a large metal filing cabinet. He opened a drawer.

"Here you are, Pete, put those castings down for a minute and take a seat. Have a look at these."

Norman explained a series of photographs. Some were old, black and white, taken at Oxenhope; more recent ones were from ploughing matches and tractor club rallies. "She's won all of these," he said proudly, showing a photograph of an array of trophies.

"They're impressive. So when did your grandfather acquire her?"

"From brand new, in 1934. I've even got the original buff-coloured logbook." He found it and handed it to Peter.

Peter held it carefully, aware of its age and fragility. He noticed that the name of the first owner had been written in dark-blue ink with a fountain pen, not a modern biro, but what caught Peter's attention was the name: William Arman Coles. He could hardly conceal his excitement. "So your grandfather was William Arman Coles, written as it says here?"

"That's right, Pete."

"The middle name, Arman, that's unusual isn't it?"

"I suppose it is, although I've never really thought about it."

"Is it a family name?"

"No idea…My dad didn't have it and I don't."

"It was Moses Jupp's middle name."

"Was it?"

"Yes, it was on his death certificate. I think you might be related to Moses Jupp."

"What? The bloke who was killed by the mowing machine?"

Peter nodded. "Yes…and the thing is I've got a suspicion that the coins were hidden by Moses Jupp. If I could prove it, and if you are related, you'll be a descendant."

"Yes…I think I'm following, but so what?"

"Well, the other day I read about a treasure case involving some gold coins discovered during work in a garden in the East End. It turned out that they'd been hidden by a Jewish family during World War Two. The family perished in the blitz and the exact hiding place was lost. At the subsequent inquest, the coroner ruled that the coins should be returned to their rightful owner. A descendant living in the United States was traced and proved as the rightful owner."

"So, you think that if I was a descendant of Moses, then I might be the owner of the coins and they wouldn't be treasure?"

"That's right!"

"And the museum wouldn't be able to claim them?"

"Right, again!"

"I like the sound of that."

CHAPTER 43

OXENHOPE

"Good morning, Moses," called Mr Turnbull across the yard as Moses came out from the cottage.

"Morning, Mr Turnbull, sir."

It was seven in the morning and Moses had hardly slept. All he could see when he climbed back into bed was the dark shape of the body sliding uncontrolled into the well, along with the sound of the echoing splash as it broke the surface of the water below. He joined the group of labourers waiting to receive their instructions.

Mr Turnbull addressed the men first. "I would just like to thank everyone for their efforts yesterday. You managed to save about a third of the straw. I don't understand what caused the fire, but if anyone has any idea please come and see me. I know the rick was last year's straw, but we can't afford to lose any more or we might be short of winter fodder." He turned to speak to Archie, the foreman, and then left the yard to return to the farmhouse.

"Right lads," Archie began, "we're on haymaking again today. It's still a bit early in the season, but there's been some good recent growth and it might give us a chance of two crops this year. The weather's looking fine for a spell, there's no dew this morning, and we need to make the most of it. Like the guv'nor said, we'll have to get as much in as we can or we shan't have enough...Alan and Henry, you carry on with the new rick in Long Lay...Michael

277

and Bob, you'll be mowing in Oak Meadow...Clifford, Ben, and Moses, you'll be turning over the windrows in Long Lay, and you two – Dan and Birchy – will be gatherin' up on the cart and taking it to the rick. Any questions?"

No one spoke. Moses was grateful not to be the fogger that morning, although he expected to be on milking duties later. He worried that he'd missed any evidence of what had taken place in the cow stalls. He went over it in his mind, hopeful that he'd cleared up thoroughly and left no traces.

"Now get your tools and your lunches and we'll be off," ordered Archie.

The sun had started to burn away the light cloud as they set off to do the tasks they'd been allocated. By the time they all started working, it was a beautiful morning.

Moses tried not to think about the events that had occurred just a few hours before. He laughed and joked with his workmates, but found it difficult to be light-hearted. He copied Clifford and used a pitchfork to turn over the lines of cut hay. The smell in the meadow was sweet and wholesome; the rustic scene so different compared to the effluent and detritus which used to float past him on the Thames. It lifted his mood a little, until a cuckoo called from the shadow of some nearby trees and its distinctive call was answered by another from the wood behind the cottages. It reminded Moses of what had happened there during the night, and he shivered.

The workers stopped late in the morning to eat some bread and cheese, and swig some water. The conversation among the men returned to the subject of the fire; the general view being a mystery as to how it had started.

Archie came to find them. "Moses, I want you to go over with Michael on the mower this afternoon. Bob's not feeling well. He's been sick and I've sent him back. You any good with horses?"

"Not really, but I'm sure I can learn."

"Well it's easy, really. Just keep 'em going straight. Michael will be doing the complicated part. Leave your pitchfork here and get over there."

Moses picked up his food and water and set off for Oak Meadow. He tried to put his thoughts in order. *It was an accident... Not my fault...I can't be blamed. Perhaps I should tell someone. No, don't think that.*

Michael greeted him. "Hello Moses, you come to 'elp?"

"Yes, Archie sent me, but I'm not much good with horses."

"You'll be all right. Come and say hello to Tinker and Dreamboat."

Michael led him around to meet them.

The horses were chewing contentedly on some hay. They both wore blinkers, but allowed the two men to pat their foreheads and necks. They seemed happy enough. Behind them, lay the sickle mower; its gleaming cutting blades looked frighteningly sharp to Moses.

"Tinker's the lead horse, but he can be a bit naughty," Michael explained. "Just hold on to his bridle, here, and he'll be fine. Dreamboat just follows him."

Moses tested himself on where he had to hold the bridle. "I've got it."

"Good. Right, I'll be sitting on the mower. I need to control the cutter. All you need to do is lead 'em nice and straight. When we get to the end, walk 'em out to the left and turn 'em so that they're lined up to cut along the headland. Then we'll come up the other side."

Moses looked up and down the meadow. The day had become hot, and so he took off his shirt, which he hung from Tinker's harness. He examined the mower once more, noting its width. He'd have to take account of that each time he began a new strip.

They started as soon as they were ready. During the following two hours, they cut a good deal. The mower was a recent addition to the farm and Michael was proud to be trusted with it. It was much faster and more efficient than hand-cutting with scythes. By mid-afternoon, the standing grass awaiting the cut had significantly reduced to a small oblong in the centre of the field.

Later, Mr Turnbull appeared with his dog and carrying a shotgun. He liked to be present towards the end of scything or mowing because gamebirds, rabbits, hares, and vermin sought refuge in an ever decreasing sanctuary. They were forced eventually to make an escape and break cover. He waited patiently with his loaded gun, for any opportunity to make a kill and hopefully bag something for that evening's pot.

Moses held on to Tinker's bridle, but his mind was not on the job. No matter what he tried, he couldn't stop himself recalling the scene in the cow stall. He tried to shake it off by looking at the ground where the grass had just been cut. He thought that he might spot another coin, but knew he could hardly drop his hold on the bridle to pick it up. He continued to torment himself with thoughts of whether he should have told someone about what happened or acted differently.

A gun went off about twenty yards behind Moses. He jumped, and his reaction was transmitted to Tinker. The horse reared his head and Moses lost his grip, causing Tinker to charge off with Dreamboat by his side. Michael fell backwards off the seat and still holding the reins was dragged along until he let go. It all happened in a split second. The mowing machine accelerated towards Moses and swept him off his feet, tossing him onto the cutter. His last memory was of incredible pain in his thighs and hands as the motion of the runaway mower bounced him up and down upon the slashing blades.

CHAPTER 44

Peter was puzzled. The 1871 Census showed that Moses and Elizabeth were living at Oxenhope and that they had no children. But by seven weeks after the census, at the end of May, Moses had died. How had his middle name of Arman been passed on?

He looked again at their marriage certificate. It clearly described Moses as a bachelor and Elizabeth Doggett as a spinster; so neither had been married before. He wondered if Elizabeth may have been pregnant when Moses died and a search of the birth records turned up an entry during the third quarter of 1871: an Emily Jupp. The registration district was Marlborough, and so Peter was certain that she was Moses' daughter. That meant that poor Mrs Jupp *was* pregnant when her husband had his fatal accident.

Next, Peter looked forward a generation for Emily's marriage. Assuming she married before she was fifty, he looked at the marriage records up to 1921. He couldn't find an entry.

Had Emily died or emigrated?

He checked the relevant records and again he couldn't find a match. It really was quite frustrating.

He sat in front of his computer, with his chin cupped in his hands, trying to think of where to go next. He tried to gauge how events may have transpired at Oxenhope. As a result of Moses' death, Elizabeth was widowed. A few weeks later, she gave birth to their daughter. He was certain he'd found the correct birth and resisted the temptation to order the actual certificate. He'd save his money and only do that as a last resort.

What would a widow, left on her own, have done at that time? Would she have been evicted?

He dug out the inquest report on the death, having recalled something in the closing lines.

Moses Jupp was not used to working with horses. The jury gave a verdict of accidental death, coupling it with an expression of opinion that only those well able to control horses should be employed in such work.

It seemed to Peter that, although not specifically named, some element of blame for the tragedy must have been felt by Richard Turnbull, Moses' employer.

Perhaps he allowed Elizabeth to stay on at the farm afterwards.

Peter decided to check the 1881 Census for Oxenhope.

By then, Richard Turnbull had died, because the head at the farmhouse was John Turnbull, aged twenty-eight, no doubt Richard's son. He was single at the time. There was one other family member, an elderly spinster aunt called Marion. The rest were servants and they did not include Elizabeth Jupp.

He looked through the other households at Oxenhope and noticed one in which an Elizabeth Tarrant was married to Archibald Tarrant. They had three children, the eldest of which was a daughter named Emily, aged nine.

A quick search of the marriage indices revealed a marriage between Elizabeth Jupp and Archibald Tarrant in the first quarter of 1873. Peter had previously noticed while checking the 1871 Census that Archibald Tarrant was a neighbour. He realised that Archie and the widowed Elizabeth must have married, deciding that it was easier and more convenient if Emily, his step-daughter, took on the Tarrant name.

Now, Peter felt that he was getting somewhere. He renewed his attempt to find a marriage for Emily, but this time he searched under Tarrant instead of Jupp. He was pleased to find that she married David Coles in 1889. She was eighteen. By the time of the 1891 Census, she and her husband had a two-year-old son named Albert.

Peter brought his search forward by another generation and this time looked for the marriage of Albert. Luck was on his side, for he quickly found that Albert Coles married Dorothy Turnbull in 1912. Their first child was named William.

Could this be the William Arman Coles who was Norman's grandfather and the first owner of the vintage tractor?

The 1901 and 1911 census returns showed that Dorothy was John Turnbull's daughter. She was the elder of two daughters. There were no sons.

It took Peter just a few minutes to order the birth certificates for Albert Coles and William Coles. He wanted to confirm that the Arman middle name was shared by both of them. If it was, then Elizabeth must have told her daughter, Emily, that her biological father was Moses Arman Jupp, and that her paternal grandfather was Samuel Arman Jupp. The certificates would prove that Emily had passed on the name.

Lastly, Peter also ordered the marriage certificate for Albert and Dorothy's union in 1912. Then, he shut down his computer and went to tell Felicity about what he'd learned.

CHAPTER 45

Three weeks after the discovery of the skeleton, the Wiltshire coroner opened an inquest into the death. Peter and Norman were there as requested. Neither of them had ever been to such an event before. It was held in a two-hundred-year-old building in which a great many trials and inquests had taken place over the years.

They presented themselves to the court usher who checked their names and then directed them to sit in the third row of the long tiered pews. They were in plenty of time, so they took their seats and waited patiently for the start.

Peter looked up at the bench and the large, carved, wooden chair from which the coroner would conduct the proceedings. It certainly gave an impression of power, gravity, and solemnity, as was intended. Above the chair, was a substantial portico, fringed with an upstand of gilded wooden mouldings and topped by the Royal Arms. A notice on the wall caught his eye:

PLEASE BE AWARE THAT MULTI-DIRECTIONAL
MICROPHONES ARE INSTALLED AND THAT
CONVERSATIONS IN THE COURTROOM CAN BE
OVERHEARD AND MAY BE RECORDED.

Several men and a woman were ushered into the row immediately below them. The new arrivals talked together in hushed tones. They had papers and electronic tablets close to hand. Looking around, Peter noticed a young lady sitting alone at the end of the row behind them; probably, he thought, a reporter from the local paper.

Behind, several rows were filling up with a steady stream of members of the public.

The nighthawk who'd fallen down the well was also there. He sat in the second row on the far side with another man. They appeared to be together.

Norman had noticed them too. "Look over there, Pete," he whispered, "it's that bloody nighthawk, and I bet that's his mate with him, the one who got arrested first. I've a good mind to point 'em out to the coroner. I mean, they were there to steal objects buried on my land, and they caused criminal damage in the process. Caught in the act and what happened? Apart from some traffic offence, they got off scot bloody free!"

"That might not be a good idea, Norman," Peter whispered back, trying to placate him. "We're not here for that. See that notice over there about private conversations? You'll probably get us slung out if you try that…Contempt of court, isn't it?"

"Yes, I suppose you're right, but it really gets my goat."

Before Norman could say any more, the court officer entered from a door to the left of the raised bench and instructed the court to rise. The coroner appeared from the same door and mounted the steps to his very impressive chair.

Peter could see that he was aged about fifty, balding slightly, and quite portly – if not overweight. He looked tanned, so perhaps he'd just returned from holiday. He was wearing a black gown, but no wig. He seemed more like someone Peter would meet at a dinner party, someone quite ordinary; although, Peter wasn't sure what he'd expected a coroner to look like. He might have an important role, but there was no reason why he shouldn't look normal.

Once settled, the coroner looked around the courtroom and put on a pair of glasses. He began by briefly explaining that an inquest was not a trial; it was not about deciding on issues of guilt, but purely a fact-finding inquiry. His role would not be to pass sentence or penalty. The session would not be held before a jury. He scanned his notes and continued. "This inquest is to determine the identity and cause of death of a body recovered from a well at Oxenhope Farm, Wiltshire." He looked down to the court officer. "Please call the first witness."

Detective Superintendent Hughes spoke first. He informed the court of his role as Senior Investigating Officer and described the circumstances leading to the discovery of human remains.

The coroner interrupted. "Was there any water in the well?"

"No, it was dry, probably due to it being abstracted by the local water company. The landowner was unaware that the well existed, and could not give any information as to when it last held water." He passed a series of photographs to the court officer for display on an overhead projector. When he resumed speaking, he periodically signalled for the next image to be shown, so that the sequence coincided with his descriptions. The images showed the area immediately around the well, the view down it, and a map of the locality and topography.

Peter listened carefully. He was slightly nervous that he would be asked to tell the coroner what he'd seen in the well or to answer any questions. He hated speaking in public.

"I shall shortly hand over to my colleague, Professor Bailey, to give details concerning the skeleton," the detective continued. "I can say that it is male, so far unidentified, and in the opinion of the forensic officer at the scene, the death may have occurred in suspicious circumstances." He indicated that he had nothing more to say at that time.

There was a murmured response within the room.

"Thank you, superintendent, please resume your seat," instructed the coroner.

The court officer looked at her papers and then announced the next witness as Professor Bailey, who stood and began reading from his notes.

"My name is Professor Ian Bailey. I am a forensic anthropologist. I carried out post-exhumation tests on the skeleton in the laboratory. Due to the absence of any soft tissue, my investigation was limited to the skeleton only." He took a sip of water, then signalled to the court officer to show a photograph of the skeleton as laid out on a white cloth-covered table. Coloured labels were attached to most of the bones.

"The skeleton is complete and is that of a European male with an estimated age at death of between thirty to fifty. Height around five-feet eleven inches and of medium build. The skull showed evidence of a penetration injury of the occipital bone, most likely caused by a metal object with width not exceeding half an inch. This would have been fatal. Death probably occurred within a short time of suffering such an injury."

"Could the death have been accidental?" the coroner wanted to know.

"It is not possible to say with certainty whether the deceased received the injury as the result of an accident or that it had been inflicted by another person or persons. I cannot be certain how the injury occurred. However, the finding of the skeleton at the bottom of a well does imply that there may have been a wish to conceal the body and, therefore, that the death may not have been accidental. It is my opinion that the head injury was sustained elsewhere and that the location in which the body was discovered is the deposition site."

The professor briefly viewed his report and continued. "The right tibia was broken. The nature of the break is consistent with a strong and sharp blow from the front. No healing of the bone had occurred, so the break probably occurred around the time of death, either shortly before or after."

"How could it happen after death?" asked the coroner.

"It could have been broken during deposition."

"I see, and do you have anything to add?"

"No, that concludes my report."

Attention turned towards the court officer once again, who introduced Professor Martin Henderson, a forensic odontologist.

"I carried out an examination on the teeth of the deceased. There were thirty-one teeth. LR7 had been extracted – that's a molar from the lower right jaw. I found evidence of dental decay including several cavities. None of the teeth had been filled with amalgam. The death most likely occurred before 1880, after which we have the emergence of what we would recognise as dentistry. The lower and upper right canines were worn in a manner consistent with clamping a clay pipe."

"Who would have extracted a tooth prior to the 1880s?" asked the coroner.

"Extractions were mainly carried out by a barbers or black-smiths."

The coroner grimaced. "Thank you Professor Henderson. Detective Superintendent, do you wish to continue?"

"Yes I would."

"Please do."

"Thank you. I would like to turn to the objects we recovered, which we believe were personal to the deceased." He passed across to the court officer a further series of photographs to be displayed. "Five Victorian coins consisting of a silver half-crown dated 1866; two silver sixpences dated 1868 and 1846; a copper penny dated 1870, and a copper halfpenny dated 1865. The 1870 penny has been classified by a numismatist as being in extremely fine condition with little wear. Being the most recent coin, we believe that the death took place fairly soon after the coin was minted during the period 1871 to 1873. The wear showing on the other coins is consistent with that period, which means that the body may have been submerged for more than a hundred and forty years..."

The coins interested Peter, especially the silver half-crown. He'd never found a Victorian one.

"A silver vesta case, hallmarked London 1850, maker Benjamin Barling; the bowl and stem of a plain white ceramic clay pipe, broken into four pieces, with no markings or distinguishing features, and a small brass pipe tamper in the shape of a naked woman; a brass warded key to suit locks widely used in the nineteenth century – they were superseded by more secure locks of better design. Lastly, we recovered a belt buckle made of cast copper-alloy. It has a decorative plate showing two knights in armour with swords raised in combat..."

Peter was startled by what he saw as he stared at the photograph projected above. There was no doubt in his mind: it was so similar to the Fontwell Fakes that it must have originated from the same source...a Fontwell fake! There had to be a connection between the ones from the granary and this man's belt. But how could there be?

"...Eighteen hobnails from the heels of a pair of leather boots," continued the detective, reading from his report. "Five brass buttons of similar design featuring an anchor, manufactured by Firmin & Sons between 1844 and 1901 – these would have been from a waistcoat of some kind – three copper-alloy trouser buttons for the fly; a larger top button from the trousers, and six small copper-alloy buttons to fit a pair of braces; two collar studs and five plain, bovine, bone buttons from a shirt."

The detective paused to take a sip of water and clear his throat before continuing. "The deceased was wearing a silver ring on the ring finger of his right hand. Hallmarks show that it was made by William Leuchars, a famous London silversmith, apparently, in 1864. It is quite large being equivalent to a size U. Despite the recovery of these objects, I regret that so far we've been unable to establish identity. We've researched newspapers and periodicals of the period 1870 to 1900 in the county of Wiltshire and the adjoining counties for reports of missing persons, but we currently have no leads. We will shortly publish, online, a series of photographs of the deceased's personal effects, as well as information on how and where the body was found. It will be in the form of an appeal to the public. We will be asking anyone who has information to come forward."

"Are you saying then that the death occurred about 1871 to 1873?" asked the coroner.

"Yes, sir, that's our best estimate."

The coroner turned towards Professor Bailey. "Do you agree with Detective Superintendent Hughes as to the period in which the death may have taken place?"

"Based on the condition and evidence of the skeleton, in my professional opinion, I would say that the date of death took place more than eighty years ago."

The coroner directed another question to the professor. "It is your opinion that the deceased died more than eighty years ago. Would you accept that his death could have occurred around 1872?"

"Yes, that would be possible."

"Thank you, Professor Bailey." The coroner turned to the other professor. "And what is your opinion, Professor Henderson, regarding the date of death?"

"In my opinion, I would say that the death occurred before 1880."

Satisfied, the coroner asked Detective Superintendent Hughes to stand down, and then addressed the court officer. "Do we have any other witnesses?"

"We have the landowner, where the well is situated, and the person who first spotted the skull on the floor of the well."

"I see," he said as looked back at his notes. "I don't think we need to hear from them."

Phew...what a relief! thought Peter. He really didn't want to be asked to speak in court.

The coroner addressed the police officer. "I assume you would like more time to see if the appeal yields any information?"

"Yes, sir, we would. I know it's unlikely, but you never know."

"Very well. I shall adjourn the inquest for today. We'll reschedule for..." the coroner looked down to the court officer for a suggestion. She proposed a date for three months' time.

Satisfied that the police officer thought this would be enough time to identify the body, or not, the coroner ended the session.

"All rise," announced the court officer. With that, the coroner descended and left the court through the same door he'd used to enter.

"What do you think of that then, Pete?" asked Norman.

"Shush..." replied Peter, briefly placing a finger over his lips. "The microphones."

"Oh, yes...Good thinking."

The two men filed out, following the team from the police and forensics; Peter hopeful that Norman would forget about the nighthawks. Thankfully, he had. A few minutes later, they had ordered two teas in a small café around the corner from the court.

"They'll never identify him you know," said Norman. "What do they expect an appeal on the internet to bring up, apart from a load of nosey so-and-sos coming through my wood hoping to gawp down the well? That's all I need, them disturbing my birds. Hey, I just thought…Perhaps I should move the cover and put a big bucket down there with some water in it. I could ask 'em to chuck in some coins and make a wish!"

Peter laughed. "I shouldn't worry. I mean, how many people are even going to know about the appeal? I wouldn't have thought it would be that many."

"And who'd have any information anyway?" Norman chuckled. "It happened a hundred and fifty years ago!"

"I might know something."

"What?"

"Remember the photo of the buckle? Don't you think it had a similar style to the objects we dug up in your granary?"

Norman considered. "Yeah, I suppose it was similar, but so what? It could just be a coincidence."

"It could be, but it seems a strange one to me. I'd not even heard of the Fontwell Fakes three months ago. Then, out of the blue, a skeleton turns up, thought to have been down the well from about the time that Moses Jupp lived at the farm…and I know he had something to do with the fakers."

"So you think there's a connection?"

Peter sighed. "I can't be sure, but when I saw that buckle, the hairs on my neck stood up. There's got to be a link. As soon as those personal items go online, I'm going to have a really good look at them to see if I can spot anything."

"Yeah, well you do that, Pete. You're good at that sort of thing. Let me know if you get anywhere, won't you?"

"Course I will, Norman."

CHAPTER 46

A few days after the inquest, the postman delivered the certificates that Peter had been eagerly waiting for.

The birth certificate of Albert Coles confirmed his mother as 'Emily Coles formerly Tarrant', and his middle name was 'Arman'. It proved that Emily had given her son the middle name of her father. She had obviously given the name Tarrant as her previous name: it was a common occurrence for that to happen if a widow with a young daughter, such as Emily's mother, remarried.

William Coles' birth certificate confirmed that his middle name was also 'Arman'. His parents' marriage certificate showed that when Albert and Dorothy married in 1912, Dorothy's father, John Turnbull was already deceased. Peter checked the death records and found that he died in the last quarter of 1911.

Dorothy had no brothers and she was older than her sister, so she must have inherited the farm. By marrying Dorothy, Moses' grandson, Albert, became master at Oxenhope and the family name running the farm changed to Coles.

Peter could hardly wait to show Norman that he was related to Moses Jupp.

Peter checked online daily, to see if he could find the police appeal for information to identify the body in the well. When it was finally published, he carefully studied the photographs of the items recovered. For him, the belt buckle was the most important clue.

Who might have worn a belt like that? Perhaps more importantly, who might have made a belt like that? Surely it had to be one of the Fontwell fakers, especially since Moses had a connection with the two forgers and, of course, eight Fontwell fakes were found at Oxenhope.

Peter still hadn't traced Eddie Milner. He seemed to have vanished from the records after 1871, and the police had the period 1871 to 1873 as the most likely date for the death of the man found in the well.

Could the body be that of Edward Milner? It fits. He was thirty-four in 1871, so the age is right. He was single and the skeleton was not wearing a wedding ring. Milner appeared to have no attachments, so his disappearance would have been less likely to be noticed. Oxenhope was a world away from London and sparsely populated, which meant that there would have been little likelihood of his body being discovered and connected to Whitechapel.

The police officer at the inquest had said the death was suspicious, but Peter couldn't explain how or why Moses might have been involved, and if he was, whether he had a motive. Ever since he'd read about the theft of some moulds by a mudlark and the subsequent exposure of the fraud, Peter was convinced that the thief was Moses Jupp.

He might have been a bit of a rogue, but a murderer seems less likely. Maybe he'd taken his payment from Redding – the collector – and ran. Maybe he wanted to make himself scarce? Maybe he wanted a new start? Can any of these questions explain why he and Elizabeth had left London and moved to Oxenhope?

Perhaps someone who'd been making money out of the fakes suspected or learned that Moses had stolen the evidence exposing the fraud? Perhaps they wanted revenge? Revenge... Milner and Nunn's business was probably ruined and Milner's attempt to sell the Fontwells in Windsor ended with him in court...

The game was up for the fakers. Billy Nunn died from

tuberculosis in April 1871. Peter doubted that he would have been well enough to come out to Oxenhope in search of Moses. That left Milner; somehow, maybe he found out where Moses was living.

That was it...it had to be...that's what might have brought him to Oxenhope to end up dead and disappeared. But did that mean that Moses murdered him? Surely not! But maybe he did?

Ideas and questions swirled around in Peter's mind, but it was all conjecture. Nevertheless, he decided that he would contact the police. First, though, he wanted to talk over his theory with Felicity. She often had good ideas and maybe she could suggest something he'd overlooked or somewhere else he could try to trace Milner, before he approached them.

During supper that evening, he brought her up to date with his notion that the skeleton may be that of Edward Milner.

"I don't think they'll take you seriously. You don't actually have any evidence, do you?"

"No, you're right. I suppose it's just a collection of historical events that I've somehow cobbled together."

"Exactly!"

"But you must admit, it would be exciting if I really had discovered the identity of the body in the well. The police must have access to far more records than I have. Perhaps if I just gave them a name, they could expand their information from that. What if they have records going back to Victorian times or sources that I can't even imagine?"

"That might be the case, but are you absolutely certain that this Milner character vanished as you say? Have you checked everything?"

"No, I must admit it's difficult to check everything. There's so much information out there now. It's almost impossible to check it all."

"Well, I think that before you contact the police, you should have another go at finding him. You'll look an idiot if the police investigate him and find him somewhere after 1871. They might even charge you for wasting police time."

"Yes, perhaps you're right. I probably have got a bit carried away with all this. I'll give it another go."

"You've got a letter from the British Museum!" Felicity called from downstairs. Peter shot down to the hall table to see what it was.

The light-grey envelope bore the impressive dark-grey logo of the museum, and the franking advertised an up-and-coming exhibition. Peter could hardly contain his delight. He turned it over and carefully opened it, extracting the contents.

He had expected to pull out a report on the hoard of gold coins, giving a detailed description and a recommendation that the find should go forward to inquest. What he actually read was a report, but with an unexpected conclusion. When he'd finished, he went to find Felicity.

"Hey, you'll never believe this!"

"Believe what?"

"It's about the hoard that I declared from Oxenhope."

"Well I guessed that...Come on, what's happened?"

"There's a report and everything, and it confirms that they are Roman aureui of the Emperor Trajan, but there's not going to be an inquest."

"That's good, isn't it? It means you don't have to prove that Norman's entitled to them."

"Well no. They're going to hang on to them because," and Peter quoted from the accompanying letter, '...*our research indicates that these coins are identical to the coins found in the same field in 1842, and due to their close proximity to that find are therefore likely to be from that same hoard. As the 1842 hoard resides in Pewsey Museum, we are recommending to the Coroner that these coins be reunited with the rest of the hoard held there...*'

"So would the museum's opinion change if you proved that Moses Jupp buried them?"

"Unfortunately not...it goes on to say that, '*the balance of probability indicates that the finder of the coins, circa one hundred and fifty years ago, failed to report them to the Coroner and therefore had no title to them.'"*

"What? They even reported them in Victorian times?"

"Oh yes...the original hoard was claimed by the Crown as Treasure Trove. The law has changed a bit, but the principle is similar. I can see where they're coming from. It's not something I'd thought of. Norman's going to be very disappointed."

"So will you and Norman get some money instead?"

"No, because they are part of the original hoard. I can't believe it. I don't think I've ever heard of that happening before."

"Never mind, you still had the excitement of finding them."

"I know, but it would have been nice to have finally found a proper hoard, recognised as treasure."

"So what are you going to do?"

"I'll have to ring Norm and give him the bad news."

When Peter phoned Norman, he could tell that he hadn't yet received a similar letter. He was far too upbeat. By the time Peter had explained the contents, he sensed that Norman felt a little disillusioned. To the farmer, it was just another case of meddlesome bureaucrats making life more difficult for him.

Still, that's Norm, thought Peter afterwards. *He'll get over it. Frankly, the British Museum is right. Those coins should have been declared and they weren't. Never mind, he told himself, it was a real thrill to find them.*

He sat staring blankly at his computer screen, thinking wistfully of what might have been. Still, never one to dwell too long on disappointment, Peter decided on one last attempt to find Edward Milner.

This time he extended his search further, looking for any parents and brothers or sisters, intending to follow them on later census returns in case he moved in with any of them. Once again he met a brick wall. Milner's parents died in the early 1860s and his only brother passed away unmarried in 1868. He couldn't find any other close relatives. Perhaps the best hope of finding him would be to make a fresh search of the marriage indices.

A man in his thirties would surely be a candidate for marriage. Searching the name Milner returned two hits, but the ages were completely wrong and the locations didn't ring true.

Peter then thought of something he hadn't tried before and he kicked himself for being so remiss. He tried variations of the spelling of the name: 'Millner' and 'Millener', but without success. Then he found a useful website that gave advice and suggestions on how surnames became misspelt.

He wrote 'Milner' down in longhand and played around with the possibilities. He looked for possible discrepancies, either made by either the original creator of the record or the transcriber to the index. In his own handwriting, which wasn't very neat, the last letter of Milner looked like an 's' rather than an 'r'. He tried 'Milnes'.

In the fourth quarter of 1878, Edward Milnes married Rosemary Stoddard in Whitechapel, London. He was forty-one, the same age as Milner would have been. Peter then remembered the couple from Whitehaven. The wife's first name was Rosemary. He searched the 1881 Census to find them again. This time, he knew he'd found the right Edward Milner. He'd previously only looked at the image of the original record, not the transcript, and it was the enumerator's poor handwriting that had fooled him. When he looked closely at the place of birth for Edward, 'Whitechapel' was written in such a scratchy way, it looked almost the same as 'Whitehaven', which was the birthplace of his wife and most of their neighbours. Foolishly, Peter hadn't noticed the difference.

So, Edward Milner was alive after 1871, but what had happened to him subsequently? The answer finally came in an obscure shipping list he managed to find in *The Whitehaven News*. The schooner, *Cassiope*, left Whitehaven on 14 April, 1883, bound for Melbourne with a general cargo, including the first elephant ever taken to Australia. Interestingly, she had been built by the Whitehaven Shipping Company. Her manifest included the names of Mr and Mrs Edward Milner.

For Peter, it was proof enough that the couple had emigrated. Reluctantly, despite the Fontwell-like appearance of the belt buckle, he dropped his theory that the skeleton recovered from the well was that of Edward Milner.

Thank goodness Felicity had persuaded him to do one more search.

"Hello Norman, how's things?"

"Oh not too bad, Pete, considering. Come in."

Norman welcomed Peter into his office. The warm fug that hung in the air from the dogs was almost sliceable.

"Fancy coming out for some lunch, Norm? Up at The Fox, my treat."

"What, today?"

"Yes, it should be quiet being midweek. I'm sure they'll fit us in."

"I shall have to get changed first. You sure, Pete? What's the big occasion?"

"Now come on, don't be cynical, perhaps I just want to buy you lunch!"

"Give me ten minutes, can you?"

"Of course…I'll wait in the car and listen to the radio. There's no hurry." Actually, Peter needed some fresh air.

When the farmer reappeared, Peter was impressed. He'd never seen him look so smart. Norman had changed his boots, put on a clean shirt and clean pair of trousers, combed his hair, and was carrying a jacket.

"I've shut the dogs in," he said, as he got into the passenger seat. "They should be all right for a while."

They chatted on the way to Wyke, just a ten-minute journey. After Peter had parked the car, he retrieved a folder from the back seat. Walking inside the pub, he could see he'd been right: there'd be no problem getting a table.

"Hello Norman," Barry, the owner, welcomed him. He was drying some glasses and paused to hang his cloth over a beer pump. "Don't normally see you up here at lunchtime."

"Ah, well, that's because I'm being treated. Do you know Peter Sefton, Barry?"

Barry looked at Peter. "Yes, I think I've seen Peter in here from time to time. Usually in the dining room with your wife, I assume, and sometimes with friends."

"You're right, Barry: the wife, but you could get me into trouble." They laughed and shook hands.

"Have you got Wi-Fi?" Peter asked.

"Yeah, no problem...here's the code." Barry handed him a card.

"Great, thank you."

Norman and Peter followed a young waiter to a table. When they were settled, Peter brought out his mobile phone and connected it to the pub's network. Noting the disapproving look on the farmer's face, he said, "Don't worry, Norman, I think it's rude to bring out a phone during a meal, but I've got good reason. You'll see why presently. Besides, it won't ring: I don't get many calls."

"That one of those smartphones?"

"Sure is, although it's quite new and I haven't completely got the hang of it yet. I've practised what I want to show you. My niece has been given me some lessons on how to use it." He brought up a website on the screen and studied it for a few seconds before disconnecting.

"What's that then?"

"You'll have to wait and see. It won't be for a while; probably after we've eaten, about two o'clock."

Norman seemed intrigued.

They ordered food, and didn't have long to wait before they could tuck in. Conversation inevitably got around to the gold coins and Peter did his best to cheer up Norman. He kept an eye on the time while they chatted.

"Have you heard any news from the police or the coroner, Norm?"

"Had the police on the phone the other day...said they'd no new leads on identification. They were pretty certain that the follow-up inquest would give an open verdict."

"That's what I assumed, seeing as they can't prove murder

and can't put a name to the remains. It all happened too long ago."

"I thought you had an idea who it might have been?"

"No, not now. I had an inkling, but it proved to be wrong."

"Never mind, Pete…Hey, do you think there'll be a funeral? If so, who pays? I hope it won't be me!"

"No idea, I'd imagine the coroner would have to give the go-ahead for a funeral. If there aren't any relatives then the local council would take responsibility. I know you wouldn't have to pay."

"Thank goodness for that."

Peter checked the time on his phone.

"What's going on then, Pete?"

"Can't say just yet…you'll have to hang on a bit longer."

They finished their meal and the young waiter came to take their plates away.

"So, can you tell me what you've got in that folder then?"

It lay on the table next to them. Peter reached over and opened it. He pulled out two birth certificates and a marriage certificate.

"I thought you might be interested in these; have a look. These prove that Moses Jupp was your great, great, great grandfather."

Norman was enthralled. He studied the certificates and listened intently as Peter explained the connection. "I'd have never known any of this if you hadn't come along with your detector."

"You're right! It's strange how things work out. For me, it was Moses Jupp's death certificate that really got me going. I've turned up things before with a name, but it was actually tracing the owner of that worn Roman bronze coin, and then to discover that he died on your farm, and in the very field where I was searching…"

"…and in such a horrible way."

"Yes, unfortunately," agreed Peter. He looked at the time on his phone. "Right, we're almost there. Let me get connected to that website again. I need to show you something that might be of interest."

Peter placed the mobile phone on the table between them and adjusted the volume. There were no other diners nearby, but he didn't want the sound too loud. When they could both see the live streaming on the screen, the two men leaned in to the phone to hear what was being said.

"Lot 186, assorted crowns and coins. Commission bids with me. I'll start at two hundred pounds...two-fifty...three hundred... looking for three-fifty...three-fifty on the internet... Any more? Hammer's up, selling to the internet at three-fifty. Sold! Lot 186."

"Where's this then, Pete?" whispered Norman.

"A live auction in central London; big auctioneers who specialise in coins and artefacts."

"What is it you want me to see?"

"You won't have to wait long, Norm, just be patient. There's only about five minutes to go."

The two of them watched with interest.

"Lot number 194, a collection of twenty-five assorted cap and uniform badges. Eighty pounds? I'm looking for eighty pounds to get us started...Militaria, someone? Surely? Nobody?" The auctioneer looked frustrated. "I'll take forty pounds for Lot 194. Come on, give me a bid, ladies and gentlemen...Forty pounds...? No bids online? No bids in the room? We'll pass it."

"This is it, it's up next," said Peter.

"Lot 195, a group of eight ancient-looking medallions known as Fontwell Fakes; highly sought after these days. Lots of interest. I can go straight in at the lower estimate of five thousand pounds...Thank you, madam...Six thousand...seven thousand... eight in the room; thank you, sir...Nine thousand...ten in the room...eleven on the internet...twelve in the room...thirteen thousand on the internet...any more? Fair warning...fourteen; back in, madam...fifteen in the room...any more? Sixteen in the room...the internet's out...new bidder in the room...Seventeen... eighteen...nineteen thousand with you at the back...Last call... all done, hammer's up. Sold! Nineteen thousand pounds."

Peter picked up his mobile, closed the website, and opened the calculator app.

Norman, bemused, watched Peter tapping at the phone's screen.

"By my calculation, after commission and VAT, there's just less than fifteen thousand pounds coming your way, Norman."

"Those were the things we found under the granary floor?" asked Norman.

Peter grinned and nodded.

Norman was incredulous. "But they just went for nineteen thousand pounds."

"Yes, not bad, eh?"

"That makes them worth two thousand pounds each. I thought you said they were worth about five hundred pounds each?"

"I did, but that was before I took them to the auction house. Their expert was really excited. He said they were extremely rare and were previously unknown examples."

"But I thought you said the fakers produced thousands?"

"They did, but I've a theory about that. I think our man, Moses Jupp, stole the moulds that the collector, Titus Redding, used to prove the fraud. What if Moses took some castings at the same time and buried them later on in your granary? They might have been new designs. After the counterfeiting was exposed, the prices collapsed. One of the fakers was arrested in Windsor for trying to sell dodgy antiquities. So the whole thing went up the swanny. No more medallions, like the ones we found in the granary, were ever produced, unlike the relatively large numbers of previous designs. That's what made those eight we found so incredibly rare!"

"Well...that sounds quite plausible to me. Not that I'm complaining, but I can't take all the money, Pete. You found 'em, and you did say the first time you came that we would split anything of value fifty-fifty."

"You remember that then?"

"I wouldn't forget something like that. Anyway, seems only fair to me."

"Are you sure?"

"Course I am."

"Thanks Norm, that's decent of you."

"I think we need to celebrate, Pete, don't you? Barry..."

Norman called across to the owner, "can we have two more drinks over here, please?"

When the drinks arrived, Peter said to Norman, "Let's raise a toast to your ancestor, Moses Jupp."

The two men tapped their glasses together.

"To Moses Jupp," they said in unison.

ACKNOWLEDGEMENTS

The inspiration to use a Thames mudlark as a leading character came from discovering that one of my wife's ancestors was listed as a scavenger on the 1881 Census. His name was Moses too.

Although this is a work of fiction, elements of fact run through many of the situations and events: shoeblacks, ragged scholars, and Madame Genevieve being examples. Tragically, an individual really did lose his life after a mowing machine accident in the manner described. He was only fourteen.

The Fontwell Fakes are my invention, but there was a scandal in the antiquities world of mid-Victorian London. Two East End metalworkers named William Smith (Billy) and Charles Eaton (Charley) were exposed as having produced and sold hundreds of fake antiquities. I would like to acknowledge in particular Robert Halliday, author of 'The Billy and Charley Forgeries' (*London Archaeologist*), whose extensive research into these two characters and the items they produced, now commonly known as 'Shadwell Shams', was particularly helpful.

I need to thank my family for their comments and advice, and am grateful to Sue Shade for her diligence and patience in helping me to improve my writing. I would also like to mention Anni Byard and Ian Richardson of the Portable Antiquities Scheme, run by the British Museum, and fellow detectorist Paul Buxey for their assistance.

Operation Chronos is the real name of the police campaign to tackle the problem of nighthawking. At the time of publication, a number of arrests have been made and punishments issued by the courts for the crime of illegal metal-detecting.

The vast majority of metal detectorists regard their hobby as a fascinating and enjoyable activity, and observe the law. Witness the staggeringly impressive hoards discovered and reported under the rules of the Treasure Act in recent years, most initially discovered by someone using a metal detector.

After twenty-five years of detecting, I've still to find my own hoard. The closest I've come, so far, was finding two hundred modern twenty-centime coins buried all together on a beach in France, presumably hidden by a parent to provide an activity for the children. I couldn't even spend them as the French franc had been replaced by the euro.

The search goes on!

Made in the USA
Middletown, DE
10 February 2020

84462343R00187